A Road To Joy

www.ARoadToJoy.com
www.AlexStacey.com

First Edition Print 2019

ISBN: 978-1-9991268-0-3

A ROAD TO JOY
Published by Fresh Pennies
www.FreshPennies.com

Cover Art by Trevor Gustafson
www.TrevorGustafson.com

ALEXANDRA
STACEY

A Road To Joy

Hamilton, Ontario
Canada

Inspired by true events.

And somewhat embellished.

This book is dedicated to

My Cracked Pots
Deb, Stash, Sylvia, and Vickie

My Soulsisters, My Tribe, My Therapy, My Sanity

Who taught me how to heal myself
and helped me remember that anything is possible.

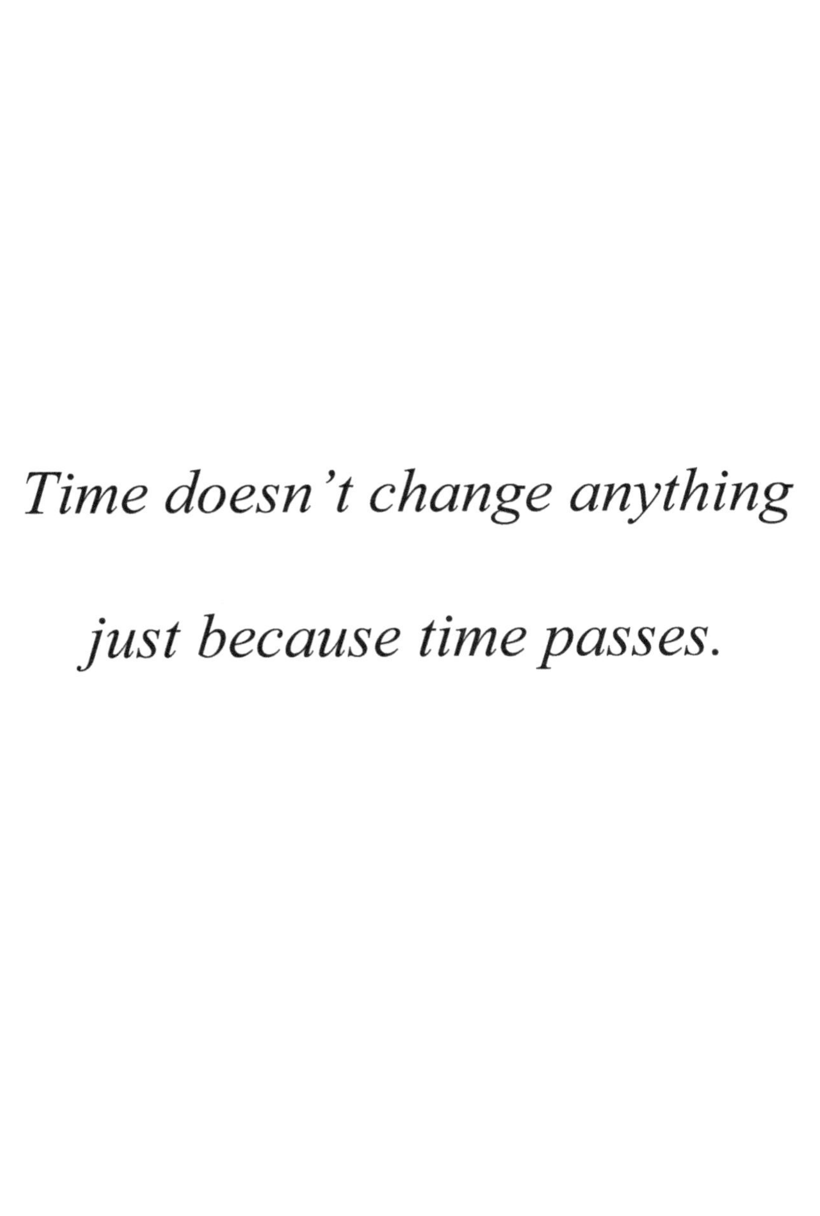

Time doesn't change anything

just because time passes.

Table of Contents

Making A Clean Getaway

It's hard to say how I knew the difference between a squish and a crunch. I couldn't say as I'd ever really felt a squish, though I did know a crunch when I heard one. Maybe I knew it was a squish more because it didn't quite sound like a crunch. There was a slight hesitation, the very merest hint of resistance, my automatic reaction of giving just a whisper of a nudge. And then, squish. Just like that.

My first reaction was one of blasé what-the-fuckedness. It was early. Too early for anyone to give a shit what I was doing sneaking out before the sun was even a degree or two above horizontal. Truth is, even in the middle of the day, I could probably walk out into the street naked with my tits on fire and still not learn the name of a single neighbour. Five years I'd lived here and still had to refer to the Notes in my phone to know which house that kid lived in or whose Piece-Of-Shit SUV was blocking my driveway again. Not for the first time I thought I should maybe throw a big bar-b-que and invite everyone over for burgs and beers and maybe get to know them a bit. The next thought was that would be too much work, and I'd forget who was who before the dishes were done.

My second reaction was that I should probably go see what it was I just ran over. I sat through ROCK 109's best guess at the day's weather, the little weird man who wanted to give me money for my gold, and a rockin' musical reminder that certain days of the week are less popular than others, all while trying to figure out a way to do that without actually getting out of the van, without having to unstick my sweaty thighs from the crap leather seat I'd just worked so hard to mold around my fat ass. On the flip side, if I were going to make a good getaway, I certainly wouldn't get far if I'd just flattened a tire.

I grabbed the steering wheel and bobbed violently in my seat. The van rocked wildly, not feeling markedly different from what I thought it should feel like.

Yeah.

Tire-Inflation-Test Results: Inconclusive.

Crap.

Ripping through a funky stream of pure unadulterated blasphemy, I tore my legs from the grip of the masochistic cowhide beneath me and slid out the door back onto my feet. *Six thirty in the morning, and the air's already too thick to breathe. I hate the heat.*

Two steps away from the van and my thighs were slipping around each other like a pair of well-lubed water balloons. My sunglasses fogged over as the heat hit their air-conditioned lenses. I pushed them up; they stuck on my forehead and pulled one hair out of my head. I took a moment to grieve, sure that there was no way it could have been one of the grey ones.

The door to the van was still open, a singer promising loudly, over a devilishly appropriate bass, to help me erase any sign of unwanted problems, as I rounded the front of the vehicle, suddenly hoping I'd put the damn thing in PARK. Nothing there.

Round the other side, nothing.

The back, nothing.

And then, there it was, as I came back round the driver's side, in all its black and white – and red – glory. The squish.

Fuck.

I hated that cat. But still...

Fuck.

The ominous voice continued on, listing his credentials, threatening deeply from the still-open door.

Nope. Thank you, Warbler Of Wrath. Handled this one all on my own.

I cautiously stepped around the results of my handiwork and climbed back into the driver's seat, slamming the door most satisfactorily.

The mom in me nagged something about cleaning it up before the kids got up and reacted in whatever surprising and unexpected fashion their little wheel-of-fortune brains would think up this time.

But the She in me, the She who had been quietly whispering in my ear for years, the She who had been pleading with me in tears as I lay in bed, night after night trying to find sleep, the She who was now standing firm and demanding to be heard, put her foot down.

No, She ordered.

Stomped it down, right there and then.

Not your circus, not your monkeys, She hissed.

Stomped it down hard.

Right on the gas pedal.

The van shot forward as only an eight-year-old minivan can shoot, squealing one tire while the other just sort of shot blood and guts all over the neighbour's brand-new SUV. Serves What's-His-Name right for blocking half my driveway again.

I peeled out of my street, around the corner, leaning precariously over on two wheels, some kind of maniacal laugh oozing creepily out of the side of my mouth in perfect unison with the rock anthem on the radio, the songster and I both deciding together, that we were perfectly okay with just walking away.

Making Enemies

It was mid-morning before I finally decided I was hungry and stopped for a bite. The view had morphed from endless walls of over-reaching buildings to sporadic industrial sites with letters for names, giving no indication whatsoever as to what the people within might actually be doing. It always irked me to read "A Leader in Logistics and Quality Assurance" or some such nonsense under a logo, as I mentally promised to look them up should I ever have need of some mysterious logistics or want to be assured of my inherent quality. *Turds.*

Driving for me had always been remarkably meditative. I'd been driving long enough to be able to keep both eyes on the road while letting my mind wander aimlessly over the mundane and random thoughts that constantly pass through my head. I love to ponder the names of streets and towns, calculate exactly how long to my destination based on my current speed, crank the tunes and sing until my throat is seared. Memories come flooding back like reruns on local television, ideas pop up like fireflies around a campfire, feelings settle into place like puddles on a rainy April day. The drone of the engine and gentle hum of the floor on my feet lulled me into a calm and happy consciousness.

Attuned as I was, however, to the stupidity of others, no trance was ever complete without the intrusion of some crazy ass driver who cut me off, or some precious sample of humanity who thought I couldn't see him foraging deep into his sinuses for that last elusive booger. And nothing ruins a mood better than some random personalized license plate that makes no sense whatsoever to anyone who can read, forcing me to spend countless irretrievable minutes trying to figure it out.

Fuck you Mr. BM BSER.

For the second time that morning, I peeled my legs from the leather seat and cringed as my weight shifted from my butt to my feet. *I really need to crack out that yoga dvd...* After a minute or two of my blood finding its way into my extremities and, thankfully *back* into my head, I headed into the crowd that filled the multi-choice of bad food choices. While I tossed around the variety of goods designed to assure a long, slow, agonizing death by consumption, I headed for the bathrooms to relieve my overextended bladder, though what it could possibly be full of at this point was beyond me.

I may have had a lot of problems, but bladder proficiency was not one of them. Though the line to the endless array of stalls was short, I stood back to let a young mom and dancing daughter go ahead of me. The woman smiled gratefully, and the wee brat stuck her tongue out at me as she passed.

Wet your pants, you little fart.

A stall door opened, and a very generic looking teenaged girl exited, head down, curtained by the straight, boring long brown hair that seemed to define this generation, phone in hand, fingers flying like sparks across its screen. I wondered how she'd pulled her pants up.

I moved to enter the stall the Ball Of Angst had just left and bumped her shoulder, sending her phone skittering loudly across the bathroom floor, into a wall, under the gigantic paper towel dispenser.

"Oh no," I started, as sincerely as I felt, watching the girl scramble to the floor to retrieve the tiny box that held her life force. "I'm so sorry," I assured her. "Is it ok?" I cringed as I fully expected to have to fork over a half-year's tuition for a new phone.

The Guardian Of The Cell Phone crawled out from under the sink, hands gently caressing every square millimetre of the golden ingot.

"Is it ok?" I asked again, bending to peek under the curtain of hair. Giant brown eyes met mine, and for a moment, my heart broke at the pain in them. Just for a moment.

It's a goddam phone, for chrissakes.

"Yeah," she admitted. "It's fine."

"I'm so sorry," I told her again.

"It's okay," she assured me, with whatever expression may have passed across her once again hidden face.

I gave up my attempt to make a human connection and locked myself in the stall to attend to my bodily function.

Sitting there comfortably – at least the toilet seat wasn't upholstered in worn leather – elbows on my knees, enjoying the blank stare that comes with the relief of deliberately and forcefully emptying one's bladder, my mouth dropped unflatteringly open as the hand, complete with phone attached, slid under the door and clicked loudly with the distinct digital fakery of an active shutter. As quickly, she was gone.

Little fucker took my picture! While I was peeing!!

And I know that my mouth had 'dropped unflatteringly open' because I have since seen that pic online as the backdrop on various memes that hilariously label me as some crazy mom 'when she finds your socks on the floor,' or 'when she hears you swear for the first time.'

Fucker.

I looked for her through the food court minutes later as I waited in line, but I didn't see her. I ended up heading back out to my van with my two large ice capps and a dozen assorted donuts, the calm serenity of my Drive-So-Far all but gone. I kicked a stone that was in my path. It shot up and put small dent in the side of my van. As I sat there in the parking lot with the air conditioning running on full to cool the van back down, a slow smile crossed my face, a small piece of chewed donut falling on my shirt, as I imagined my sweet young photographer *squished* somewhere over in the truck parking lot behind the restaurant.

Just for a second. I would never wish that on her. It was just a thought. It went away. Mostly.

I drove for another hour before I realized I had no idea where I was going. That realization didn't slow me down at all, but it was interesting to think that I had awakened that morning, hours before, threw some shit in a bag, and left, with no plan, no destination, no direction. I just drove.

I hadn't told anyone I was leaving.

Now *there* was something.

I'd been gone for more than five hours without a single text, no phone calls, no one wanting anything, when I was suddenly swept with a wave of woebegone obsolescence. I quickly realized that they were all probably still asleep. Without me there to drag them out of bed, they would likely sleep until bedtime. I could be dead in a gutter for hours more yet before anyone needed money.

But I was clearly up in cottage country now, the highway lined with alternating trees and sloped granite walls scored with the scars of blasting crews a century gone. The air was easier to breathe, sweeter, cleaner. I opened the window and let the wind have its way with my hair. Every hill and turn in the road unknotted one more muscle. Every car that turned off my path was another person removed from my planet. Every deep breath I took reached farther and farther into the nooks and crannies of my mind.

As the van rambled on, my thoughts quieted, my emotions settled, and the glaring white of my knuckles began to look pink on the steering wheel. I don't recall much of the drive that afternoon but wasn't surprised to realize I was now heading straight on into an early evening sun. I hadn't noticed a sign for hours and had no clue where I was, but figured I was likely still in the province. I started watching for signs of civilization where I could grab some gas and a bite of real food. The donuts were long gone.

An old worn "Welcome to Bl er" sign hinted at the possibility of human inhabitants. No idea what or where Bl er was. I saw a stop light in the distance, which meant that there was at least one intersection. So, there might be a store. And food. "Population 4053." *Ooh! And a liquor store!*

Making A Great First Impression

As the sun dipped below the tree line, I stood at the tailgate of the minivan slugging my backpack up over my shoulder and cramming the bags of groceries and wine into one big blue reusable IKEA bag. Holding my purse strap in my teeth, I managed to pull the door down forcefully on the second try, clocking myself in the head as I did so. Falling forward into the basket of wiper fluid and jumper cables, I gasped for breath while the stars that were dancing wildly behind my eyelids slowed and dimmed. I must have been standing there, bent over into the back of the van with my ass sticking out, for a bit, because the next thing I remember hearing was a careful, "You okay there, Ms. Bullock?"

Somehow realizing the voice was talking to me, I gritted a terse "I'm fine, I'm fine," through teeth that seemed to be flossed with purse strap, while smearing the cold patch of drool, that had collected between me and the cheap vinyl bag, all over my face. I struggled to stand straight, turning to gaze into the motel guy's three eyes.

"You sure? You're bleeding a bit there," he pointed.

"Nope. I'm good. Just trying to get inside. Thanks."

Get lost, Motel Guy, leave me alone.

I hitched up my burden once more, slinging the shoulder strap of my purse around my neck, and pulled the door down, stumbling more than adroitly stepping out of its way. Feeling impressed with myself, I moved past the kind but repulsive little man with a deft but definite hip sway, countered only by the mostly alcoholic ballast in my other hand.

Oh yeah, I got this.

"Okay then, I'll just be back over there in the office if you need anything."

"Thanks again --- there," I choked as the purse strap cut into my throat. One heaving step to haul myself and stuff up onto the sidewalk from the pavement of the parking lot and I was standing in front of my room for the night.

Number 4 of 13 bright yellow doors lined up along the sidewalk like obedient people at the bank begging for their money. Three other cars were sporadically parked in front. Motel Guy moped back the way he'd come, old faded jeans drooping from his non-existent ass, and not in a young studdly kind of way. I'd always wondered who stayed in these little nameless roadside motels. Now I knew.

My key cackled loudly as the hand-sized worn plastic tag hit the concrete, its tiny key clinking as a timid afterthought.

Of course, I decided. *It's going to be like that, then.*

I bent to pick up the key, only to be slammed in the back of the head by the overstuffed pack on my back. Cutting my losses, I felt up the door with my one free hand, found the doorknob, and forced the key through the jagged little slot like a prisoner on Viagra. The door popped open easily with a slight turn of the knob, and I fell into the dark drab room with the grace of a tased drug addict, lassoed perfectly by my purse strap caught firmly on the doorknob. There was the sound of breaking glass, and as I lay there wondering why life hated me so very much, I was enticed by the pleasant aroma of a freshly cracked bottle of my favourite Chardonnay.

Call it a win, then.

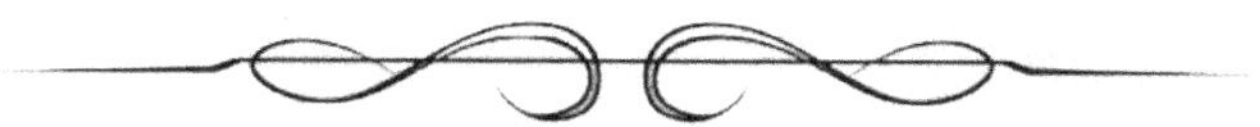

The room wasn't half bad once I'd found all the lights and turned on the television. Channel selection was virtually nil, but I quickly found their streaming service and decided a night with Blanche, Dorothy, Rose and Sophia was just what I needed. It still astounds me that I was now the same age as the youngest Golden Girl, and I'd have ditched them because of that if they weren't so damn funny. So, I left the tv turned up loud while I settled in and unpacked.

A shower was definitely in order; I stripped down and headed to the bathroom, revelling in the feeling of being naked in a room with lights on. How long had *that* been? Two? Three? Decades?

The idea that there could be a webcam in the place suddenly dawned on me, and I grabbed a towel, wrapping it the full three-quarters of the way around me that it allowed. *Leave a little to the imagination,* I muttered to the perv who was surely listening.

I flipped on the bathroom light and shrieked out loud at the face that was staring back at me in the mirror. It took about a half second to realize that it was me. But that's a long time to be scared to death.

Pushing my hair, long as it was, out of my face, it looked like it had been glued to my head in handfuls, shocks of antiqued copper, bland brown, and dirty snow. My eyes were squinting suspiciously back at me, questioning my intentions. Eyebrows, suddenly exposed, were waving at me like fingers on a hand cramped by severe hypothermia. There was chocolate frosting on my chin. And dried blood smeared across my temple.

Good lord. When did I turn into the Wicked Witch of the East?

I took my brush and the thumb-sized bottle of the motel's mystery 2-in-1 shampoo into the shower and brushed and scrubbed and stood until the hot water ran out.

As I was drying off, I opened the cut on my head again. It was bleeding pretty bad, so I threw my t-shirt and shorts back on and ducked out the door to the van. Even in the dark shadows of the parking lot, I easily found Tool Box #2 amid the wiper fluid and jumper cables. I carefully closed the tailgate and tiptoed barefoot back alongside the van to my door and the brightly lit laugh track inside.

"Wow. You look human," I heard – no, *felt* - in the deepest, smoothest molasses, dripping warmly down my back.

O. M. G. I've just been dunked in warm cream.

I stepped out of the light of my doorway toward the voice and found him sitting two yellow doors over, leaned back and relaxed in one of the two Muskoka chairs out front, beer bottle in hand, feet crossed casually in front of him.

"Excuse me?" *Yeah. Real cool.*

"I said, you look human. You weren't looking so good earlier."

"Oh," finding and releasing my inner bitch. "And that was a problem for you?"

He hmphed the most seductive hmph I'd ever heard. "No, not for me. Don't care much what you look like. Just thought you looked like you'd been through quite the battle."

"Ohh, and you felt sorry for me, the poor little damsel in distress?"

"Hah! Hell no!" he barked deeply. "You looked like an Amazon warrior. I'd have come and helped – at least offered you a beer – if I wasn't sure you had a sword in that bag." He drank deeply.

I stared blankly at him while somewhere in the back of my consciousness Sophia was giving Dorothy shit for something.

"Seems you're still in fight mode. No beer for you." He looked at me coolly, my last chance to say something intelligent.

"You might be right," I admitted. "If you hear a lot of noise and yelling, just ignore it. That way no one gets hurt."

He hmphed again, dismissing me.

I took my Tool Box #2 inside, closing and locking the door loudly behind me. There was a tearful group hug on the screen as I opened an intact bottle of wine and settled myself on the chair in front of the mirror. I took off the lampshade, instantly turning my reflection into that of one that shouldn't appear there, opened the black plastic case, and, finding the bandages, butterfly tapes, alcohol swabs, and cotton balls, set to work fixing my head. Once found and cleaned up, the gash in my scalp was easily 'stitched' by braiding thin locks of hair across the wound to hold it closed. I marvelled at my ingenuity, deciding I liked the look of my medically functional cornrow. I sang along with the television, ancient and long-forgotten memories filling in lyrics that defined the true meaning of friendship, looking at me in the mirror. Putting the lampshade back on its perch, I decided, yes, I did look better. Mr. Melt-My-Bones Elliott was right about that.

I poured myself a juice glass full of wine, brought the bottle with me, and climbed into the lumpy, bouncy, surprisingly clean bed. Leaned back against the headboard, elixir at hand, the Girls baring their souls to me, the tears began.

I cried and I laughed and I drank until I saw light peeking through the crack in the heavy vinyl curtains. Every inch of me ached. My head throbbed in perfect time to my heart. My eyes had swollen so much that the rim of the glass touched my eyelids before the bridge of my nose. I don't know exactly when I fell asleep, but in the hours that followed, I didn't move. I didn't dream. I didn't think or worry or wonder or regret or threaten or hate or fail.

For the first time since everything changed, after so much work and effort, after all the pressure and expectation, I slept. And I escaped. For a few hours, there was nothing. And I don't think I have ever felt so relieved. So grateful. So happy. At some point in the middle of that night of despair, I knew that there was no way I was ever going back.

I slept on and off until I was finished, done, and couldn't imagine ever needing to sleep again. Thankfully, at some point, I had my wits about me enough to turn the tv off; there is nothing worse than sleeping with the news on. When I'd finally grown tired of being mostly unconscious, I began the slow and painful process of returning to the business of living.

Collecting three empty wine bottles from the floor as I went, I found a fully melted ice capp I'd left on the air conditioner. Pretty much the only thing in the room that was cold, wet, and virgin, I took a cautious sip.

Meh, I've had worse.

I nursed the cool caffeine-laced concoction carefully, wondering why my throat hurt so badly. It felt a bit better once revived, and my ability to swallow improved quickly, and thankfully, as the hunger kicked in.

Cracking open the box of Pop Tarts, I nibbled, sipped, and stretched until my body agreed to catch up to my mind. I padded around the room barefoot, tidying up the mysterious array of clothing and garbage I'd somehow managed to toss about in my stupor. Iced cherry pastry clenched between fingers barely wrapped around the flimsy plastic cup of java, I multi-tasked like the Pro I Was and started to slowly feel mortal again.

Until I caught a glimpse of myself in the mirror.

Except for the length of my hair, I was rocking a pretty good impression of Rocky On A Bad Day. Eyes that looked like pregnant slugs, cheeks that had somehow morphed into someone else's, lips chapped like a dead lizard in the sun. My shoulders were slumped, and I'm not altogether sure the hint of the birth of a serious hunchback was just bad lighting. No wonder crying had such a bad rap; it certainly had a way of bringing out the ugly. It suddenly occurred to me that something should be registering as painful. I found some ibuprofen in the Tool Box #2 and choked them down with the Pop Tarts, just in case.

I sat on the edge of the bed falling into a blank stare at the wooden chair in front of me. For a while, there were two of them. Then they snapped back into one whole seat again. But with eyes focused on the lopsided heart cut into one of the back ribs, I indulged myself in the emptiness of just sitting. My breathing slowed, deepening until I couldn't resist the urge to crack my toes. My gaze remained locked on the heart, but my awareness began to spread. I could see the desk behind it, the tv beside it, the trash can underneath. I noticed the print on the wall: a sailboat on an anxious sea, the moonlight casting it in silhouette. My shoes sat on the floor, heel to heel, in a stance that I could never master as a preschool ballerina. The bathroom was out of range of my peripheral, but the light from the doorway cast an odd shadow across the floor and up the wall looking remarkably like a giant ax ready to kill the chair with a single strike. The heart blurred and my eyelids, heavy with abuse, closed peacefully.

The first real thought that came as I floated slowly back into my body was that I had packed my bags. I was leaving. No idea where I was *going*, but, apparently, I had decided it was time to go. I stood carefully, slung purse and backpack over my shoulder with an ease that surprised me and dragged the considerably lighter IKEA bag off the counter. Key in hand, hand on doorknob, I glanced back around the room out of habit, making sure no one left behind, and headed out to the van.

It took a moment to get my bearings. The vehicle before me was unrecognizable; the black looked yellow reflecting the light beside my door, but that was definitely my license plate. I was the MOMNATOR. Looking past the van through my squinty eyes and skeptical brows, I realized that everything else was black.

What the hell?

I dropped my bags to the sidewalk at my feet and fished for my phone. For all my poking and prodding, it might as well have been a rock. Of course, it never occurred to me to bring a charger.

Pretty sure I felt the 'hmph' of judgment before I heard it.

Gawd, that man could mumble sexy!

Glancing to my left, I caught the flash of shock on his face before he quite expertly rearranged his features into a bland look of disdained concern.

"What time is it?" I asked him bluntly.

"Ten-thirty," he oozed.

"PM," he confirmed.

And while I was cataloguing that information, "Wednesday," he added, just in case.

He opened his mouth to add something, but I somehow managed an expression that shut it quickly, though I don't think it was actually the expression I was going for.

"I checked in on Monday," I muttered.

"Yes, you did."

Two days. I'd slept for most of two whole days. If I'd known that while I was doing it, I would have enjoyed it more.

Well then. I couldn't very well resume my travels in the middle of the night. I stood dumbly wondering what Plan B was going to be.

"I'd offer you a beer, but it might not go well with the crack – or heroine – or truck – that did that to you."

I tried the look again. He'd adapted.

"You could have a seat if you like. Maybe think things through a little before you take off."

That might work, except ...

"Before I sit down, I just want to know one thing."

"Okay," he agreed, looking at me slyly.

"Are we going to be having sex?"

He did me the courtesy of hesitating. "No. We're not."

"Good." I plopped down in the matching Muskoka chair, bleached white in the moonlight, leaving my bags on the sidewalk and my door ajar to the dark and vacated room within.

"Good," he agreed. "Glad we got that out of the way."

He finished his beer while we sat quietly, and I didn't feel like I had to explain anything. When he went back into his room for a refill, he returned with a dripping cold bottle of water for me. As the fresh wetness splashed down my throat, a wave of cold tickled its way through my flesh, intimately, but with an aftertaste of an emotion I didn't quite recognize. At once both amazed by a drink of water as if it were my first and saddened as if it were my last. I was confused and aware, alert and dazed. Overwhelmed, but in control.

I looked at the label. *Just water.*

"So, are you at least feeling a bit better?"

I thought about that. Nodding, I decided, "Yes, I think so."

"That's a plus, I suppose."

It was.

"Have you been sitting in that chair for the last two days?"

"Yep."

I liked this man.

"Just to be clear. You're not really Sandra Bullock, right?"

"No. No I'm not." Checking in under a fake name had seemed funny at the time. I didn't expect to be called on it.

"Good. I don't do celebrity very well."

I snorted. "You know you're a dead ringer for Sam Elliott."

"I'm better lookin'," he drawled.

I turned to look at him. He was serious. And right.

We chatted like old friends for quite a while. None of the small talk and bullshit that drives me crazy. More of the stars and aliens and politics and books. He asked no personal questions, and I didn't feel obligated to share. I felt completely and totally anonymous. But oddly, not invisible. *Definitely not invisible.*

I noticed it. We'd been out there for hours as if it were perfectly normal to have a most intense and deep conversation with a total stranger, in the middle of nowhere, in the middle of the night. I felt no need to tone down my opinions, no instinct to hide my true self, no inclination to guard my words. We talked of nothing important, yet everything we shared was vital to the easy conversation we created between us. We sparred and agreed equally, each opposing the other's ideas as freely as water washing over rocks, and then finding common ground in the next sentence. It didn't matter what we said, it only mattered that we said it. We talked and we listened, as if we would be asked to transcribe every word later on. Yet, looking back, I can't remember the details of our dialogue. I can only remember feeling bonded to this stranger as we sat touched by the same breeze, sharing the air around us. It was an intimacy that I accepted to the very depths of my being. I invited him into my most honest existence and felt him open his secret self to me. I'm pretty sure that if we had had sex, God Almighty Himself would have been impressed.

As unknown as this man was to me, my encounter with him was familiar, comfortable, almost predictable. He was at once my favourite pair of jeans and a brand-new pair of shoes. This feeling I knew too well: the one that says I'm home, I'm safe, I wouldn't have it any other way. But just as I was lulled into the soothing calm of it, familiar exploded into recognition with a searing flash of pain, a blinding, burning agony that stopped my breath for a moment that lasted a lifetime. The memory of something as simple as being one with another human being, deeply, truly linked together on some inexplicable mythical level, a privilege I hadn't enjoyed in three years, stopped my heart cold. And, as I had countless times before and since, I wished with my entire soul that it wouldn't start again. *Please, I want out. Please...*

But life is cruel, and distraction is its minion. We were interrupted quite abruptly by a giant fat raccoon that waddled across the parking lot in front of us. We both stopped and watched, without comment or surprise. The mid-sized beast traipsed by with an air of entitlement that had me thinking perhaps I should at least offer a slight head-bow of acknowledgement. In the minute it took for him to pass in silence, there were three of us in the world: me, the man, and the raccoon. At once, the most insignificant and most indispensable beings ever created by Nature: three nameless creatures, aware of each other, together in the same space and time, connected on some level. But separate. Interacting but apart, affecting each other, but leaving no lasting change. A moment in the history of the universe that would never come again, couldn't be repeated, that was both inconsequential and memorable. Anonymous. But not invisible.

As suddenly as he'd arrived, the wee beasty was out of sight, returned to the darkness, and the moment vanished with him.

Without another word, I simply got up, gathered my things, and returned to my room. I closed the door, lay flat out on the bed, and slept, weightless, dreamless, motionless, straight through til morning.

When I woke, he was gone. I came outside to find door number 6, open and blocked by a cleaning cart, the sound of muffled curses within from whoever was restoring the room for the next random traveler. Without much thought about it, still dressed from the night before, I loaded my stuff and me into the van and let the vehicle creep its way slowly along, listening to the popping of the gravel under the tires as I went, to the driveway that would take me back to the two-lane highway that had brought me there three days before. Without hesitation, I turned right, into the unknown.

Making Memories

I was well past, what was for me, uncharted territory; I had never been north of Barrie, and Barrie was a couple days ago. Any trips we'd taken as a family were camping trips to local conservation areas. When the kids were small, a forty-minute drive in a packed car to Valens or Turkey Point was all the adventure we could tolerate. Five of them and a dog against the two of us was a crap-shoot at best.

Nate and I always seemed to be on the same page when it came to the kids. We were naturals against the Divide And Conquer scheming our begats began to test us with. We never fell for their conniving little tricks - except maybe where Gilda was concerned. That Little Pumpkin had Daddy wrapped around her chubby little finger from the moment we found out she was a girl. She could do no wrong.

It never mattered that I could prove that she had planned and manipulated to get what she wanted. Some expert along the way told us that her extra twenty-first chromosome would prevent her from being able to reason at that level: a myth I would soon see eradicated from our existence. But as far as Dad was concerned, her halo was golden and that was that. The fact that she was indeed the sweetest soul ever to grace humanity just meant that we all loved her more for it, and none of us ever begrudged her the special bond she had with her dad.

I worried about it for a half a minute once, asking the boys if it ever bothered them that Dad was such a pushover for their sister. They assured me that, no, it didn't. After all, they had no problem using her to their advantage when they wanted something. So, it was all good.

As parents of five kids within five years of each other, we were lucky that we never seemed to quit on the same day. One of us was always All In. And I think that made it all work.

It didn't, however, make it all easy.

There were moments of perfection. Immeasurable pockets of time where the stars aligned, the universe calmed, and I was witness to the closest thing to Heaven I could imagine. Seconds, minutes, sometimes even a day or two, where everyone and everything was exactly as anyone could have ever hoped, happy, loving, living in a utopic bubble of rapture. I think of these moments sometimes. And I am awed by the sheer power of them to take me back to that place and time, in that moment, when everything was right in my world. I can visit any one of these treasures and find my peace. But like the moments themselves, too soon, the trance is shattered when the Proverbial Shit once again hits the Fucking Fan.

So it was, the day of Gilda's Big Adventure.

We were camping. Not so much because I *liked* camping – I mean, who wouldn't prefer a cruise? But it was cheap and doable, and I didn't really mind it. I was fortunate that Nate and the boys decided early on that most of the *work* of camping was man's work, and there were plenty of hands for that. Tents went up quickly, stuff was unpacked readily, plans were made swiftly. Nate loved the chance to really get down and dirty with his sons, and any time we could get away like this ultimately made for some good stories after the fact. They would go fishing and hiking, exploring and learning, always returning filthy and hungry and busting with news of their adventures.

Of course, while they'd be off meeting the world, I enjoyed the peace and quiet of time with Gilda, especially when she was younger. She was as curious as any of her brothers, but the learning was slower, more intense. Time with her one-on-one was time that almost stopped with the tedium of repetition and simplicity. I'd learned that advertisers will repeat their message six times for the average person to get it. The average child retains it after sixty reruns. Gilda needs six hundred. Me, being a Person Of No Patience, found that the reward of seeing that cherub face light up with understanding made the expense of time and effort on my part worth every tear I shed for her. Watching her try until she physically could no longer hold her little body upright, and then wondering at her determination when she would continue where she left off upon waking again, I realized that I could put in no less effort. I had no idea in the beginning how much our combined struggles would pay off; I even look at her sometimes now, second-guessing whether I could have pushed her harder. But I suppose the facts that she reads and writes and has friends and school and a job, and is now bugging to get her driver's license, add up to some kind of success. For both of us.

While Nate had the boys out, Gilda and I would tidy up the campsite, make ourselves a special lunch, go for a walk, take a nap. The fresh air and peace of the forest always felt mystical to me. Gilda, with her rosy cheeks, chubby hands, and tiny little elven ears added to the magic. She was always her own 'moment.'

We were roasting wieners over the fire, the boys rowdy and reliving the afternoon's fishing adventure that was the reason we were having hot dogs for the third night in a row, when I realized that Nate had not only leaned over on my shoulder uncomfortably from the chair beside me, but had fallen asleep. Peeking through the wilderness-caked spikes of his thick dark hair, I could see the fan of Gilda's soft dark eyelashes on her cheek as she slept deeply on Nate's lap. I watched quietly as the boys began to slow down, and one by one, stop talking, stop eating, and finally give up.

I asked Dan to take Gilda and put her to bed. He was only about ten at the time, but she was a small five. He lifted her gently and carried her off to our tent to sleep. I sent the rest of the boys to bed before waking Nate.

"Hey, where'd everybody go?"

"I sent them all to bed. You tuckered them out."

He turned his face up to me, his full lips stretching into a lazy smile framed by his dark camping beard, eyes still closed. "Other way around, Babe."

"I'll trade you tomorrow. I'll take the kids. You hang out here."

"Mmmm. Somebody wants brownie points."

"Nah. Someone else already took them all."

He nodded. "Me."

"Yeah, you." I kissed him. He let me. "Go to bed Big Man. I'll get the fire and stuff."

He stood up in stages, and shuffled off to bed, but not without a quick, low, unmistakable "Hey!" at the boys' tent, effectively turning the volume down from giggles and yips to whispers and snorts. I packed the food into the car and doused the fire before zipping myself into my tent with my husband and daughter.

A moment.

I woke the next morning, early, with Gilda's pudgy bare foot wiggling sleepily against my right cheek. I grabbed it firmly and planted a big Mom Kiss on the bottom as I started playing with her little piggies. By the time one of them was eating roast beef, she was sitting up and smiling at me, excited to see what this amazing new day would bring.

I put my finger to my lips telling her to be quiet and not wake Daddy. She giggled and hugged herself with the conspiracy. We gathered our clothes as silently as a mom and an enthusiastic cherub can do in a tent and zipped ourselves out.

I let her go wake her brothers while I dished out the cereal and Pop Tarts. Squeals of laughter, not all Gilda's, nearly brought the tent down around them, but one by one they all popped out like champagne corks, complete with noise, mess, and an air of celebration. I packed their lunches while they ate and explained that I was the tour guide for the day.

We were set to go less than an hour after waking, and though I'd warned them to stay quiet and let Dad sleep, they all insisted on hollering a hearty "Bye Dad!!" as we trekked off.

Any hike with Gilda is a lesson in patience for me and the boys. But they had long since mastered the Perpetual Circling that kept them in motion at their own speed while Gilda toddled along at hers. She would squeal in delight as one or more of her brothers would sneak up from behind when she was sure she'd seen him disappear into the trees ahead of her. They never complained about having to slow down around her, and she adored them. Eventually I realized that her trying to keep up with them was what fuelled her determination.

We walked for a while, the boys bringing tiny forest trinkets for Gilda to tuck into her backpack. Acorns, leaves, twigs, pebbles, all made great gifts for Gilda. She would empty the bag and go through her treasures every night at the fire, learning the word for each item, and identifying the brother who gave it to her. It was a game they all enjoyed: one of many they'd come up with on their own to include her.

At last the trail opened up onto the beach where the canoes were kept. There were only two tied to the dock; I'd wanted three so that John, who was now seven, could paddle along with his eldest brother Dan. The canoes were small, two-person craft, and the pond was shallow and just big enough to be able feel like you were lost at sea – if you were a child. When Nate took them fishing, he'd take them out on the lake in a motorboat. They were all good swimmers, but not ready to canoe a lake. I directed them to the shed and got them into life jackets. They barely sat still long enough for my dock lessons before the four boys, Dan the oldest with John the youngest in the red boat, and the twins in the green, were paddling far better than I'd have expected, out into the middle of the pond.

I sat on the dock with Gilda, watching, my heart breaking as it always did when she was sad.

"Me go too," she said quietly beside me, more to herself than to me. She never complained. "Me go too," she whispered.

"Mommy and Gilda go next, Dumpling." I held my hands out, palms up, and wiggled my fingers. "Wait."

Her little pink hands copied mine. "Me go too."

With one eye on the boys, I entertained her while we waited by splashing my feet in the water. She couldn't reach, but never stopped trying. The boys paddled away for quite a while, only needing two reminders that canoes are not bumper cars, until Gilda decided she was hungry. Tapping her lips with her fingers and thumb clenched together, she squealed loudly at her brothers and informed them that it was lunchtime.

They paddled in to the dock quickly and accurately, because, apparently, bologna sandwiches are incentive to mastering a new skill. They ate quickly in their respective vessels, not wanting to waste too much time at a standstill, but as they ate, I gave them the option of choosing which canoe would be traded off to Gilda and me for a quick ride. Poor John looked like he would cry if I tried to remove him from his perch, but Gilda piped in and explained, "Me go too!"

To my surprise, the twins offered up their canoe.

"Do we have to stay right here on the dock, Mom?"

"No, but you have to stay where you can hear me."

"Awesome!" they chimed in perfect unison. The twin thing is real.

Dan and John cast off as the twins climbed out of their boat. I was just getting Gilda strapped into her life jacket when I heard the splash. I looked up and two wet heads bobbed up out of the water with identical expressions that were a cross between, 'we didn't do it' and 'what the heck just happened???'

Moment gone. Adventure begun.

"Are you guys okay?" I called to them.

They both realized they were swimming and safe, but were quite far out, with a canoe that was now upside down. "Yeah!" Dan was laughing. John was still deciding between laughter and tears.

"Can you swim back to me and pull the canoe?"

"We'll try." Dan encouraged John as best he could. I watched while they swam their skinny little hearts out, but the canoe had other plans.

I thought through my options quickly. I could swim out and help them tow it, but that would leave Gilda by herself on the dock. I could leave the canoe and have the boys swim in. But chances were, I'd still have to at least tow John in. I could paddle out and... Well, that plan didn't go any further. I was going to have to get in and teach the boys how to flip a canoe.

I called the twins back to me and explained the problem. Not knowing how long it was going to take, I decided my best bet was to send the twins back with Gilda to let Nate know we were a little stuck. Backup and three kids out of the way seemed like a good idea.

I showed them the way back to the campground road; they just had to round the dock behind the shed and the gravel road was right there. We'd come through the trails on this side and taken hours. I'm sure they thought we were miles and miles from home, when, in reality, we were only a five-minute walk down the road from our site.

"Take Gilda back to our campsite and tell Dad what's happened. I'll get the boys and the canoe out, and we'll be back in a little while."

"Okay," they agreed together.

"Can we go play then?"

"Sure. Just take Gilda to Dad and tell him I said it's okay. And make sure you stay close enough that you can hear Dad. Don't wander off. Or you won't get supper." That threat was a good as a chain leash for these two.

Gilda was not impressed.

"No, me go boat."

"I'm sorry Sweetie. Next time. We'll come back tomorrow. Boat ride tomorrow, Gilda."

"No Mommy. Me go boat."

"No Peanut. You go see Daddy."

"Mooommmmm." Determination with a hint of threat. It was hard not to laugh when she was both so adorable and so angry.

"No. Go with your brothers." I shot them a quick look of 'make it look like fun dammit!'

"Come on, Gilda," they started running around her. "We'll race you!"

Her little pout loosened up a touch.

"Come on, Gilda, we'll 1-2-3-Wee you!"

And she was gone. I watched as a pair of bookended 8-year-olds grabbed their little sister by the armpits, counting 1-2-3 and lifting her forward about a half a foot on the Wee! It was enough. They headed off behind the shed.

I turned my attention to the heads still bobbing happily across the pond. No help for it, I jumped in and swam easily to them, and proceeded to show them how to right a canoe by yourself in seven easy tries.

I'd forgotten about the fork in the road and realized too late that we'd taken the long way back, so the three of us sloshed into our quiet, empty campsite cold and hungry as the sun dipped below the tops of the trees. I was sure that once they were fed and warm around a fire that night, John would be the lead storyteller with his Tale Of The Tippy Canoe.

I sent the boys to their tent to dry off and change while I lit the portable propane bbq that was our stove. Without waiting for it to preheat, I dealt out a dozen burgers across the grill to cook while I found some dry clothes. After a lengthy – mostly because it was a rare *private* – trip to the outhouse, I unzipped my tent, loudly cursing Nate for leaving his shoes right in the way.

My cursing was promptly drowned out by Nate's cursing for my landing square on top of him as I fell over his shoes.

One minor but fervent wrestling match later, we crouched, breathing heavily, staring at each other with classic WTF Faces.

"What are you doing jumping on me like that?"

"Since when do you ever sleep in the middle of the day?"

"I went in to town to the store. When I got back, no one was here, so I took a nap!"

"I tripped over your shoes again! If you would put them away…!"

"You know they're always there! If you would look where you step…!"

At this point, autoplay took over. We'd had this conversation a thousand times.

I started rifling through my bag for warm, dry sweats while he tried to maneuver out of the way. He finally seemed to notice that I was wet.

"Go for a swim?"

"Not on purpose," I muttered trying to get my fat head back out of my sleeve.

"Fall in?" I could hear him smiling.

"Nope. Your sons did. They tipped the canoe, so I had to right it and tow them and the boat in."

"But, did you look good doing it?"

"I did," I grinned, still buried in my shirt. "Once I started swearing that mofo flipped right over for me. I think they're impressed."

"With your skill or your language?"

"Shut up," I managed clearly as my head popped out through the right hole, admittedly looking more like Cousin It than me. "Burgers are on, and I'm starved." I could hear Dan and John rooting through the cooler just outside.

Nate stood hunched between me and the door. "I got this." He poked through my hair like he was shucking corn and kissed me happily before zipping loudly out of the tent. I finished dressing, thinking how lucky I was. I saved my kids. And now they and their Dad were getting food ready for us to eat. A moment.

Shit, meet Fan.

Dan and John had the table set before I got out there. Nate was turning hamburgs into cheeseburgs. I pulled the covered tray of fixin's out of the cooler and filled water glasses. Nate was singing quietly – or trying to - flipper in hand. Poor Gilda had inherited his complete lack of musicality. For someone who loved music as much as he did, Nate was destined to forever be the audience. Gilda, however, loved to share and did so as loudly and as often as possible. Her brothers had discovered that they could pass great gobs of time locked in a minivan trying to Name That Tune as Gilda sang happily with her headphones on.

I hugged Nate from behind, sliding my still ice-cold hands up under his shirt and stealing his heat. He startled as he always did but didn't push me away.

"Call the twins, will you?"

I felt the sound of his voice as he bellowed in his sternest Dad Yell, "Eugene! Martin! Supper!"

"Gilda too," I reminded him as I moved to stand beside him.

"Gilda! Supper! I'm surprised you let them take her," he leaned on me, his arm across my shoulders.

"I'm surprised *you* let them take her."

"I didn't *let* them anything. They were all with you."

"I sent them back to you when Dan and John fell in the pond. They were supposed to leave her with you."

"I never even saw them. I thought they were with you the whole time."

We looked at each other as something very big started rearranging my insides.

"Martin!! Eugene!! Gilda!!" he hollered, handing me the flipper and moving to the middle of our campsite, peering closely into the bushes around it.

A loud Ouch! and its responding giggle pulled our attention to the bushes between the tents, after which we were promptly rewarded with the sight of our darling pair of twins, both covered in dirt with twigs in their hair. I watched the bushes as they approached. The monster in my belly had a friend.

"Where's your sister?" I asked them, terrified.

"She's with Dad," Gene assured me.

I looked at Dad. He shook his head.

"What do you mean she's with me?"

"We put her in the tent with you for a nap," confirmed Marty.

I ran back to our tent, searching like an idiot through the sleeping bags. She's tiny; maybe we missed her.

No Gilda.

I couldn't breathe. The tears were instant.

This wasn't the first time we'd lost her. But it was the first time we didn't have store clerks or a nursing staff to help find her.

The next two hours were the most excruciating of my life. Nate and I split up, each taking two boys, searching campsite by campsite, frantically asking the few campers who were there in the middle of the week if they'd seen her. Every one of them dropped what they were doing and joined the search. But after a half hour, we realized we had no clue where she was. I lost myself in some kind of Purgatory Of Insanity as my thoughts jumped from killing myself if she were hurt, to wondering how easy my life would become if she were dead, to Nate leaving me and never forgiving me for this, to my spending my life in jail for letting this happen and never seeing my boys again, to trying to remember what my last *moment* was.

Nate called 911.

Within twenty minutes, officials were arriving.

Volunteer firefighters, park officials, police, neighbours, random people who'd seen the commotion from the highway. Before I even realized how truly horrible our situation had become, there were dozens of people, calm, rational people gathering together, talking, planning, moving, searching for my baby girl.

And all I could do was hold my breath and promise her that I would never be impatient again. I would never fall short. I would never let her down. I would never let her out of my sight. I would never swear or sleep late or slack off. I would never give the easy answer. I would never not take the time. To help. To explain. To teach. I would never breathe again.

I was swept into a search party of six people. We took the trail the kids and I had taken earlier to the pond. The police officer with us wanted to know every detail of our afternoon. What had happened in her day? What was she thinking?

I laughed at that. It was hard enough staying one step ahead of four boys who were always going in four different, but childishly rational, directions. Gilda didn't work that way. Her thoughts were more like fireworks on Canada Day. You never knew what the next one was going to be. Sometimes a dud. Sometimes spectacular. Always colourful. Always exciting.

I could hear dogs barking in the distance.

We came out of the trail at the pond where the kids and I had been that morning. I tried not to think about how many hours she could have been gone already. While the others combed through the bushes and searched through the shed, I relayed our escapades of the day. The boys. The canoes. The boys tipping the damn thing. I should have kept her with me. I should have kept all of them with me. I should have let the fucking canoe go. I should have been a Mom.

I peered through my tears at the pond and tried not to imagine my Sweet Pea lying in the cold mud at the bottom. I tried not to hit the cop's shoes as I puked.

The people gathered, and we headed off toward the road behind the shed, as I'd seen the twins do with Gilda a lifetime ago. I stopped, realizing this was the last place I'd seen her, laughing with glee as her brothers Wee'd her. She'd forgotten she was angry as soon as she'd focused on them. Now she might never have her canoe ride.

"Come on, Mom, they're leaving," Dan pulled my hand gently.

Fucking canoes. What was I thinking? I turned to look back at them, the green one still tied to the dock where we'd left it. The red fucker, the one that had tipped, floating defiantly on the far side of the pond because it had no intention of either staying put or staying afloat. I should have left it for dead.

I let Dan lead me out to the roadway, dazed. I could hear the cop talking, maybe to me, maybe to someone else. I never did find out his name. He was asking something. But in my mind, I was having my own conversation. I was talking to Gilda, asking her to forgive me. Asking her to come home, to sing, to cry, to do something, anything, so we could find her and keep her safe.

All she'd asked for was a canoe ride.

And suddenly I knew exactly where my baby was.

I ran like I've never run before. Back along the road, past the shed, down the dock, and dove hard into the pond. With the strength that is the myth of a desperate mother, one who just dove into a pond wearing a thick absorbent sweat suit, I swam across that pond to the red canoe. Treading water with fire in my legs, I reached for the gunnel of the boat, terrified, unable to breathe. Pulling it down gently, carefully, peeking over the edge, I sobbed as I saw her, her tiny body expanding and contracting with each soft breath, the dark fan of her eyelashes on her cheeks, burnt pink from the sun. I took the rope and towed her back to the dock.

A thousand hands reached down to me and pulled me from the water. The canoe was lifted on to the dock, and the cop dipped into it, lifting my sleeping daughter up into his big strong arms. She snuggled into him, dozing soundly as only Gilda could.

"Look Mom," Dan said, handing me her little backpack from the canoe, along with her teddy bear. I looked past him, seeing two empty Pop Tarts wrappers and two empty juice boxes. "She took Jerlet on a picnic." *Jerlet*. Gilda for *Charlotte*.

"You're a good Mom," I felt the hand on my shoulder and turned to the cop.

I just shook my head. I didn't think so.

"But she's wearing a life jacket, Mom. It's upside down, but it's on."

And with that I lost my shit.

Cell phones clicked, whistles blew, dogs barked. All around me people were talking, cheering, crying.

Then Nate was there, holding our daughter, holding me, our boys all clinging to us.

By the time we climbed into our sleeping bags, it was well after midnight. And we were understandably exhausted.

"I love you more today than yesterday, you know."

I didn't think I had any more tears. "But I lost our daughter."

"She was never lost, Babe. She knew exactly where she was the entire time. She had herself an adventure. Just like her brothers. All we've ever wanted was for her to be just like the other kids."

"Careful what you wish for…"

We packed the next morning and headed home, having had enough adventure for a while. A month later, Nate came home with a giant black beast of a dog. A year-old Newfoundland rescue. We named him Appa, because the boys liked the way Appa looked after The Avatar. Nate trained him and had him certified as a therapy dog. And Gilda was never alone again.

I'd driven another entire day lost in thought, grateful for the library of truly good memories we'd created as a family. It was easy to lose myself in the happiness of my old life. Easy and addictive. I'd been spending a lot of time there. The therapist said I was avoiding. The therapist said a lot of things I didn't want to hear.

From the day that everything changed, *my* life was gone forever. It was hard to explain to everyone; their lives pretty much went on as they had before. The kids kept their friends, their jobs, their schools. Their futures would scroll on very much the same as they had before. I would make sure of that.

Our friends and family would carry on, thinking of us as we passed through their busy lives and minds, only feeling the heartache when they stopped to think about it.

My life, however, was completely, suddenly, and inextricably derailed. My entire future, every single minute of my days, weeks, years, was changed. One minute I'm working away at the business of living: running errands, cleaning house, tracking kids, paying bills. And in the time it takes to breathe a deep breath, Nate's last, everything I knew and loved and expected and wanted and hoped and enjoyed was gone. In the span of a heartbeat, I lost my friend, my confidant, my protector, my supporter, my co-conspirator, my comedian, my strength, my lover, my love. The 'til death do us part' clause in the vows was now a reality - with the finality of an atomic bomb. For all the condolences and sympathies and thoughts and prayers, there is no one who fully *gets* the depth of my loss. I am more alone than I have ever been in this life.

It's so much more than the loss of the person. It's the loss of everything *he* loved. The movies, the big family gatherings and parties, the camping trips, the concerts, the fun. I don't eat peanut butter anymore. I don't go to IKEA. I don't watch football. There are no more Christmas shopping trips to the specialty store to splurge on all the flavoured K-cups for the holidays. No more reunions with the old neighbours. No more nights out making a donation to the casino.

But it goes deeper than that. Without my connection, I became a tolerated presence around the television station where he worked, eventually realizing that all I was doing was triggering everyone's grief. They could escape it, remembering him on key days. They would post and comment online. They seemed genuine. But the truth is, when I lost Nate, I lost all of his people, too.

For a while I was busy with the business of closing a man's life. The paperwork and phone calls, the lawyers and doctors. Transferring accounts and property into my name, cancelling his credit cards and social media. For about a year, it was a full-time job.

The distraction of being busy kept my grief at bay while I helped the kids through theirs. But at the end of a year, that magical year when all the movies have the widows looking for new husbands, I had never even crossed over to the other side of the bed. I was still setting the table with an extra place setting. The radio in the car was still set to his favourite station.

A year in, and there was no marital 'parting' for me. I'd accepted that I would be married to a ghost forever. I would still talk to him regularly even though, despite everyone else's conviction that 'he's still with us,' I'd never 'felt' him around. But it made me feel better having someone to yell at.

But I didn't just lose my husband. I lost me.

I had no idea what I liked anymore. Or what I wanted. Or what to do or how to move forward or whether I even wanted to. To be perfectly honest, there have been many times when I've resented my kids for anchoring me to this life against my will. I figured if I just backed the van into a snow bank and went to sleep with the windows up and the engine running, maybe I'd never wake up. And it would look like an accident, so they'd be okay. I set a date to give it a try, picking a date not too close to holidays or bad weather, settling my affairs and getting everything organized and ready in the meantime. I'd see how I felt when the time came. In the last two years, I've postponed five times. My next scheduled appointment with The End was three weeks after this milestone birthday. Far enough apart so the kids wouldn't be connecting my beginning with my ending.

I still have the work of running a family. And it keeps me busy. But I began to wonder if this is all there is. I can't stand the idea that my life, the one and only, the greatest gift of all, is only worth this petty servitude to my children. And if that's the case, what the fuck am I going to do when they're grown and gone? Even Gilda will move on one day. Then I will not only be alone but finished. *That* date is penciled in.

And it's getting closer.

Dan was already finished school and working in an engineering firm. The twins would be going into their fourth year of university in the fall. John would be starting and was already gone most of the time working and squeezing in as much time with friends as he could. Come September, it was just going to be Gilda and me and Nanny in the house. At 82, Mom's memory had started to fail, and I was getting a good idea of what kind of child she'd been. She moved in with us when the twins left for school. Nanny not only had no filter, but she had the discretion of a sailor on leave. Made things interesting if I was up to it. But mostly, I was beginning to have little guilt-filled fantasies of Life-After-Nanny. With just us girls in the house, I felt like all of my fun had been taken away.

The days began to feel darker, as if every day was cloudy. Spring had held no hope for me this year. I didn't bother planting the flowerbeds. I hadn't opened the pool. And the whole house had started to reek of old. Old people. Old furniture. Old musty dreams.

I was cleaning shit out of the carpet. The smell had actually wakened me. Somebody had diarrhea. In the living room. And as I scrubbed through the tears, I realized I didn't even know whose shit it was. Gilda, Nanny, or the dog?

I sat looking at the pile of dirty rags and bucket of shitty water. The crack in the blinds took that moment to allow a dull but annoying pinpoint of light to stab me in the eye. Morning then.

It was my birthday. I was now fifty years old.

An hour later, I was killing a cat in the driveway.

Four days after that, I was standing in a Walmart in Thunder Bay trying to decide which charger to get for my phone, while in the back of my mind, there was an odd little tingling feeling as if something were trying to get my attention. A feeling more than a thought. If I had to describe it physically, it was like a penlight seen across a mirror calm lake on a moonless night. It was moving, trying to get me to focus on it. But the more I tried to look at it, the harder it was to see. If I had to name it, I'd call it – luck. But that didn't make any sense at all.

Making A Statement

I found everything I'd wanted at Walmart. I actually grabbed some fruit and a case of water. I didn't know it was possible for anyone to get sick of Pop Tarts and wine, but there you have it. Some sandwich fixin's and a cooler with ice. A sleeping bag, air mattress, and mosquito net so I could turn my van into a tent and save the motel money.

I'd been switching back and forth between what I'd worn when I left and what I'd brought, rinsing out the spare in the bathroom at night. Not wanting to waste the time and money on one tiny load of laundry, I decided I was going to buy myself a whole new wardrobe. *Because, W! T! F!*

I found my favourite XL white cotton granny panties and a new white sport bra. *I'm okay with the uniboob look.* The men's 3-pack of large white t-shirts and store brand athletic shorts in black, blue, and grey. A new pair of sneakers and a 6-pack of white ankle socks. I felt absolutely decadent!

Some trash can liners to control the mess in the van, my preferred one-ply toilet paper, wet wipes, and a phone charger, and I hit the limit of my mental budget. I reached the checkout, not sure if I was disappointed or relieved to find that long lineups at the cashiers were the norm across the country. I picked the shortest line and resigned myself to wait.

I was fourth up. Number One Guy was almost ready to pay, and Number Two Chick was putting her things on the counter, when a pretty young woman – girl maybe, about eighteen or nineteen - cut in front of me. She didn't ask permission or make eye contact, she just tucked in. I was in no hurry, and she had nothing with her; I just figured she was getting a magazine or something, so I said nothing. No harm in being the nicer person, I thought.

Everyone moved up one, and as I was about to cross the threshold into the official cash line aisle of Impulse Purchase Hell, the front of my cart was bumped noisily to the side by what I can only describe as The A-List Star of the People Of Walmart YouTube Channel. This decrepit, hunched old fart, with more fingers than teeth, pushed his way past me, his cart overflowing and rejecting boxes and bananas to the floor as he went, muttering on about his bad back, and sore knees, and assuring everyone within earshot that he plainly did not give a 'flying fuck' what anyone thought of him, so we could all just 'fuck the fuck off' and get out of his way.

As I was the one immediately affronted by this Piece Of Shit, I stood up straight, arms out, and in my most intimidating Mom Voice, simply and loudly commented, "Wow!"

I am the mother of five teen and twenty-something kids – a total of one-hundred-and-three concurrent years of parenting experience. I know how to use my voice to control virtually any kind of riotous behaviour in an instant. I have a Stink Eye worthy of any prison's Medal Of Honour. But here, on this day, in this place of all places, I met my match.

I hate to call him a man and insult every decent man on the planet by association, but, technically, he had a pair of basketballs in those baggy ass filthy jeans.

He turned on me, with no effort to keep our conversation private, and ripped a stream of vile at me that stunned me with both surprise at its venom, and, on some deep level, awe at its force.

"Wow? Wow?! You fucking cunt of a whore think you're better than me?! Fuck you Bitch! I don't owe you anything! You don't count for shit! FUCK YOU!"

My eyebrows were locked up in my hairline. In my entire life, I have never been speechless. Not that I didn't know what to say. Oh, plenty of options were popping up. I felt like a freaking Terminator as they scrolled through my mind!

'Oh, I'm sorry, I didn't realize how old and pathetic you are. You have no time left to waste, please, go ahead.'

Or, *'Apparently, you've forgotten a little thing called manners. I'd have let you in, and you wouldn't have had to make a complete ass of yourself.'*

Or, *'Awwww, did we get our little pecker caught in our zipper this morning?'*

I just couldn't pick one.

"I don't know you! I don't know any of you!" he tried to engage the entire store. "I'll never see you again, so I don't give a fuck what you think! Fucking bitch," he mumbled to the girl, whom I now assumed to be his granddaughter, sent to hold the place in line for him. She hugged him and my heart softened a touch. My mom is older now, her memory fading worse by the day. She is not the same person she used to be. It happens, and I could only hope that when my time comes, people are as patient with me. I was glad I hadn't risen to his challenge and tried to sting him back. I moved over an aisle into the next line.

"Yeah, fuck you Bitch!" looking right at me past other shoppers who all had the same look on their faces as I did. "I'll never see you again, right?"

You're asking me a direct question, like you want me to participate in this little nightmare of yours?

"Right?!" he demanded.

Feeling compelled to answer as he waited, I matched my grin to his and simply told him, "I certainly hope not." It was satisfying to hear muted, though useless, snickers around me.

I'd turned myself away from him so as to avoid any accidental eye contact but couldn't resist a sneak peek at what he was up to a minute later.

If I thought I was unprepared for his attack on me, it was nothing compared to the shock of witnessing him, body pressed close up against – oh please, don't let it be – his granddaughter, her face cupped in his hands, as he bent to her and kissed her – on the mouth!!! – as if they were home alone with a bottle of Dom in front of the fireplace. Something tried to crawl up out of my stomach.

I moved over another lane.

As I buried myself within the walls of chocolate bars, razors, batteries and magazines, I caught the eye of the baby in the cart ahead of me and all was forgotten as she and I played a resounding game of peek-a-boo, to the clear and obvious relief of her frazzled mom. The little butterball waved bye as her mom pushed her toward the exit, and I turned my attention to the checkout screen, because checkout accuracy is everyone's responsibility.

Cringing a little at the idea of spending almost a hundred and eighty dollars on nobody but myself, I decided I was okay with it. I was so okay with it that I punched in for another hundred dollars cashback. I left with the final satisfaction of passing ZipDick on the way out, still bagging his groceries.

I arranged my stuff into the back of my van. loaded up the cooler, and grabbed the bag of grapes for the drive. I started up the engine and, while I waited for the air-conditioning to kick in, I cracked open the phone charger and plugged it in. I sat deciding whether or not to plug the phone in as I cooled down, and realized it was buried in my bag in the back. So, I left it there.

I pulled forward through the empty parking space in front of me and turned left out into the laneway to leave. Three cars up from where I'd parked, there was a half-filled shopping cart sitting all alone behind a little red sports car. My first thought was that someone might have fallen or had a heart attack and was lying on the pavement between the cars. I slowed to a crawl and looked as carefully as I could but saw no one. I passed the cart carefully, thinking there must be a couple hundred dollars' worth of groceries in it.

Well, not my circus, not my monkeys.

I rolled past about another twenty cars when I spotted him. Wrinkly ass sticking glaringly out of the faded dirty jeans, the top half of him was hidden in his trunk, the car bouncing more than even ancient shocks should allow as he moved things around. He stood and turned, reaching for more groceries from his cart, but it was gone.

I couldn't stop the smile.

He looked around, angry, obviously searching for The Someone who'd taken it.

I had the van at a crawl as he spotted his stuff, a good hundred yards behind me. I could see the bright green watermelon in the baby seat through my mirror. He stomped off after it, his mouth cursing whatever Grocery Gods had seen fit to abscond with his goods. Before I'd even decided, I did it. I pushed the button and the auto-open had the window all the way down before he got to me. I couldn't hear his stream of verbal filth because *someone* was laughing so hysterically that the sound filled the sunny summer day like a good whiff of fresh baked bread. He looked at me as he passed, and I saw recognition spread across his face. Recognition and an anger that should have had me trying to find Holy Water to douse him with. He was about to say something - I can only imagine what more he could possibly have to share with me - when he broke into a lopsided run behind me. I watched through the rearview mirror as the cart began to move again, encouraged by the impressive power of the invisible air around us. The basket cooperated almost eagerly, wobbly wheel and all, reaching break-neck speed down the aisle. Whether it hit a stone, or a wheel just gave out, the cart hitched loudly, left the ground for the split second it took to tip it on its side, and crashed to the blacktop, skidding with a tooth-shattering clash of metal on asphalt. Plastic bags do not make good seatbelts. Milk, bread, maxi-pads (*whew!*) flew through the air. Cans of soup cracked with the dead weight of new dents on nearby cars. It was bedlam!

Trying to drive through the tears, I rounded the aisle at one end and had no choice but to drive down the next for one more look. The scene unfolded like comic outtakes after the credits: an addled man who could have been eighty, or Forty-On-Crack, belching obscenities, arms flapping like a crazed gorilla, feebly kicking the shit out of an upturned shopping cart, its wheels spinning in the sunshine, spurring him on with their squeaky peals of 'Is that all you got?', random groceries puked out of ripped plastic bags, splayed across the laneway in a delta of pantry sediment, and a giant watermelon rolling steadily down the aisle, making a quiet getaway.

It was late afternoon, too late to continue on, but I didn't want to stick around, still feeling the nasty aftertaste of my Close Encounter with Mr. Despicable. I stopped for gas and asked the young man at the cash if he knew of a good place within an hour or so to camp for the night.

He mumbled something like 'Kaka-kaka,' and asked me if I'd like anything else. Wondering if he maybe had some kind of stutter or something, I bought a scratch ticket and decided to wing it. Waiting for an opening in traffic to pull out of the gas station, the asshat behind me honked, because, apparently, his judgment was infinitely superior to mine. So, I opted for a considerable increase in my comfort level for Acceptable Merging Distance and pissed him right off. Of course, it was a childish attempt to regain some iota of control over what was quickly becoming my own virtual Hell On Earth. I'd had nothing but fuckedy fucked-uppedness since I'd left. And I was tired of it. At least, tired enough to throw some good old passive aggressive bullshit back at it.

I made my left turn, and the God in the Orange Camaro roared out right behind me. I signalled and changed lanes safely to the outside lane, as I saw him do likewise in my rearview. I settled into the right lane, and he pulled up alongside me to my left, levelled up with me, and opened his window. I looked over at him, made eye contact, and blew him a kiss.

I have no idea what his actual reaction to that was outside of the stunned expression that popped up on his face, but he gunned his engine and took off. Within about three seconds, he was out of sight. I shrugged to myself, confident that if this little bit of road rage ever ended up before a judge, no one could fault me. I was just trying to keep the peace.

Fifteen minutes later, I noticed a big green sign promising the Provincial Park Peace and Tranquility of Kakabeka Falls.

No stutter then. Just confused hearing.

I pulled in and set up camp in the minivan, finally remembering to plug in my phone. I ate slowly and settled in for a night's sleep in the fresh breeze and hypnotic din of a lot of water falling over a high cliff somewhere close by.

Packing up in the morning was as simple as gathering up the mosquito netting and closing the van's rear hatch. I stopped at the park house on the way out to wash up a bit and change my clothes and snapped a few pictures of the most surprising landmark I'd ever seen. The falls were far bigger than I'd thought, and powerful. All the majesty of Niagara without the crowds and city. I stood for a long time, watching the water leap over the edge. I picked a small piece – a crest or a dip or a fold – and followed it over and down for as long as I could see it. Mesmerized, I started again, following the flow to the limits of my vision, and again, over and over, until my breathing seemed to harmonize perfectly with the life of the river before me. My mind emptied, enjoying the rapture of nothingness until at last a shiver snaked its way from the crown of my head to the backs of my knees, the cold dampness seeping deep into my bones. I looked around. It was an overcast day, but I couldn't tell if it was drizzling or if I was just coated with the spray of the falls. Either way, I was the only person in sight. It's a wonderful sensation to have the entire world to yourself by choice.

I drove away reluctantly, the van's heat system warming me slowly, curious as to what other new things I would see on my travels. I took the calm of the solitude with me. And I wasn't in the least bit surprised to see that, on starting up my phone for the first time in five days, there was not a single missed call. No texts. Nothing that required my attention, and so none was given. I breakfasted happily on a fresh fruit bowl and bottled ice coffee as I headed west.

Making Good With The Neighbours

I rolled into Winnipeg around suppertime. Early suppertime with the time change. I now had access to my data on the phone, so finding a campground was easy enough. I decided on a reliable, predictable, franchised campground just off the highway right on the Assiniboine River. When I checked in, the guy told me I could have my pick of sites since the place was basically empty.

My expectations for a pleasant stay dropped a notch, but not because I wanted a crowded resort: more because I wondered why the place was so unpopular. It was July in Manitoba and it turned out that I was one of five visitors in this huge campground. *Oh well, how bad could it be?* I set up my makeshift tent in the back of the van and tidied up my mess from the neglect of a full day of living and driving. I collected a bag of garbage and dutifully took it back up the road to the last garbage can I'd seen on the way in.

The campsites, if you could call them that, looked more like slots at a drive-in movie. They were lined up between and along the sides of two parallel roads that ran the length of the dirt and stone field that made up most of the camp. I assumed the two paths joined out of sight at either end creating a racetrack of sorts that would be great fun for the teenaged boy who grinned at me mischievously through a mouth full of braces as he passed on an ATV. *I love teenage boys. Not in a creepy way. Just because they can be so damn funny.*

On the way back to the van, I was greeted firmly by a robust ball of a woman who was just stepping out of a midsized RV parked three sites up from mine. "Hello there, Neighbour," she commanded with the full expectation that I would stop and talk with her. "I'm Nancy. We're from Saskatoon," she continued, adding a few more O's to the word than was absolutely necessary. "Where are you from, Hon?"

"Hamilton," I mumbled dumbly.

"Oh, I love Hamilton. Yeah. Beautiful city. Doesn't smell as bad as everyone says. Flew in there once for a wedding. Nice place to get married I suppose. Too bad your football team stinks so bad though." She winked at me, I guess assuming I was a fan and not wanting to offend me too badly. I had no idea how they were doing these days; I didn't watch anymore.

"I like it, it's home," I offered, not sure whether I wanted this conversation, nor whether it even was one.

"Roger!" she called back over her shoulder. "Come meet the Neighbour Roger!" She turned back to me. "You'll like Roger, my husband. He's a funny guy. Likes to talk. Just tell him to shut up when you've had enough." She winked again. Maybe it was just a twitch.

"I was just going to get a bite to eat," I started, trying to make a getaway.

"Oh, nonsense Hon. Who are you with?" she peered around the end of her rig, spying my van through eyes squinted so tight she couldn't have possibly seen anything.

"It's just me," I admitted.

"Well then, that does it. You'll eat with us. You can't eat by yourself. We've got plenty. Roger'll love to have someone besides me to talk to. He's a talker alright. Just gimme a wink if you're too polite to tell him to shut up yourself. I'll quiet him down. Roger!!" she bellowed again over her shoulder.

"No, really, I've got my dinner all ready," hitching my thumb toward the safety of my van.

"Ther's no way it'll be better than whatever Roger's cooked up for us. That man can cook. Cook and talk he does. Worth marrying him just for that I'd say. That and – you know," she winked again. "Doesn't hurt that he's good at that, too."

That forced a smile. Nancy might not have had the manners or grace of a rabid dog, but there was a kind soul in there somewhere, and I couldn't help but like her. Before I even knew what was cooking, I agreed to join them.

She led me over to the picnic table they'd set out for meals, where dishes were stacked neatly in a bin on the end of one bench. We sat opposite each other and set the table as she filled me in on what had scared away all the travellers.

"Yeah, so the waters have already crested and started leaving Saskatchewan. They should be here starting tomorrow. That river there'll probably rise higher than last year, and that was a bad one. Getting worse every year now." She pointed out the water damage I hadn't noticed before: a distinct and obvious line that marked every tree and building in sight as if they'd been sited with a laser level, about five feet above the ground. I tried to imagine the entire campground submerged under a rushing river, the sight of which, right now, seemed as impotent as a leaky juice box. In the distance down the road, I could see the boy with the braces carefully stacking and chaining picnic tables to trees.

"The Army's here now, helping folks sandbag their houses against the flood. Even knowing it's coming, it's still a huge job. Poor families having to go through this year after year. They can't even sell and move. Who'd buy in now?" She was shaking her head in commiseration.

I began to understand the magnitude of it all. These people's lives were here. Their property, their homes, their friends and families, jobs. To just uproot and leave was too much to ask of them. Better to take their chances fighting the inevitable. I felt Nancy's sympathy.

Until the door to their camper burst open with a crash and a grunt, and Nancy jumped up with a spryness I hadn't expected to help her husband carry our dinner out to the table.

Roger was much older than I'd expected. Tall and straight, but grey and limping terribly. If I hadn't known he was her husband, I might have guessed father!

Nancy took the tray from his hands and set it on the table, while Roger hobbled over to seat himself beside her. Once settled in and facing me, I saw that he was nowhere near as old as I'd first thought. His face was lined and tanned from years of working outside, his bright blue eyes twinkled with a mischief that instantly piqued my curiosity about him, and when he smiled, I was greeted with a wide warm smile full of gorgeous even white teeth. I'd have bet dentures for sure if his right upper canine wasn't sitting perfectly perpendicular to the rest. Roger was a very handsome man.

Nancy introduced me as The Neighbour From Hamilton, and Roger nodded warmly, accepting me to his table. I found myself grinning back at the two of them. He took my plate and spooned a huge helping of something that looked quite potatoey and smelled deliciously beefy onto it, carefully plunging a generous chunk of some soft warm magical bread into the mix. I was suddenly starved for a good meal and accepted the company gladly as I listened to Nancy prattle on about practically every topic known to man.

I learned that they'd been married for 38 years. Their three children were grown and had given them seven grandchildren. The pair were recently retired and had decided to let their son move into their house with his wife and kids while building a new home for themselves. Two months into the plan, and Roger and Nancy had thought it better to leave the kids there and travel for a bit. They were prepared to be away until Christmas.

The meal was as satisfying as it promised. At one point, with my mouth happily filled with gravy soaked bread, listening to Nancy describe the process of sautéing the beef before stewing it, for, from the look on Roger's face, what must have been the millionth time in their relationship, I felt that tiny little hint of a feeling again. The light across the lake. It was jostling about a bit more slowly, teasing me, but still not letting me focus on it. As quickly as it took the form of the word *lucky*, it was gone, and my vision cleared once more in time to see Roger nodding seriously, apparently agreeing to sauté from now on.

I watched them, this couple who sat comfortably together, interacting as if they'd been created that way. What a history they had.

I remembered conversations I'd had with Nate. Long talks that had gone on well into the night. About everything. About nothing. Phone calls and text chats. Laughter and arguments. Silence.

A flash of regret washed over me as I remembered more than once letting my anger seethe in the quiet festering of affront. How many times had I stopped talking, giving up because I felt like I wasn't being heard, or because I just didn't want to hear what he had to say? What I wouldn't give now for one minute – one moment, face to face with him, just to tell him I was sorry. *I'm so sorry. I'm sorry I yelled. I'm sorry I went quiet. I'm sorry I doubted. I'm sorry I let you down. I'm sorry I wasn't a better wife. I'm sorry I let you die. I'm so fucking sorry. I'm sorry for all the conversations we missed out on because I was a fool.*

Before I could take another breath, the wind tickled a stray hair from my head across my cheek, under my nose. My face twitched at the itch, and my head tilted to one side, ear to the sky, and I heard the whisper in the breeze as it passed.

We never missed anything. It was one. Not many. Just one.

Nancy's voice reached my mind once more. I wanted her to stop talking.

It must have shown on my face, because it was Roger who put his hand on Nancy's to quiet her and nod to me. If Nancy's expression instantly melted into a reflection of my own, I must have looked a sad sap.

"Oh my, Honey. What happened to you?" she asked, point blank, straight on, with no room for retreat.

I took a deep breath. "I kinda ran away from home," I whispered in my best attempt at deflection.

"No one looking for you?" she asked, while her husband nodded encouragingly.

Four eyes intent on my answer. I felt obligated to respond after we'd shared a meal together. I'd always explained to the kids that a stranger is anyone we've never had supper with. As soon as we've sat at a table and eaten together, they became friends. Worthy of our trust. Invested in our well-being.

Crap.

"Kids'll probably think I ran away. They'll manage. They're capable. I did a good job." I blathered on. "They know I'm mad. They'll avoid me as long as they can."

"How old are they, Hon?"

"Well. Dan's 23 now. The twins are 21. John's 20 and Gilda's 18."

"Ohhh," they agreed, as if they understood completely. *With three of their own, they probably do.*

"And where is their father?" she asked bluntly. "You're divorced then?"

Whoa. That hit a nerve, searing and scratching like a hair dragged across your eyeball. I'd never said it out loud before. I'm not sure why I felt the need to say it now. Was I ready to admit it? I'd been lying these past three years to anyone who didn't already know the truth, who needed to ask. *Yes, yes, I'm married. To a wonderful man. Yes, happily married. Of course.* I hadn't changed my Facebook status. I'd never checked anything but 'Married' on a form. To say it would make it real, wouldn't it? And final. Once I confessed it outside of my own mind, it would be out there, not my secret anymore. I'd never be able to take it back. Why, suddenly, did I feel I had to be honest with these people? I would never see them again.

It was one word. How much punch could it have?

But it's such an ugly word. I never liked it much before it described me. Now it just felt so cold. So separate from the rest of the world. It made me different. It made me a ghost among the living, neither alive nor dead. Someone to be avoided, someone marked, cursed.

The word invited sympathy and discomfort. It sucked the life out of people.

I searched their eyes for understanding, for support for this giant leap of faith I was about to make. If anyone would accept me, surely Nancy and Roger had the capacity and the wisdom to help me through this ridiculous and intense step in my journey into the unknown. Eyebrows rose expectantly.

"Widowed," I squeaked timidly.

And there it was. Hanging in the air between us like a grenade with the pin pulled. I waited for the boom.

"Ahhh, I'm sorry," Nancy nodded as she stood and started clearing the dishes.

I stood to help, but she reached across and patted my hand. "No, no dear. You sit and relax. This is nothing." There was something in her tone that made me plunk my butt back on the bench. She cleared the table in no time at all and ducked inside. I heard the water running feebly in the little kitchen and turned to Roger.

I think he tried to hide it, but I saw the pity. Exactly what I didn't want.

"So where do you think you're heading from here?" he asked, too sweetly, finally permitted to speak in his wife's absence.

"I don't know. I'll decide as I go."

He just nodded, as if that sounded like some kind of sane plan.

We sat in silence listening to Nancy whistle her way through the clinking of dishes and the splashing of water for quite a few minutes.

No questions. No comments. No 'how long has it been?' No 'what happened?'

Because none of that matters.

Because you can define a whole person with one fucking word.

Widow.

Tells you everything you need to know.

Makes every conversation from now on awkward, sad, depressing.

Nancy came back out. "You'll be wanting to go hunker down about now," she suggested. "Another half hour and you won't even be able to walk from here to your place without giving up a pint. These mosquitoes could carry a baby away."

Disappointed to be so abruptly dismissed, but relieved to be able to have my thoughts back to myself, I thanked them both for the meal and their company, wished them good travels, and left them to their evening.

I lay on my air mattress, the air heavy with the summer heat, thinking of the strange duo I'd just met. I imagined the decades of stories they'd written as a team, together, apart, the good, the bad. They'd had their sickness and health. They'd been both richer and poorer. Better and worse. The only bridge they hadn't crossed was the parting of death. My throat closed painfully at the thought.

There is no parting.

In the quiet of my thoughts, I heard the words again. *We never missed anything. It was one. One whole twenty-three-year-long conversation.*

A tiny piece of me, a piece buried so deep inside as to have simply become a part of me, filled and floated like a miniature helium balloon through my heart and into my mind, where I could see it clearly for the first time. Regret. No, not regret. Worse. Self-loathing. For every bad word said between us. Despair, knowing I could never take any of it back. I could never add to it. I could never fix it. Wounds and scars that would never have a chance to heal now. Remorseful memories of mistakes forever left to rot in my memory.

But if it was only one conversation – one long continuous interaction – then every unkind word, every accusation, every disagreement was actually countered with a loving, supporting, genuine commitment. For every 'goddam you piss me off' there were ten 'you know I love you with my whole hearts.' For every minute of anger, there were a hundred of happiness. For every hour of 'life's too busy,' there were days of 'it doesn't get any better than this.'

Over a lifetime together, the good outweighed the bad by a margin that I suddenly realized made the bad all but disappear. If it was really just one long conversation, then we got it right. So very undeniably perfectly right.

The tiny balloon floated away, into the night. I watched it sparkle through tears of relief and release, a microscopic flash of light dancing through my perception, impossible to catch, until it popped, forever freeing my regrets to the universe.

I closed my eyes, surrendering to the wave of feeling that shook me to my soul. A feeling I still couldn't recognize. Couldn't fully identify.

Fucking lucky.

I rolled onto my side and tried to sleep. Through the confusion that filled my mind. Through the disquieting feeling of the air around me. There was no quiet, and in fact, the darkness seemed to amplify my thoughts, my feelings, even the sound around me.

Throughout the night, Nancy's warning took on a sense of reality I hadn't believed possible. The collective buzz of literally millions of the little flying demons was deafening. It droned on for hours, alternating between the silence of being able to ignore it, and the crescendo to intolerable levels of decibelic torture every time it entered my conscious awareness again. Sleep came and went with the cycles, bringing disjointed dreams and the unsettling emotions they left behind, until the sky began to lighten in the east, and I slept deeply at last.

The Widow. Alone. Relieved. Pathetic. Peaceful. Contagious. Lucky.

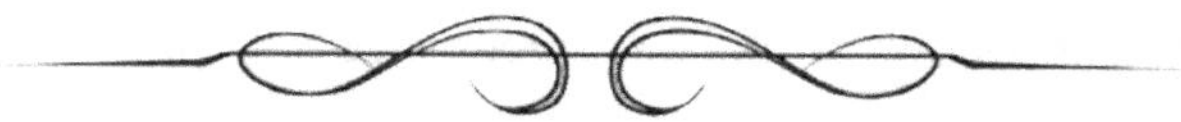

When I woke, I was instantly overcome with a feeling of panic; something wasn't right. I sat up, fumbling awkwardly for my eyeglasses, pushing handfuls of uncooperative hair out of my face. If anything had actually awakened me, it was the silence.

The air was still and heavy, the humidity sticking thickly in my throat making breathing an effort. The trees along the river stood perfectly still, at attention, like soldiers focusing for battle. I listened closely but could barely make out the sound of the river. The night before, I had heard it clearly rushing past, confidently making its way through the park with no concern for the human inhabitants nearby. Now, it was eerily quiet; I thought I could hear it but wasn't altogether sure.

I wondered if maybe Nancy was noticing the subtle changes around us as I peered through the window toward my nearest neighbour. Thinking I'd got myself turned around through the night, I stumbled out of the van to get a better look.

They were gone.

Not just Nancy and Roger.

Everyone. Gone.

I was the only one left.

Feeling a little like Dorothy in Oz, I turned on my heel trying to get my bearings. The park was empty except for my van. And as my head began to clear and I recalled the warnings of the floodwaters coming, I realized that one of the two roads leading through the campground was gone, too. I suddenly had a waterfront campsite.

Shit!!

Following the new shoreline back up toward the exit, I guessed I didn't have long at all before I wouldn't be able to get out.

I drove through most of the rest of that day in my pajamas and bare feet, glad I'd awakened when I had and not an hour later. Glad that the van had started, even though I'd had no reason to think it wouldn't. Glad of the warnings that let me figure things out while half asleep and groggy. Glad of the circumstances that saw me driving safely into the prettiest little municipal campground in Gladstone Manitoba that afternoon.

That night, as I fell asleep in the dry security of my van-tent, a small tree grove away from a surprisingly popular train corridor, I thought of the light across the lake. It was brighter now. Maybe a real flashlight, moving rhythmically back and forth, begging my attention. Trying to tell me something. Trying to make me *see*.

Lucky.

Making A Fool Of Myself

Without having to speak to another living soul, I packed up and left about mid-morning after cleaning up a bit and absent-mindedly eating something bland and cold. I continued west but with a northerly tilt as traffic had been diverted the day before because of flooded roads. Looking straight ahead, the land was so flat I was hard-pressed to figure out how the water could puddle at all, never mind overflow its path. As it was, when I had thought I'd be heading west to Regina, I was actually aiming more north for Saskatoon.

Most of the day alternated between the monotonous endless uneventful forward motion of the prairies, and the nerve-wracking crawl of trying to pass oncoming trucks on less than two visible lanes of roadway without getting run off into a newborn lake. I didn't think even my well-stocked Mom Van could keep me going long if suddenly expected to float.

By the time I reached Saskatoon, I was in dire need of a bathroom and a coffee. I pulled into the first Tim's I saw and headed inside, wishing I could have just opted for the drive-thru. I passed a table where three very beefy men in fluorescent orange shirts and giant heavy work boots were laughing heartily, and accidentally made eye contact with one of them. Some ancient habit made me cringe inside, but Nature Called, so I trudged on into the bathroom.

I will never understand the design considerations that result in a toilet stall that forces an only-slightly-larger-than-normal woman to sit on a toilet, without adequate room to spread her legs far enough apart to allow for proper wiping because one knee is wedged under the gigantic never-ending toilet paper holder, that always seems to be empty, stuck, or otherwise too much work, and the other foot is trapped under the stall divider around the automatic feminine hygiene disposal unit that opens obediently if it thinks one's ample buttock might want to throw something in there. *Seriously guys, if I have to stand on the toilet seat to open and close the stall door, you're in the wrong line of work.* Regardless, after showering myself with a faucet that saw fit to shoot hot water straight out at my navel while leaving my soapy hands untouched, wrestling the paper towel dispenser for a second sheet, and trying unsuccessfully to repair myself enough so as not to offer myself up as another Internet Meme on the way back out, I decided to skip the counter and hit the drive-thru anyway.

As I got to the construction workers' table, a giant foot stuck its way out on the floor in front of me. Glad that I'd been moping, or I might not have noticed it, I eyeballed the owner with my best Stink Eye.

He was actually kind of cute. Rough, messed up from a hard day's work. Long eyelashes and bright green eyes. He was grinning in a cheeky way that hit a nerve I didn't want to feel.

"Hey," he started in a friendly enough way. "Cheer up. It's not that bad."

There was a tiny part of me that wanted to laugh at the irony of the sentiment. But that tiny part was instantly squashed like a ketchup packet under a boy's size 5 boot.

"Can I buy you a coffee, Gorgeous?"

Okay. First off. *Gorgeous?* Fuck off. Who was he kidding? At my best I'm not bad looking. But I have never been 'gorgeous.' And I was certainly *not* at my best at that moment. And second, *um, no.*

"No, thank you," I smiled as warmly as I could. My mood was still in the toilet along with my dignity and enthusiasm. And as cute as this guy was, he didn't even register on my Scale Of Interest.

As I stepped carefully over his foot, I heard him mutter to his friends.

"Bitch."

I stopped dead, still straddling his boot.

Just walk on, urged the voice in my head belonging to The Controller Of The Mental State. *Just walk away.*

I hate that little fucker.

I was tired. Physically, emotionally, tired. It had been days since I'd actually spoken to anyone. A week since I'd seen anyone I knew. A month since I'd had a decent conversation with anyone who knew my name. Years since I'd connected with anyone who cared. I didn't give a shit about this guy. I didn't want to be gorgeous. I didn't even want to be noticed. I *wanted* hide. I *wanted* to run away. I *wanted* out. The frustration, the anger, the growing lump of stone in my gut were weighing me down, drowning me. *This,* I thought miserably, *is why we have gun laws here.*

Mr. Green Eyes was about to understand exactly what the word 'bitch' meant.

"Okay Asshole. I was polite. I *said* 'No, thank you.' All you had to come up with was, 'Okay, sorry if I bothered you.' You might even add 'have a nice day,' you know, if you were leaning that way. Or you could have tried, 'Maybe another time.' That would have got through. Respect. Kindness. Now me and every other person in here thinks you're a douche. You wanna call someone a 'bitch?' Go look in the goddam mirror."

I left.

I was about three steps from the van, ready to drive away and off a cliff – if I could find a bloody cliff in the middle of fucking Saskatchewan – when his calls finally registered.

I turned to find him jogging over to me, hand out between us to ward off my next attack.

"Look," he started before he stopped in front of me. "I'm really sorry. That's not me," he defended pointing over his shoulder with his thumb. "You just looked so, I don't know, broken. There was something about you, I just wanted to help you. Or something. I don't know." His hands were waving in the air between us as he spoke, trying to shape his words. "You just seemed so lost. I forgot where I was and who I was with, and realized too late I sounded like an idiot, and then I guess I tried to save face. And you put me in my place and I'm sorry. I'm not a douche, really." He smiled in the most genuine and harmless way, I couldn't help but feel like I'd overreacted and made a fool of myself.

I tried to answer, but my throat closed and threatened to choke me dead on the spot. *No, no, no, don't cry, DON'T cry, DO NOT cry.* I bit my lip hard. One lone tear broke free and shot down my cheek with the speed and finesse of a finger sneaking a taste of a freshly iced cake. He saw it. I saw him see it. *Fuck. I give a Super-Hero Mic-Drop-Worthy Rant, and then I have to turn tail and run like a weak little woman.*

In that instant, I thought he might just grab me and hug me, and I knew that there was nothing I wanted more than to feel those big strong arms wrap themselves around me, pull me close and hold me. I wanted that kind warm voice to kiss the top of my head and tell me not to worry, everything was going to be okay. I wanted to feel his heart beat against my cheek. A live beating heart thumping with purpose and hope in my ear. A hard chest against my body, holding me up, keeping me from crumbling into the heap of sadness I'd become. Warm breath seeping through my hair to heat my skin, to make me feel like, somehow, I was still alive myself. To bring me back from this dark pit of despair where I now lived. Where the sun never shines, and the birds never sing. Where death now ruled. *Just tell me I'm okay. Just tell me I matter. That you love me. I'm so fucking alone. Please...*

I'd been staring into his chest, the reflective X on his shirt coming into focus. He stepped back, tipping his head forward to get my attention from under his brow. I looked into his eyes; they were kind, concerned. But I couldn't just unload on this stranger here in the middle of nowhere. I managed a nod, offered a slight smile of forgiveness, and turned to get into the van. I saw him watch me drive away and wondered what he must have been thinking about me, forgetting all about the drive-thru and my coffee.

I was glad that the roads in Saskatchewan are as flat and straight as they are. It's easier to drive while you're crying.

Making Things Harder Than They Have To Be

My contact lenses gave out just outside of North Battleford, so I pulled into the Provincial Park to camp for the night. I chose a site tucked as far away from the beaten path as I could get and within an hour, had a fire going under the last two hotdogs in the cooler. I feasted on the last Pop Tart, the last banana, and the last half bottle of wine. I'd have to stop for more groceries in the morning. Whoever had camped there before me had forgotten one of their folding lawn chairs. I cleaned it up and parked myself in front of the fire until it was nothing but coals that a few handfuls of dirt put an end to. I went to bed, exhausted, eyes swollen once again, and fell into the stupor that had become the escape at the end of my days now.

My mind played over the day, and I tossed and turned trying to find something better to fill it with. Sleep played with me, teasing me, blurring the lines between dream and memory.

It was our wedding day. I was puttering around getting ready what I could. My hair was pinned up, I was wearing my favourite baggy old sweatshirt and the matching sweat pants that I'd cut off into shorts. Seated cross-legged on the upholstered bench at the foot of the bed, I was slowly, carefully, going through the process of making up my face, taking care not only to colour inside the lines, but to avoid the temptation of overdoing it and walking down the aisle looking like Bozo The Clown In A Wedding Dress. The mirror was propped up on some pillows on the bed, and it was easy to lose myself in the routine of a million mornings.

My mom's endless patience was on point that day. Every step of the maquillage process was punctuated with my repeated pestering of 'how's that?' 'is this okay?' and 'too much?' And every time I asked, Mom leaned back through the doorway with a smile and a 'yes dear, that's perfect.'

It seemed that everyone was there. It was a huge hotel suite, and the busy of the morning filled it. I thought it was unusual that both my parents were there getting ready. Of course, my sister and bridesmaids were all there. At one point I looked up and caught a glimpse of my soon to be brother-in-law shaving. That was only odd in that I didn't think it so.

But all in all, we were happily preparing for the day ahead, content in our own tasks, aware of each other, but each of us preoccupied.

About the hundredth time I looked up, I caught sight of Nathan in the bathroom, wearing an oversized plush white bathrobe, carefully putting on a pair of generic hotel slippers. He hadn't seen me yet, and it startled me that he was there.

Glancing over at my mom, she tipped her chin up in a silent what's up question.

"Is that him?" I asked her, my mouth moving, but without sound.

She peeked her head around the corner into the bathroom and looked back over her shoulder at me, nodding.

"It is him, isn't it?" I asked her silently.

She stood dead still, watching him.

At that point, his brother, wiping the excess shaving cream from his face stepped back into the room with us. I saw him ask me what was going on.

"Look," I nodded toward Nathan.

Robby followed my stare, dropping heavily into the chair behind him. "I'll be damned," he whispered.

The room went suddenly silent. There must have been a dozen people in there, and every one of us stopped to stare, the question on everyone's lips, "Can you see him?"

Yes. I can.

He looked up and noticed me for the first time. And the smile that spread across his face lit up the room as if he'd just pulled open the heavy draperies to blind me with morning sunshine. My heart stopped. I couldn't breathe; I didn't need to. His eyes were locked onto mine, and the only thought in my mind, filling my soul, was the shear and overwhelming love I felt for him. I felt a warmth melt over me, physically oozing over my skin, embracing my entire body in comfort and joy. I couldn't move. Locked in place, at once ready to explode from both euphoria and terror, I just watched him.

He came toward me, slowly, smiling, and everything and everyone in the room faded from my perception until it was just him and me, inches from each other, here and now, in the same place, at the same time, for the first time, and the last.

He sat carefully beside me as I turned into him, his arms reaching for me. My body reacted out of years of knowing him, melting into his, reaching for his strength, his protection. A flood of emotion, relief, elation, and just as palpable, surrender.

His arms encircled me, enveloping me as he pulled me in, as my body grew heavy. Sinking, weighted. The light from him suddenly began to dim, and my vision began to narrow and blur.

He was right there, about to hold me forever, one more time. But he was fading; I couldn't *feel* him.

And with the sudden realization of what was happening, I felt my heart shatter into dust, my soul screamed to the depths of infinity. I have never felt such searing agony: pain on a scale that eclipses anything a human being is capable of feeling. If it were only my body in torment, it would be bearable. But it was my spirit, the part of me that would never survive this torture. It was my life force that was ripped from my earthly form, torn from me, in the most cruel and barbaric way possible.

I heard myself pleading, crying. *No, No, No. Please, no. Please please pleeeeeease , noooo.*

I was still crying, begging, bargaining with my very soul, as I felt myself waken, only to find myself alone, lying in the dark, again. Losing him all over again. And again.

He was so close. He was right there. Why did I have to wake up? What kind of merciless God takes him away in the first place? What kind of ruthless Almighty lets me get so close to him, only to wake up before I could hold him one more time? To tell him how much I love him, how much I miss him?

There is no God. And if there is, He's an Asshole.

Making Promises

I woke early and was driving before active thinking actually kicked in. I was going on autopilot and, given the feeling of residual gravel under my eyelids, it was some minor miracle that I both managed to move forward in some acceptable fashion and did so without killing anybody.

By the time the sun started peeking in through the front windshield, hours of non-stop tears had cleared most of the debris, though my face once again looked like it'd been hit with a brick. My stomach growled loudly as I passed through Edmonton. A half hour later, it was eating itself. So, I drove through a Dairy Queen in Devon and ordered a large cookie dough Blizzard for lunch. I added a Royal caramel milkshake, complete with whipped cream and a cherry. And a banana split as a side to make it a combo. There's real fruit in a banana split.

I pulled into a random parking area that overlooked one of the multitude of Albertan rivers I was discovering, and nursed my aching soul.

Apparently, ice cream is the Elixir Of The Spirit. If you feel bad enough, there is no amount of the freezing sweetness that can be considered 'too much.'

The last time I had ice cream was the night before Nathan died.

It was his thing. He started it. And as the cold slid down my throat and seeped into my heart, I thought back to him and the first time he'd taken me to The Dairy.

We'd been dating a couple of weeks when he found out about my List. I never intended for him to know about it, but I let it slip, and he ran with it. We were sitting in his car, parked on the Brow, the edge of the Niagara Escarpment, at Sam Lawrence Park overlooking the city. There was still snow on the ground well into Spring that year, but the night was fresh and clear. The leaves hadn't filled in yet, so we had an unimpeded view and could see the skyline of Toronto and the CN Tower across the lake. We sat sipping our coffee watching the lights Down The Mountain, enjoying one of those all-night-chats that come so often during the first weeks and months of an exciting new relationship. Whether we had to get up in the morning or not, whether we had anything in particular to do or anywhere to go, we could spend hours upon hours just talking about something or nothing, sharing our stories, creating a new one. The seeds of fresh love were planted and tending the garden that would be home to our new life together left no room for boredom or fatigue. Neither one of us ever hesitated at the chance to spend time together. Things that he liked to do that I had no interest in were suddenly intriguing when seen through his eyes, and he always seemed as curious about my interests. It never really mattered what we did, as long as we were doing it together. From the beginning, it was easy.

As we sat that night, talking, laughing, sharing, the conversation turned in a way that would set the tone for our entire relationship.

"So, we've been out together pretty much every night for almost three weeks," he started.

I gave him a clear 'Mmm hmm,' in a firm but non-committal tone, not knowing where he was going to go with that one.

"I was thinking…"

"Good to know…"

I saw him grin in profile. "Don't mess me up here."

I grinned back but stayed quiet.

"So, I'm thinking, I'm really liking hanging out with you. A lot. And I was wondering what we call this. What we're doing."

"Mostly it's talking," I offered.

"Stop. No. Like, what do I say to people? Are we dating? Is it serious? I want to make sure I get it right."

"Wait, you're talking to people about me?"

He looked at me, a little startled, suddenly worried. "Yes?"

"Oh. Good. 'Cause my sister was asking me the same thing."

He relaxed a bit. It was so easy to mess with him.

"Well?"

"Well what?"

"Are we dating then?"

"I guess it looks that way, yeah. Is that okay with you?"

"Sure!" he sounded as excited as I could have hoped, then quickly composed himself. "If you're okay with it?"

"Well. So far so good. You haven't bumped off The List yet."

"The List?"

Whoops. I'd never mentioned The List to anyone. Well, not true. Not to *anyone I was dating*. My friends and sister all knew about it. They all thought I was nuts, but I was a firm believer in my plan.

"Um. Yeah. It's just a stupid thing. It's nothing really."

"No, it's not nothing. Tell me about The List."

I looked at him carefully. He wasn't going to let it go.

"It's just a silly thing. I kinda wrote, like, a list. Just what I like and what I don't like."

"You mean you actually wrote down criteria for your dates."

"Well, that sounds a little harsh," I cringed. "But, basically, yeah."

He turned fully in his seat to face me, obviously choosing his next words carefully.

"And what, exactly, is on this List?"

No help for it, he was about to tackle a number of those criteria…

"I can't tell you."

"Yes, you can."

"Okay. I *won't* tell you."

"Why not?"

"Because then you might act different. And I wouldn't know if you're real or not." *Good lord, that wasn't it at all…*

"So, you're saying, it's a test!"

"No!" *Certainly not! Well, yeah, maybe it was.* "Well, kind of…"

"Explain this List to me."

"It's kind of a visualization thing, really. I got sick of wasting my time dating guys longer than I should have just because I felt bad dumping them. And I got to thinking that I should probably decide exactly what I was looking for and call it quits as soon as I was sure it *wasn't* what I wanted."

He squinted hard at me.

I guessed his next question was going to be, 'And how many guys have you put to this test?' But I was wrong.

"And what's the longest anyone has ever stood up to The List?"

"Eight weeks," I told him.

He continued his squint. And finally, "Okay."

"Okay? That's it?"

"Yeah."

He promptly changed the subject. And while he seemed to spend the rest of the evening as if the conversation about The List hadn't even happened, I wondered if I'd gone too far and really screwed up a good thing.

But he asked me out again the next night, and the next, and the next.

I thought he'd forgotten about it.

Until about a month later, when he took me down to The Dairy for ice cream for the first time.

It was warmer and we were sitting outside at one of the round concrete tables happily licking away at our giant cones. The sun was setting. It was a beautiful night.

"So, you know what today is?"

I back-pedalled fast: nothing special as far as I could tell. I shrugged, smiling apologetically through my brain freeze.

"Sunday?" I offered, index knuckle pressing hard between my eyebrows.

"Our *ninth* Sunday."

I looked at him blankly. "So, what is that one? Paper? Stone?"

He laughed. "Good one," he admitted. "No, our first date was 8 weeks ago today."

I had to take his word for it; I was never good with dates.

"Really? Wow." *Seriously, wow. How could two months have gone so fast, and yet I felt like I had known him forever.*

"Yep," he licked on. "So how am I doing against this List of yours?"

I almost choked. I tried to Cough And Avoid, but he was serious and waiting for an answer.

"Um. Pretty good, I guess." I hadn't given The List another thought. In fact, I think I'd decided about a month before that I was going to marry him. "You're still here."

"Good," he said with finality. "Everything okay? Any problems? Any complaints?"

"Nope," I assured him. "All good."

"Good," he declared. "Wanna do another week?"

My turn to squint at him. Except it was more of a smile than a leer. "Sure," I agreed.

"Good."

"Good."

He let it drop, and we enjoyed the rest of our evening walking along the beach.

We'd begun to fall into a routine of sorts. He was calling me at work on my lunch hour. I was checking in with him when I got home. We had a standing date for dinner every night, some nights staying in, others following through on plans, still others just winging it. But every minute with him was fresh and exciting and fun and meaningful.

Until the following Sunday.

We were driving around and somehow ended up coming into Stoney Creek from Grimsby. The next thing I knew, we were ordering cones at The Dairy again. Sitting and licking, he started.

"So. Everything okay?"

He caught me mid-lick.

"Yeah. Everything's good," I smiled.

"Any problems? Any complaints?"

"Nope," I shook my head as a drip of chocolate mint hit my finger.

"Wanna do another week?"

"Yeah, I do."

"Good."

Yes, it was. Very good. Most every single week. For the rest of his life.

He asked me to marry him at The Dairy.

"So. Everything okay?"

"Yeah. Everything's good."

"No problems? No complaints?"

"Nope."

"Wanna get married?"

"Yes. Yes, I do."

"Good."

We honeymooned in the Bahamas. He took me for ice cream the night before we came home.

"So. Everything okay?"

"Oh yes. Everything's good."

"No problems? No complaints?"

"None."

"Still wanna be married to me?"

"Very much."

Every week.

Until the kids came along. We couldn't always make it out of the house once we had babies in tow. Sometimes he'd bring home ice cream. Or a coffee. Sometimes we'd have our weekly chat crashed out on the couch after the kids had gone to bed. Once at the hospital while Dan was getting stitches in his elbow. And more than a few times in the car in the driveway so we could actually hear each other talk.

I had to laugh as I remembered the shittiest one.

The twins were still in diapers and we never did figure out what it was they'd eaten at the birthday party the day before to give them both a case of diarrhea that would rival a pig farm. I caught wind of it first and was chasing down Martin, who had stuck both hands into the Leaking Bucket Of Shit he was wearing, while screaming at Dan to run outside and get Daddy as I continued my pursuit.

It was like trying to swat a fly.

A pesky housefly that consumes your attention until something finally snaps!

You know you want to kill it; it's been torturing you for hours, buzzing around your head, landing on your sandwich, laughing at you. You've shooed it away repeatedly, upping the anger-meter a level every time. Until finally you decide, *ENOUGH!! That's it you little mother fucking fucker, I WILL KILL YOU!!* And some primal instinct deep, deep inside purrs at the idea of being the predator who will now end a life. You don't even bother with the fly-swatter, because you are a Hunter. You are *the* Hunter. And you will be the Master Of The Food Chain because you are the Supreme Life Form on this planet and that little Son Of A Bitch has it coming. How dare he taunt you, the Queen Of The Kill, this way!! You are going to kill it with your bare hand!

You wait. Your mind clears. Your heart rate slows. So slow you can hear it. Ominous. Threatening. A death toll.

You sit motionless, your breathing almost imperceptible. Shallow, but invigorating. You are Zen.

It'll come. It'll fall into your trap. Only your eyes are in motion, guided by your ultra-keen ears, following the sound of the little pecker's wings as he wends his way to his doom.

Until finally, your patience is rewarded, and the little beast lands on the table. Right beside your plate, stalking a breadcrumb, completely oblivious to the threat that awaits him. You visualize your attack. You see the arc your hand will make, clearly etched through the air in front of you, as if drawn by a Master Shifu. You instinctively know the speed you'll need to succeed in your mission. You are ready.

Your brain switches to autopilot. Eons of human experience take over as you watch the event on a timeline that only true animal instinct can achieve. Your hand comes up and over the target zone. Speed, agility, and purpose of The Hunter. And it slams down onto the table, with a force that bounces the plate, sandwich, and full glass of water loudly, violently, toppling them into a mess of battlefield destruction on the floor.

Too late, you realize, that you have failed, and the fly flies free of your assault, free to live another day. Because in the midst of the blitz, somehow, for just an infinitesimal fraction of a second, your civilized human intelligence interfered. In the time it took for light to cross the room, your mind forced you to hesitate, imperceptibly. You sabotaged your quest, because, well, let's face it: Bug Guts. *Ewww.*

Catching a shitty toddler is much the same thing. You know you want to. You know you need to. You know things are only going to get worse the longer you delay. But, ewww. Shit. Everywhere.

I managed to grab a piece of t-shirt as he ran past, chased enthusiastically by his replica. As he squealed with the excited terror that only a person whose age is still measured in months can do when caught by a frustrated parent who is the only one in the room *not* playing the game, I heard an extended insistent grunt, accompanied by the unmistakable rumbling, bubbling rupture of an exploding anus that did *not* belong to the wriggling shit-soaked armload I had just captured, who, upon hearing his brother, broke into ab-crunching peals of laughter that only served to eject what remained within, out, and into my waiting hand.

As my endless whiny *Noooooooooo!* found its way through the house, I heard the backdoor slam and Nathan's booming 'Babe!! What's going on?' precede him up the stairs.

I felt how I imagined people feel when their house is on fire and they hear the sirens coming.

"Catch Eugene!" I hollered as I bolted for the bathroom.

A Far More Adept Hunter Than I, he met me in the bathroom with Shitty Twin #2 a minute later.

A full half hour of washing, rinsing, and repeating later, we had two shiny clean kids locked in the playroom with their brother and the baby monitor on guard while we stood looking at the manure pile that was our bathroom.

"Hey," he nudged me with his elbow. I looked up at him, wishing he could manifest some kind of magic wand to get us through this. Pretty sure my eyes were bleeding from the stink at this point.

"So. Everything okay?"

I looked at him. He was grinning with mischief.

"Yeah. Everything's good," I smiled, obviously ignoring the obvious.

"Any problems? Any complaints?"

"Nope." How could I possibly complain about anything when I had a husband who would dive into a mountain of baby feces for me?

"Wanna do another week?"

"Yeah, I do."

"Good."

Yes, it was.

There *were* times when I did have a problem. Or a complaint. The first time it happened, I decided to see how it would go.

We'd been out, at Nathan's brother's place for dinner. While our nieces and Dan and the twins played happily out back, we sat and enjoyed drinks with Robert and Elaine as a couple of couples on the deck overlooking the yard. I was pregnant with John, so wasn't drinking. But Nathan had a few more than usual and happily, and explicitly, sang the praises one of my particular bedroom skills to our listeners. Maybe my hormones were flaring, but I was mortified. My brother-in-law laughed as any supportive friend/husband/father would. My sister-in-law just sat looking bug-eyed at me, eyebrows in her hairline, blinking loudly, her knowing expression saying, *I'm so sorry, I'll miss you*. She quickly gathered the wherewithal to excuse us to the kitchen, where she was able to talk me down from my murderous reaction. And truthfully, it was nothing, really.

But the next day I was still upset about it. More than I thought I should have been.

The day after that was Sunday, and when he asked if I had any problems or complaints, I went for it.

"You know the other night when we were at your brother's?"

He looked at me, surprised that the conversation had suddenly, after five years, changed.

"Uh, yeah?"

"And you saw fit to tell them that not only do I give great head but that you'd hire me out if we ever needed the money?"

He did me the courtesy of cringing.

"Yeah," he moped.

"Well, I think I have a bit of a problem with that."

He turned to me and took my hands in his. "I'm so sorry. It seemed funny to me at the time. I don't even know why I said it. I shouldn't have. You don't deserve that." He took my chin in his hand, forcing my stare into his. "It won't happen again."

"I know," I admitted.

He kissed me, with purpose, as if trying to convince me of his sincerity. As if a kiss could actually seal a promise.

Turns out it could.

We talked long into the night after that. I think we needed to reconnect. It wasn't lost on either one of us that it truly had been a conversation that we'd been having for more than half a decade, and that that had been the first time one of us had had a complaint. It scared us a little. Was this the beginning of the long end? The process of the marriage becoming blasé and predictable, something to be tolerated? Was life now going to just keep rolling along, taking us with it? Were we to resign ourselves to a relationship that would slowly erode over time into something that we just accepted as existing for the sake of existing?

Something changed for us that night. We decided, without really realizing what we were deciding, that we would do whatever we could to make sure that our marriage didn't just survive but thrived.

He was always the solid one. He was always up, happy, energetic. I was the one with the temper, the foul mouth, the shortage of patience. I was the one who would doubt. But he was always there with the right words, at the right time.

He was always reminding me that we were a team. When things got to be too much, there was always a voice in my ear, a squeeze of my shoulders. 'I'm on your side. I got you.'

Days when I felt I just couldn't keep up with him, he'd always step up his game. I remember watching him vacuum the floors and clean the kitchen and do the laundry, all while feeding the boys, day after day after day while I tried to nurse Gilda through her first year. I worried that it was too much for him, coming home from work to a filthy house and crazy kids, while all I could do was sleep. But he never faltered. He never slowed down. He never complained.

"It's not 50/50 Babe. It's 100/100. You'd do the same for me."

And I knew he was right.

We were a team. A great team.

As the years passed life got busier. There were weeks, sometimes many in a row, where we missed our Sunday Night Check-Ins. I don't think either of us realized at the time how much we needed them; we'd coast along, drifting slowly, almost imperceptibly apart. I would start to feel overwhelmed, overworked. He would start to get testy. The kids acted up more. Even things like bills and chores seemed to pile up. But when we were lost in the middle of the detached fog, we never really knew what the problem was; we figured it was just life.

Until something would happen. Either a break in the crazy, or something to push us both over the edge. Nathan would eventually kidnap me – usually kicking and screaming over the mess I would return to! – and *force* me to stop. Stop worrying. Stop rushing. Stop thinking. Stop doing.

Somehow, he had this mysterious way of hitting my reset switch and setting me straight again. We could talk for hours once he got me to let go. He'd push me to tears, hold me, and then get me laughing. With my guard down, without the protective armour I'd created to help me plow through the battlefield of daily life, I could connect with him again. Our parallel paths would join once more and all of the frustration and worry and anger would just melt away. With my guard down, I was able to accept him back into my heart, body, and soul. He would lend me his strength and sense of purpose so I could conquer the world. With Nathan on my team, I was truly invincible.

I wish to hell I had realized at the time how fucking lucky I really was.

The kids were older. Gilda was fifteen already. We would sneak out for dates again and enjoyed doing that whenever we could; even if it meant date night was grocery shopping and a carwash.

We snuck out on a Sunday night. He took me down to The Dairy – it had just opened for the summer, almost 24 years since the first time we'd been there.

"So. Everything okay, Babe?"

"You know it is."

"No problems? No complaints?"

"Not a one."

"Would you marry me all over again?"

"In a heartbeat."

He licked my cone, and I gave him shit.

"Why do you do that? You know it grosses me out."

"You let me lick you everywhere, but this grosses you out."

"That's different."

"No, it's not."

I looked at him. Sometimes it startled me how handsome he still was. There was some grey in his beard. Laugh lines topped his cheeks at the temples. He had a few new rogue eyebrow hairs. But his smile was as boyish as ever, and it reached deep into his eyes. He hadn't changed much at all.

"Do you still love me?" I asked him, knowing exactly what he was going to say.

"I'm still here, aren't I?" And with a rare bit of punctuation, he kissed me fully in a way that left room for no more questions. A way that was as convincing as it was irresistible. A way that said I am yours, you are mine. We are us.

The next morning, he was dead.

Making A New Life

I hopped back on the Yellowhead and continued west, rolling into Edson, Alberta two hours later, badly in need of gas and groceries. There's a Walmart in Edson. Part of me was still a little apprehensive about giving that another go, but the rest of me decided I could be back on the road in an hour.

I was still roaming around the aisles as the third person I'd encountered in the two hours since I'd entered was happily chattering away about the latest local happenings in the small town. Against my natural inclination to avoid such interaction, I found myself listening raptly to these people who saw a new stranger as someone in need of care and attention. *Does everybody take a course in Friendly here?*

By the time I checked out, armed with the recommended extra bug spray, light-blocking sleep mask, and new pair of decent hiking boots, on top of the groceries I'd stopped in for, I had a list in my phone of four best-price gas stations, two must-see museums, three unmissable restaurants, and one emergency phone contact. I loaded my things into the back of the van as a nice old man stopped to ask about my Ontario plates, wished me good travels, and took my cart back into the store for me. When I went in to pay for my gas at the first of the suggested stations, I bought a lottery ticket.

I decided to stay for the night and splurged on a room at the Lakeview Inn next to the airport, indulging myself in a long hot shower and warm cozy bed. I ordered in the over-the-top chicken pasta dish that had been so highly recommended that afternoon. And as I nodded off into the kind of deep sleep that only comes buried in crisp mounds of bright white sheets that I didn't have to launder, I decided that, if the day ever came when I could settle down by myself, with the luxury of freedom, without the obligations of family, with anonymity, without invisibility, this is where I would go. There was an energy here that spoke to me on a level I couldn't understand, but that I could feel. *Maybe one day. After they're all gone.*

I turned off the Yellowhead at Hinton, my first genuine encounter with the enormity of The Rockies. I lived 'On The Mountain' in Hamilton. The epitome of understatement, I was sure I'd never use the phrase again without feeling like a complete buffoon. But whereas the Trans-Canada continued west, up and over the mountains to the Pacific, I decided on a whim to turn north to the Yukon. I'd come this far…

Coffeed up and on my way, I was astounded how a mere two days before, travelling across land so flat I could hardly believe the planet was a ball, I would have never imagined the landscape morphing into mountains that made every picture I'd ever seen of them a lie. And I was still in the foothills!

I spent my day driving north along the eastern ridges, windows down, breathing in the sweetness of air virtually untainted by man. Invigorating, every breath seemed to be a gift from Nature, calming my thoughts and fuelling my spirit. As the miles passed, rivers came and went, forest opened and closed around me, and shadows shrank into their origins, going home to hide from the intense midday sun, peaking out the other side as the day wore on, eventually stretching to their full length, reaching for the ends of the Earth itself.

The road wended its way over and through and around, as if it knew where it was going, having done this a thousand thousand times before this day. I followed the endless black path, trusting its experience, letting it guide me to wherever it wanted me to go. I listened to the wind as I sailed, a lone craft on a journey to parts unknown.

Three times in twice as many hours, I was passed by a car more intent on its destination than I, reassuring more than interrupting my solitude.

Civilization was becoming more and more patchy, so I stopped briefly in Grand Prairie for supplies and gas understanding on some level that I was soon going to run out of convenience stores. A short while later I felt quite a thrill as I turned onto the Alaska Highway north from Dawson Creek. I decided I was now, officially, an explorer!

Entranced by scenery beyond anything I'd ever imagined, I drove a full two hours past my decision to stop for the night, in search of somewhere to stop for the night. I gave up a little past a place called Buckinghorse River. I pulled off the highway to see if I could access a map on my phone, but there was no service. I didn't really care because, with my well-stocked van, I could pretty much stop anywhere, but I was curious as to how far from Alaska I was now.

To my surprise, I had found a roadside campground hidden behind the tree line. These gems were, in my mind, the golden nuggets of the West. They provided room to park a handful of RV's in marked campsites, usually equipped with fire pits and picnic tables, bear-proof garbage cans, and, with luck, an outhouse! Vacancy was as available and free. Campers' only responsibility was to leave everything as clean and put together as they found it. I had passed several of these open campsites throughout Alberta and now into British Columbia and was surprised at the concept. This would never fly back home. Western campers are an exceptionally responsible lot!

I pulled in and set up camp, got a fire going and settled in for dinner.

There is something about being the only person around for miles that frees the mind. I sat watching the flames, listening to the wind through the leaves, mouth watering at the scent of my burger sizzling on the grill. Feet planted firmly on the ground under my chair, my attention was drawn to the sensation, not of my feet pushing down on the rock, but of the rock pushing up against my shoes. Curious, I slipped off my shoes and socks, wiggling my bare toes against the rock, sealing the connection between me and the earth. My feet tingled almost imperceptibly, as if reaching for a vibration they could sense but couldn't actually feel. I moved from my chair to sit on the ground. Legs straight out in front of me, hands in the dirt to my sides, eyes closed, yes, there was something. Not a vibration, but a movement. My breathing slowed, quieted. My heart calmed; my ears listened. The wind sighed. The breeze came and went. Came. And went. In. Then out. Like a breath, wafting over me, passing over the ground, through the trees, fuelling my little fire. It pulled back, leaving a temporary stillness around me. And then it came again. My own breathing fell into rhythm with the wind. In. Out. Breathing as one with the Earth. The rock expanding with each breath. Contracting as it exhaled. In and out. In time with the universe. Since the beginning of time. Until forever more. Life. Breath. Relentless. Insistent. Uncaring. Whether I wanted it to or not. In and out. Without my assistance, without my permission. Living, breathing. Greater than me. Stronger than me. I am but a speck on its surface. I mean nothing. Without me, it goes on. Breathing. Living. With or without me. Because I don't matter. What I want doesn't matter. My future had vanished. My entire existence had crashed down around me. Time stood still in my own little world, where nothing moves, nothing grows; there is no change. There is only pain. Only dark. And the world keeps breathing. Keeps living. Taking me with it whether I want to go or not.

My new normal, he'd said. "This is your New Normal. Get used to it. Learn it. There is no going back. You have a daughter who needs you. She needs you to be strong. For her. The sooner you accept this, the better off she'll be. The better off you'll be."

Nobody asked if I *wanted* this.

"Can I ask, did you know? Did you have the test? Did you know she has Down syndrome?"

"No." I shook my head numbly. *No, I didn't know.* At my age, the chances of a test causing a miscarriage were infinitely higher than the odds of having a birth defect. I didn't want to risk the baby. And I didn't want to have to make a choice. So, there was no test.

"So, you didn't know?"

"No," I said, but I was nodding.

No, I didn't know it was Down syndrome.

"But you're nodding. Did you *know*?"

"Yes." *I knew. I knew it was something. I didn't know what. But I knew.*

Nathan looked at me. Anger flashed in his eyes and was gone before I was sure it was there.

"What exactly did you know?"

I took a deep breath, searching for strength that had all but abandoned me. "I knew there was something wrong. I didn't know what, but I knew. I mean, I knew she'd be okay. But I knew there was something."

"Did you mention it to the doctor?"

"No. That'd make it real. It wasn't something they could fix. At least, I figured if it was that bad, or something they could fix before she was born, they'd have told me. But they didn't say anything, and I didn't want to jinx it. So no, I didn't tell. I hoped maybe it was just paranoid hormones."

"I'm curious. We're studying that, you know. And we're finding that in almost every instance, the mother knows. She may not know she knows, but in hindsight, almost all of them realize they knew. Not just Down syndrome, but that there's something wrong."

Great, I thought. *Good for me.*

The doctor went on as if I wanted to hear what he had to say. "Her future is limited only by your expectations. Her success is up to you. And by you, I mean you, Mom. Dad hasn't heard a word since I said the test came back positive. You'll be the primary caregiver. You'll have to know everything -- every procedure she's had and will have. She'll need surgery to repair her heart. Her development. Her diagnoses and prognoses. All of it. There will be names for conditions and medications and treatments. You'll have to learn them all. Write it down. You are her advocate. She needs you. And you can't let her down."

I sat looking at the floor. The only thought going through my head was an endless loop of *Why Me?* Countered by the obvious answer, *Of course, me.*

But certainly not her.

Why would God let this happen to her? What could she have possibly done to deserve this?

God. The first time I ever doubted Him. The first time I got angry.

"God doesn't give you more than you can handle," the Social Worker tried.

I looked up at that. *Really? Really??? Are you fucking kidding me? What is it about me that makes you think I can handle this? Because, I call bullshit. Bull Shit!! If that was true no one would ever have depression or do drugs or kill themselves. Lots of people get more than they can handle. All the time.*

"You'll see, Mom. You'll get used to it and she'll be fine," she added cheerfully.

There are few times I've ever felt as angry and hopeless and helpless as I did in that moment. I was a hostage, without control, without strength, without choice. I was trapped. And seething with a fury that had no outlet. No relief. No amount of crying or kicking and screaming or throwing things or hurting anyone could begin to assuage the fire burning through my mind.

It was the first time I had ever wished for death. For me. For my baby. (The guilt over that and more would come later. And it would become a permanent part of me.) Or for the fucking Condescending Piece Of Shit sitting across from me in one of the half dozen painfully uncomfortable vinyl upholstered chairs, spaced strategically around the stuffy little 'Meeting Room' with the bland décor designed to keep me calm while I hear the worst news I've ever heard. I looked down at the inadequate box of cheap-ass one-ply tissue they'd given me and imagined scrunching it into a rock-hard ball of unsympathetic cardboard and jamming it into her eye-socket. (There is no guilt over that thought, however.)

I was numb. Physically disconnected from my body, I was adrift in the room, seeing pieces of it, but unable to focus on anything in particular. Disjointed as if just bitten across from shoulder to rib by a gigantic shark who had made off with the rest of me, leaving just my head and one arm; enough to know what I'd lost, not enough to want what was left, enough to ensure my will to survive, not enough to be able to. I was bobbing in the water waiting for the pain, waiting for the joke to be over, waiting for God to come back and take the rest of me.

"God never gives you more than you can handle," she had said.

Yes. Yes, He does.

"What doesn't kill you..."

Sometimes just breaks you.

The helplessness was all consuming. The loss of control. The brutal despair. The knowing that I couldn't fix any of this for Gilda. I was her mother and I couldn't protect her. She was three days old and I had already failed her. I knew in that moment that there was nothing I would ever be able to do to make this up to her.

"…makes you stronger."

I don't want to be strong. I don't want life to be extra hard for my new baby girl. I don't want life to be extra hard for me. I don't want this. I don't want to learn new shit. I don't want to know any of this. I don't want to be her mom. I can't do this. I. Can't. Do. This.

Anger. Frustration. Fear. Sheer impotence.

The tears came despite my confidence that there couldn't possibly be any left, falling wetly into my lap in front of the fire. I wept for my darling Gilda, who was my life's heart. I wept for my weakness. I wept for all the times I'd let her down. I wept yet again for the daughter I thought I was going to have: the one who would excel and win and succeed, who would grow up to be a wife and a mother and happy. Gilda could have and be all of those things, but never in the way I had expected, hoped, or dreamed. Never in a way that wouldn't require my full effort and dedication. I wept for myself for feeling that she was less than she should be. I wept for me. For my pathetic, unworthy, loathing self.

Warm as the air was, the cold of the rock beneath me was seeping through my ass. I forgot about the breathing and the wind and the trees and the Earth as my bowels decided that being cold was their cue to Carpe Diem. I got up stiffly and limped off to the outhouse, mildly encouraged by the luxury of surprisingly clean, if less than comfortable, facilities, until I realized that the experience would have been far more enjoyable had I stopped at the van to grab a roll of toilet paper.

By the time I got cleaned up and back to my chair, my burger was long since cremated, and the fire wasn't worth saving. I doused it and went to bed hungry, angry, and bitter, remembering, as I fell into a deep sleep of disturbing dreams, that I had a date coming up soon. It would all be better then.

Making Of A Mom

I woke to the sound of voices. Sitting up suddenly, I was disoriented, stiff, and annoyed. I'd been in a deep sleep, a relief from the self-inflicted torture of the night before, filled with dreams now scattered as abruptly as my awakening. I peered suspiciously out the windows, easily spotting the vehicle responsible for delivering the owners of my wake-up call.

A van somewhat larger than mine was parked next to the outhouse with two young men leaning casually against its side sharing a cigarette. They looked as annoyed as I felt, though I couldn't imagine any reason being more prevalent than mine.

"Hurry up, Ash! How much can one little girl puke for fuck's sakes?" The pair smirked at each other with righteous indignation.

"Shut up, Brad!" called a high-pitched voice from beyond my field of vision. "You know she gets sick in the car. If you just let her sit in the front…"

"I'm not sitting in the back," Brad whined, passing the cigarette back to his friend.

"Then we'll have to keep stopping like this," argued Ash's friend.

"Jesus Christ, if I thought I could get through the whole weekend without getting laid I'd leave her here," Brad confided to the friend, loud enough for me to hear him clearly.

My insides burned. It took every ounce of control I had not to go get Ash and take her with me.

Brad's friend decided to choose this moment to throw a bomb into the parking lot in the guise of the single most ill-timed, idiotic question I have ever had the displeasure of hearing. "You don't think she's pregnant, do you?"

I'm not sure whether it was a bone in Brad's hand or Buddy's cheek that cracked loudly with the impact, but between the amount of blood suddenly covering both of them and the caterwauling that was now echoing back to us from across the mountains themselves, my money was on both.

A pretty blond face looked out from behind the outhouse with an expression that would make her an excellent mother one day. She strode over to the pair with a wiggle and a purpose, taking instant charge of the situation by simply standing firm with her fists clenched tightly on her tiny little hips.

"Are you kidding me, Brad? Did you hit him? What is wrong with you? God, you're such a child. Let me see your hand," she ordered, looking carefully without touching the proffered limb. "Yeah, you did *something* to it…" With a firm grunt of disgust, she pushed both men down to the ground by the shoulders and set to work fetching clothing – t-shirts from the look of it – and ice from a very large cooler in the back of their van and made ice packs for each.

"Let me see your face Will." Will looked up at her, blood-covered hands hiding his nose and mouth. With no concern for his comfort, she reached down and pulled them away, peering closely at the damage.

"I think your nose is broken. Hold the ice on it."

Brad and Will sat pouting like a pair of busted three-year-olds, gripping their ice packs tightly.

"I don't know what you said to him this time, Will, but you probably had it coming again. You should both probably go to emerg," she decided.

"Are you kidding me? I paid $300 for my fucking ticket! We're going, Shawna!!" Brad wailed. I got the feeling that Will agreed with him, even if he couldn't do so as adamantly.

"Well, neither one of you can drive," she pointed out, arms crossed, standing over them, daring them to argue.

They didn't disagree.

The door to the outhouse slammed and a second tiny blonde girl, who looked remarkably like the first, right down to the stomping wiggle-walk, reached the group and matched Shawna's stance as if choreographed.

The two girls seemed to come to the same decision at the same time.

"Get in," Ash ordered, pointing far more sternly than I'd have expected for someone so tiny. The boys stood painfully, muttering their complaints loudly as they climbed into the back seat of the van.

"Guess you're sitting in the front after all, Ash," Shawna declared, opening the door on her side.

"Guess so," Ash agreed rounding the front of the van and climbing into the driver's seat. She started the engine and pulled through the parking lot slowly. Once out of sight, the squeal of the tires as they hit the pavement was buried under the bass cranked high enough to literally turn the vehicle into a rolling speaker. I could still feel the beat as I lay back down in my bed thinking, without any doubt, that this was worth waking up for.

Making Up

I lazed about for another hour or so, wondering what time it was. I was still tired and probably could have slept through the day. My phone was dead again, and I couldn't be bothered climbing through to the front seat for the charger. The sun was shining brightly through the window now, so I guessed it was mid-morning. My stomach growled demanding attention, and suddenly there was no denying the Call of Nature.

Ugh. Some days the requirements of body maintenance make me crazy. All the filling and emptying, washing, wiping, shaving, plucking, grooming, clipping, dressing, exfoliating, exercising, painting, primping, fixing, and non-stop attention to this human shell I own makes me wonder how I ever have any time left to *use* it, let alone *enjoy* it. And the enjoying of it involves even *more* primping and cleaning and dressing and exercise. Which, if done right, only leads to a whole new job list of *advanced* filling and emptying, washing, wiping, shaving, plucking, grooming, clipping, dressing, exfoliating, exercising, painting, primping, and fixing; much of which ends up requiring the assistance of a loved one. Until eventually things come to a head and there's the explosion that results in a second tiny little helpless body whose owner will be completely incapable of caring for it for *years*, even *decades*. And so now, you're responsible for the constant filling, emptying, washing, wiping, plucking, grooming, clipping, dressing, exercising, and fixing of someone else's human shell until such time as they can assume the responsibility themselves.

Good lord. Can we not just skip to the Morphing Into Pure Energy stage of Human Evolution?!

I found myself replaying the punch Brad had nailed Will with. The speed and force of it had caught me off guard; I'd never seen someone hit someone like that in real life. I couldn't help but feel – impressed. I was pretty sure I could do it. I could definitely break my hand on someone's face. As I puttered about the vacant campground like I owned it, I went about my business wondering how long it'd been since I hadn't felt angry.

Even *I* was beginning to get annoyed with living in a constant state of agitation. I'd been told regularly that I was stressed, and that it was understandable, given my circumstance. After all, who wouldn't be?

'Oh, you're so strong,' they said.

'I couldn't do what you're doing,' they assured me.

'I don't know how you do it. I would fall apart,' they admitted.

'You're such an amazing mother. Your kids are so lucky to have you,' they rattled on.

Where do people come up with this shit? And for the record, I want to know how this 'falling apart' thing works. How, exactly is this done? How do I 'give up' and 'fall to pieces?' Seriously, I need to know. Because I'm losing my shit every five minutes, and I'm still standing, and I'm getting bloody tired. What is this Nervous Breakdown everyone keeps talking about?

But nobody is listening. Nobody seems to *hear* me when I say, 'I can't do this anymore.'

They think I'm exaggerating when I tell them I am angry *all* the time.

I have a godson who's lived his life mostly on the other side of the line that none of us are supposed to cross. He's a sweet kid but has a real knack for getting in over his head and finding some serious trouble. His parents try to help, but they really just end up making it easier for him to go sideways again. I like running into him. A little bit because I go home looking at my kids with a little more respect and hope. But mostly because I honestly enjoy talking to him. He speaks with a truth and sincerity that is hard to find. He doesn't make excuses for his behaviour; it just is what it is. He doesn't expect approval from anyone. He knows he screws up, but he accepts that as part of who he is. And somehow, he still thinks he'll turn out okay.

"I'll figure it out one day," he's told me.

"I hope so, Sweety."

"I got this. I'm still hanging in," he'd grin with mischief I couldn't begin to imagine.

The last time I saw him was a while back. I was dropping off some of Nathan's recording equipment for his dad, but David was the only one home. He invited me in and made me a cup of tea.

It's funny how kids grow up right under our noses, but it takes some kind of event for us to notice. David's making me a cup of tea was that event. That and the conversation we had.

"I wanted to talk to you, actually, about Uncle Nate."

I cradled the hot cup between my hands, holding it close under my chin trying to warm up after being outside in the late winter cold. I looked at him across the table from me, his hair too long, his beard as raggedy as it ever had – and probably ever would – be. His tawny eyes squinted at me suspiciously; a new habit he'd learned as an adult that was never there as a kid. Leaning on his elbows, he looked down at the table trying to find his words.

"I wanted to tell you I'm sorry."

Not what I expected. "Sorry? For what?"

The tears started suddenly and with force, but his voice remained strong, though quiet. The house was empty and silent, except for the two of us.

"I wasn't there. I missed everything. And I should have been there."

Oh.

Guilt.

I hate that fucker.

"I see," I started slowly, tapping into the eons of experience I now had in talking to people who were hurting. I reached across the table and took his hands in mine. They were stained and calloused, crooked and scarred from too many years of abuse in his young life. "Can I ask you something?" He nodded solemnly. "If you could go back and change it, would you?"

He looked startled at the idea and nodded, freeing a fresh wave of tears.

"Do you know what you would change?"

Nod.

"Would it help?"

He stared into my eyes for a long time.

"Probably not," he whispered.

"Why not?"

"Because the only thing that would help would be Uncle Nate not dying. And I can't change that."

"No Babe, we can't. No matter how much we want to."

His head dropped in earnest sobs.

"David, we all do the best we can with what we have, with what we know, in the moment. It's easy to look back and beat ourselves up for not doing better. But the fact is, we had one chance, and we did the best we could with what we knew and had at the time. You have to believe that. You have to forgive yourself. Or you'll end up hating yourself. "

He hmphed and blew a snotty bubble out of his nose. I laughed at him and got him some tissue.

"If it helps at all, in my mind, there's nothing to forgive," I assured him, sitting back down. "We're good, you and me. And so was Uncle Nate. He loved you. He understood you. There's nothing to forgive."

"I didn't get to say goodbye," he whispered.

"Nobody did, Darlin'. But that's okay. People go around saying stupid shit like 'live every day as if it's your last.' Well, you know what? You can't do that. Nobody can. Because we're human and we do and feel human things. Not every day can be our best day. Not in real life."

He sniffed loudly, nodding, still looking at the table.

"But when your people know you love them, no matter what, you don't need goodbye."

He wiped his nose on his sleeve, an old habit I recognized.

"David. This has been bothering you for a while?" He nodded again. "Sweety, you know you can talk to me. Any time. You have my number."

"I know. But you're busy. And I didn't want to make you sad talking about him."

My turn to hmph. "I kinda wish I could get sad. I seem to be stuck on angry."

He looked up at that, surprised. "Angry? At what?"

"Pretty much everything," I admitted.

"I know *that* feeling."

I was sure he did. "It's exhausting."

"Yeah. Especially when you're not sure what you're mad at. Or who."

"Right?" I agreed. He understood it too well. "I think that's a big part of it. I have no one to be mad at. So, I just have to swallow it 'cause I can't exactly let loose on the kids…"

"No, that'd be bad. With your temper and all," he smirked.

"What temper?" I defended.

He laughed at that. "Please. I grew up with you. You're my second mom. Jeez, I remember you losing it on me at the cottage 'cause I couldn't cut a watermelon!"

Oh yeah. Not my proudest moment.

"Bet you can now, though," I winked.

"You bet I can! Mom lets me use knives now even if the courts don't."

He smiled widely, and I was uncomfortably happy to see that despite his troubles, he'd still managed to take care of all his big beautiful white teeth. I'd have sworn he was born with braces.

"I love that you can still laugh, Babes. I worry about you."

"I worry about you, too. I wish you didn't have to be angry."

"Yeah. Me too. Maybe if I could just punch someone. Really hard."

He laughed. "Someone who deserves it I hope?"

"Of course! I would never hurt someone for *no* reason."

"Want me to find someone for you?"

"I'll let you know!" I laughed, hoping he was joking. *Sort of.*

"Say the word. We'll head downtown and roam around until we find a real Piece Of Shit and you can have a go at him."

"Okay, deal. Just promise me one thing?"

He cocked an eyebrow at me.

"If I'm ever beating the crap out of someone, and I look like I need help, maybe give me minute or two before you jump in? I think I'll probably be able to manage on my own."

"You got it!"

I don't think a day has gone by that I haven't considered taking him up on his offer. And as a middle aged, stressed-out, widowed mother of five, I figure I've got at least one freebie coming. Although a six-month stretch for assault kind of has its allure.

I spent the rest of my day driving along winding roads through sunshine and wilderness, the smell of campfire in the air, daydreaming about the myriad ways of running into some undesirable Piece Of Shit who needed a good beatdown.

Making a Decision

I stopped in Fort Nelson for a walk and a coffee transfer – coffee in, coffee out - and bought a map at the checkout to see how far north I was. Only another hour or so and the 77 would meet the 7 north to Fort Liard in the Northwest Territories. I decided to take the detour across the border and keep driving until it got dark.

I'm sure my dismay at being turned away at the turnoff, because it was closed due to a forest fire three hours ahead, was selfish in light of the fact that the people who actually lived up there were in danger of losing their homes. This explained the smell of campfire I'd been enjoying for the past four hours; it must have been a pretty big fire. Nevertheless, I was sorely disappointed that I wouldn't be able to at least say I'd been there.

Determined to at least get to Yukon, I followed the Alaska Highway as it paralleled the Liard River north, and then west, teasing its way along the south side of the border until at last it crossed over to continue north to Watson Lake.

Two things I noticed about Yukon.

They're not big on road signs. All of the roadside directional info, how far to go, speed limits, everything, was one big guessing game. Eventually I realized that, if one only has the choice of going this way or that way, with both choices being exact opposites of each other, the chances of getting lost are indirectly proportional to the certainty of ultimately getting to where you were going. One road. Take it or take it.

And the quiet. Noticeable, disorienting, surprising quiet.

My plan to drive until dark in Yukon, in July, was not a good one. By the time I rolled in to Watson Lake, I could barely keep my eyes open. My dashboard clock read 10:35. I supposed it was PM, but I had been changing, or forgetting to change, it as I went, and was now three or four time zones away from home, so without my phone, I had no idea what time it was. All I know was the sun was blinding through the windshield, and squinting was quickly turning into dozing.

I found a campground in Watson Lake buried in the bush quite a ways off the main road. Even more surprising than the free campsites I'd found so far, this one was not only a paid stopover, but the receptionist was a pole with a metal box nailed to it where visitors were asked to fill out an information card and leave their $16 cash. From the looks of the inside of the box, it was a popular campground for incredibly honest people.

I burrowed my van into what I assumed was my campsite: a somewhat cleared area not much bigger than a parking space with a circle of rocks around some blackened, shrunken logs tucked into its corner. What it lacked in space, it made up for in vertical view. I looked up to my own private window of sky and decided to sleep under the stars tonight.

It's embarrassing to admit my obvious oversight…

I cleaned up, used the natural facilities, and rearranged my bedding so that my head was in clear view of the sky above through the open sliding side door. More comfortable than it looked, I snuggled in to watch the sky dim to sunset. Imagining that the stars this far north would be spectacular, I harboured a deep desire to finally see the Northern Lights. It was clear and fresh and cool. I breathed deeply, my lungs rejoicing in the reprieve from the work of constantly filtering city gunk.

I slept deeply, but in short spurts, waking once to muted voices, and more than once to the shuffling of tiny feet through the brush nearby. I hadn't previously taken notice of all of the noises of the night; my slumbers had so far felt like sleeping with the bedroom window open. But here was different. The underlying silence amplified every sound. It would take some time, I imagined, to become accustomed to the volume of my own breathing. Even the gentle breeze through the trees had a different sound to it, perhaps because there were far more needles than leaves, or perhaps because there was a certain magic in the air, left behind by eons of Nature dominating Man instead of the other way around.

As it was, every time I did approach the merest hint of consciousness, I had the sense enough to search the sky for my elusive aurora. I spent hours drifting in and out of sleep in the hopes of witnessing just a glimpse. Until I finally realized that, not only was I not going to see the Lights, I wasn't even going to see any stars. If it did indeed get dark at all, it did so with absolute stealth during an hour or two while my eyes were closed.

Maybe I'll come back in six months…

With no one to answer to, I slept until I was finished before I made my way back out to the main road to see what Watson Lake had to offer.

Far more touristy than I'd expected, I discovered an Outward Bound base camp that promised exciting Nature Tours through the area, a museum of native artifacts and local history, an extensive gift shop, and the Tags Convenience Store, Snack Counter, and Laundromat.

I pulled in to the last place, deciding to run a load of laundry and grab some lunch. The building wasn't fancy, but it was new and clean and modern.

And expensive! Shipping costs to this area would, of course, be exorbitant, but paying more than four dollars for a can of pop really brings it home!

As I sat eating my lunch, I could clearly overhear a conversation between a customer and the man at the counter. Turns out the place that had been here for a hundred years burned to the ground about seven years ago. I couldn't imagine any urban-quality firefighting services nearby, so I wasn't surprised. But there was an underlying pride in the man's words that told me the rebuilding hadn't been easy. I looked around a little more closely and found an appreciation for the efforts the locals have to put forth just to do things that come so easily to us back home.

If my fence blows down, I can just pop into the lumber store and grab what I need. Here, while I'm sure their local store would stock much of the standard things everyone needs every day, I imagined most of what they'd need to build an entire building would have to be ordered and shipped. At considerable expense. I shuddered; I can't stand waiting a day for a book from Amazon - or paying for the privilege!

The trade-off was the peace and quiet, the safety, the community, the freedom, and the connection with Nature.

I watched the people come and go as I ate. Nobody bothered me. Respect and privacy seemed to be in abundance here as well. Anonymous and invisible.

When at last my clothes were dry, I ducked into the bathroom to change while they were still warm, and, as much as I wanted to crawl back into bed, I felt compelled to continue my journey. I had every intention of driving up to Dawson so I could have a drink with the Dead Toe in it. Or maybe just watch someone else do it.

Pulling out of the parking lot, I was hard-pressed to figure out which direction would take me where I wanted to go. I was searching in vain for a direction sign for assistance when I noticed the cacophony of colour across the street. Curious, I turned in.

And I now knew where every sign in the territory had ended up.

The Watson Lake Sign Post Forest began in 1942 when a soldier was told to repair a directional sign and decided to add to it a sign pointing to his hometown of Danville, Illinois, 2,835 miles away. There were now over 77,000 signs in the forest. All of this, I learned, of course, from a big sign posted at the entry.

I parked and went in for a walk.

It was fascinating to think that this many people had passed through here, all leaving everything from product signs to road signs, street signs to license plates, to be forever remembered in this tiny empty corner of the world. I wandered through the maze much the way history buffs wander through a cemetery. Every sign represented a person's journey here. I was enthralled.

Standing in what I presumed to be the middle of the 'forest,' one license plate in particular caught my eye. It was an Ontario plate. From my home, my people. A personalized license plate that said 7BROWNS.

I stood looking at it, trying to imagine the family who had left it here. A family named Brown. There were seven of them. Two parents, five kids, just like us.

With a painful hitch in my throat, I was suddenly overwhelmed with the hope that there were still seven of them.

Because there were only six of us. We were no longer seven.

I was standing, as I had been that day three years before, feet glued in place, trapped in my mind trying desperately to understand what was happening around me.

They'd called me from the station. Nathan had fallen, and they'd called an ambulance for him.

My first reaction was that apprehension you feel when you know someone just pissed off your spouse, but the person doing the pissing has no clue. And next chance he gets, you're going to hear all about it.

"Oh, he's not going to be thrilled with that," I leaked.

"He asked us to call." My blood ran cold. "You need to come." The voice was shaky.

"I'm on my way."

I ran through the house with the list forming in my head as I went, barking instructions to the kids.

"Okay, boys, the new fridge is coming this morning. Get the old one empty and clean. Call Nanny and get her over here to help." Grab Nathan's travel pouch out of the closet. "Make sure the guy takes the old fridge. I do not want to come home tonight to two fridges." Fill pouch with medications, toothbrush, his extra eyeglasses, grab my backpack. "The fridge is paid for. You don't have to do anything with the guy. Just be nice and help if you can." Stuff extra underwear, socks, slippers, phone charger, into the backpack. "Make sure all the food goes back in the new fridge." Contact lens stuff and my glasses, my meds, cash. "And get the guy to make sure the new fridge is plugged in and running properly." Brush teeth and hair, go for the fast ponytail. "Where's Dan???" Back to the kitchen, granola bars, juice boxes. "When did he leave?" I'm pretty sure I can still catch him on the way. "I will let you know as soon as I know anything." Coat on, keys, phone. "I don't know anything more than Daddy fell down, and they called an ambulance. I'm sure he'll be fine. I'll let you know as soon as I do. Now phone Nanny. I love you!! Close the door behind me!"

Backpack slung over my shoulder, I trucked out to the driveway mentally reviewing my list, trying to make sure I had everything I needed. It had been more than a dozen years since we'd had to do a hospital run for Gilda. Heart failure is a process, not an event, and we spent the better part of a year either going into hospital or coming home, every two weeks. We got good at the process of transition days, and I was counting on that muscle memory now.

Standing in the driveway, keys in hand, it took more than a few seconds to figure out where the van was. Nathan usually carpooled to work, but with the younger kids all off school that day, he'd taken the van. I was supposed to be home all day welcoming a new fridge after all.

Shit!!

My mind refused to scroll through possible options while it focused solely on the idea that I would never let him strand me at home without the van again.

I heard a car coming up the street. Without rational thought, I ran out into the road and stopped it, opening the door before I could explain what I wanted. I had no idea who the man was, but he seemed to be able to listen fast enough to understand what I was trying to say and drove off before I had my seatbelt fastened. We passed the school on the way, and I spotted Dan easily, crossing the campus lawn. My driver stopped so I could jump out and flag down my son. Confused but alert, he ran to me, accepting that an explanation would follow. We both got back in the car and our new neighbour, as Dan would be so kind to tell me later, zipped us down to the television studio in record time. I jumped out without thanking him, thinking I should have at least said thank you.

Dan and I raced in past reception, random people automatically pointing us in the right direction. When we reached Nathan's dressing room, we had to push our way through the throng of people crowded in there.

One of the producers, who was sitting on the couch looking terrified, looked up at me and mouthed a silent apology. I had no idea know why.

I found Nathan, surrounded by bulky firemen, on the floor beside a stretcher. His head was bleeding. He had thrown up. But he was sitting up, leaning on a chair.

"Okay, Nate," someone in charge directed. "We need to get you up on the stretcher now."

They grabbed for him as he tried to roll onto his knee to stand.

"Oh no you don't, Buddy. We'll lift you."

I looked at them and looked at my husband and thought, they probably could. But I was the only one in the room not surprised when Nathan pushed them back and pulled himself up onto the stretcher.

Someone was asking questions and I realized I had answers. From among the crowd, I replied loud and strong and the sea of faces parted to look at me. I simply pointed to the top of my head and declared, “Wife.”

Things seemed to calm down for a minute then. Paramedics asked every question imaginable. Yes, he takes a blood pressure med. No, no blood thinners. No, no diabetes. No, no, he didn’t fall – he cut his head shaving it this morning, again. We all smiled because, well, that’s funny. No, no history of heart and stroke. No, he was fine this morning. No, no seizures.

And with that, my giant pillar of strength, love, and compassion, the man I’d leaned on and depended on for half my life, turned to stone before my eyes, his back arched off the gurney, feet pressed at an ungodly angle, his head pushed back to face the wall behind him, eyes rolled up into his head as if looking at the floor beneath him. I couldn’t breathe. I’d never seen anything like this before in my life. He vomited again and a dozen experienced hands flipped him on his side like a newborn.

I felt a hand on my arm, a whimper in my ear, suddenly realizing that Dan was standing right next to me. *Fuck!!*

The seizure passed and they laid him back on his back. He was disoriented, couldn’t speak, and worst of all, terrified, his eyes darting from face to face in panic.

I pushed Dan back away from him.

“Baby, you have to go.”

“Mom, no,” he looked as frightened as his dad.

“No Dan. You have to go home. Take my keys, get the van. Go home and look after the kids for me. I need you there.”

“Mom,” he tried again.

“No Sweety. I guarantee you your dad would not want you to see this. I will call you as soon as I get to the hospital. You can come see him tonight. I promise.”

He just stood shaking his head.

"Dan, please, don't let him see you here. He wouldn't want this. Go." I pushed him, and slowly, he moved out of my field of vision.

I turned my attention back to Nathan. He was more aware, answering questions with nods and shakes, but didn't seem to be able to talk.

"Okay, we're taking him to emerg now." They'd packed equipment on his legs and had him strapped in.

"Wait!!" I demanded, pushing my way through.

The only part I could get to was his head. I bent over him, hugging him fiercely, my cheek upside down against his, my words in his ear, for only him to hear.

"I. Love. You. I got this. You go with them. You do what they say. You look after you. I got everything else. You don't worry about us. I got your back." He'd grabbed hold of my forearm at his neck and was squeezing tightly in reply. We held each other for the three seconds more they allowed, and then the chaos swept back around us.

I followed the crowd outside to the ambulance. As they rolled the stretcher into the back, I heard the paramedic asking him if he had kids. I heard him answer, 'Yes, five,' and felt a wave of relief wash over me. The driver slapped me on the shoulder with a quick 'You're up front with me,' and, happy to just do as I was told, I joined her in the front seat, picking up Nathan's shoe from the ground on the way.

She drove with confidence and determination, talking to her partner in the back, asking me more questions. But a few minutes in, she flipped on the sirens, explaining that traffic was bad and people were idiots. Indeed, I was astounded at the number of cars that just didn't see or care. I would find out later that he'd seized again in the ambulance.

We got to the hospital. It seems that nine-thirty on a Monday morning the week before Spring Break is a good time to go to emergency; there was no one there.

They pulled him out of the back of the transport and wheeled him past me toward the door. He spotted me and was awkwardly trying to swat the oxygen mask off his face.

I yelled at him, told him to behave himself and leave it on. Or I would tell his mother on him.

That was the last time I saw him alive.

Inside, I hit the waiting room, grabbing a clean garbage bag out of the bottom of a trashcan for his jacket, shirt, shoe and hat. They would need washing before they were going to visit my backpack. I settled in to watch the endless news loop on the television while I began what was sure to be a long wait.

Soon after, a young woman who I mistakenly assumed to be a nurse came to talk to me.

"We have some questions for you. Do you mind?"

"Of course not," I agreed.

"So, your husband, Nate?" I nodded. "He's Big Nate from the tv?"

"Yeah, that's him." Big Nate. Everybody knew him.

"Does he have a history of any kind of illness like this?"

"No. Not at all. But there's a small part of me that's hoping this works as a little wake up call for him. He needs to lose that fifty pounds. I think he's ready."

"And you have kids?"

"Yes." Don't ask me about my kids unless you've got time for the answer that will go on forever. Apparently, she did.

We were finally interrupted by a man who was more obviously *not* a nurse, who motioned to the young woman that we were to move over there, he pointed behind him.

To a door.

To one of those fucking Social Worker rooms.

The ones where they ruin your life.

And it hit me. I'd fallen for her distraction. Suddenly, with a force that quieted my mind, stopped time, and took my breath, I realized that something was wrong beyond anything I had considered so far. By the time I sat down in the ugly little vinyl upholstered chair, in yet another ugly little room, with the too-small fucking one-ply tissue, I knew that my life was about to change in ways I couldn't yet comprehend.

The only thing I knew for sure was that I wasn't going to like it.

Mr. Social Worker, who was the supervisor of Miss Student Social Worker, sat opposite me, and in his best calming tone, began to explain to me what was happening.

"Your husband is in emergency right now. The doctor and the team are working on him. They're not sure what's happened. But his heart has stopped and they're doing CPR hoping to get it started again. The doctor will come see you when he has more news."

I almost laughed out loud at the look on his face that said, 'That is enough of an explanation. Now if you'll just sit here patiently, we'll get back to you shortly.' This is why they lock you in a little private room: so no one out there can hear how ridiculous they sound in here. This is a failed plan, because no one would be able to hear me throttle this twerp, either.

"His heart has stopped," I heard myself ask for clarification.

"Yes."

"So, he's dead."

"They're trying to restart it."

"I got that. But right now, he's dead."

"They're doing everything they can."

"But he's still dead, right?"

"He's in good hands."

"You're not very good at this."

"If you'll just be patient."

(Picture the expression on the face of someone in the nanosecond between suddenly *seeing* a living breathing tyrannosaurus rex standing in front of them and *realizing* said t-rex is biting their head clean off, and that might come close to what I imagine I looked like. *Dumbfounded* is not an adequate word.)

"Bring me the doctor."

"I'm sorry, I can't do that. He needs to be present with your husband."

"He has a team. Bring me the doctor."

"Please calm down."

This is when I noticed for the first time that the furniture is bolted to the floor.

"Bring me the fucking doctor or I will kill you and go get him myself."

"I will have to call Security if you threaten me like that again."

"Good luck with that. Get the doctor while you're out there."

He stood, actually had the tiny little balls to *hmph* at me, and left the room.

I looked at poor Miss Student Social Worker. She was terrified.

"I'm not going to kill him," I assured her. "I just want him to think I might."

She stared at me with no clue as to how to respond. But she stayed; I'll give her that.

A short couple minutes later, the door opened loudly to admit a handsome, energetic man, hair messed by hands that were used to performing miracles, dressed in drab green scrubs and bright white sneakers. He perched himself across from me on the arm of a chair, feet on the seat, looking perfectly comfortable squatting on the flimsy piece. He leaned forward, elbows on knees, and looked right at me.

After introducing himself, not that I would ever remember anything much about him, he started talking, and I did my best to listen hard.

It was looking like Nathan was being attacked from the inside by a blood clot in his lung. No idea where it had come from; he hadn't complained about any pain or discomfort. But it had hit his lung and resulted in a series of massive seizures, ultimately causing the heart attack that had now stopped his heart. They had given him as many blood thinners as they dared, and then some. In fact, that was causing problems with the gash on his head now bleeding uncontrollably. *Yeah, that was me laughing at that this morning...*

So basically, they were doing CPR, trying to get his heart going again, otherwise…

"So, he's dead," I nodded, starting to wrap my head around it.

"Right now? Yes."

"I need to see him. I have to be there."

He looked at me for what felt like forever, his gears clearly working through thoughts unknown to me.

"It's not hospital policy," he started, his hand coming up automatically to fend off my response.

I took a deep breath.

"I am not some emotional wreck. I am not the one to go off screaming and making a scene. I saw my daughter through open-heart surgery. I had to DNR my father. And my grandmother. But I have our five children at home. And his family. And I'm going to have to convince them all that we did everything we could to save his life. I can't just take your word for it."

Something I said connected. He took a deep breath and agreed. "Let's go then."

"But Doctor, you can't. You know she threatened me. You'll have to answer for this."

The Doc just took my arm and led me out of the little room and down the hall. As we walked, he told me exactly what to expect. He told me Nathan was unconscious, unresponsive, laid out on the stretcher, shirtless, there was an IV in his arm, heart leads all over him, and a team of five doctors taking turns pumping his chest.

He pulled the curtain and we stepped into My Own Little Purgatory.

Standing at the foot of the bed, I looked around. There was a black and white analog clock ticking solidly on the wall behind him; it was 9:48. Nathan's right arm was hanging off the stretcher to the side, violently bouncing in time to the compressions a strong young resident was forcing into his chest. I worried that his arm was going to be really sore and wished they would tuck his hand in under his butt to stop it. He was only wearing one shoe, and the sock I was looking at had a big hole in the toe.

I could feel the doctor standing directly behind my right shoulder, talking the entire time, telling me things, answering my questions. I would never remember what he said. But I would remember later that he told me everything I needed to know.

I felt a hand on my left arm and turned to see my sister standing beside me, tears in her eyes, holding me up, or leaning on me, I'm not sure which. Her husband was behind her. I had no idea how they knew to come or how long they'd been there.

I pulled out my phone and found the most adorable picture of Nathan and Gilda, squashed together into the screen, cheek to cheek, both laughing. I held the picture in my hand, willing Nathan to see it, wherever he was, and come back.

Of course, he had to come back. There was no choice. If not for me, if not for the boys, for Gilda. That little girl was his purpose in life. He was her champion, her protector, her guardian angel. He would never leave her. And if I had to stand there like an idiot in a hospital emergency room with my phone out to remind him of that, then so be it.

For Gilda, Nathan. You have to come back for her. She won't understand. She will break. Her world will shatter. You can't leave me to deal with that. Don't you dare make me tell her her Daddy died. Don't you dare!

I watched as the next man stepped in to relieve the last, now soaked from shoulder to shoulder and neck to navel with sweat from the effort of pumping Nathan's heart for him.

And the next man.

And the next.

As the doctor talked to me the whole time.

And I begged silently.

Somewhere in my mind I heard the doctor tell me that twenty minutes was the limit. If the drugs didn't clear the clot and the heart didn't start again in twenty minutes, there was no hope. I looked at the clock. It was 10:32.

I realized they were all looking at each other. There was a silent conversation going on in the room. I felt the fatigue growing. I felt the hope waning. I felt the fear seeping in through my skin. In my heart, I already knew. I knew that Nathan was already gone. And I knew that he wasn't coming back.

"What happens if this works now?" I asked the doc quietly. "If he comes back now, what does he have left?"

He moved forward to look directly at me and shook his head.

No.

No.

I looked at my Nathan in the picture. With Gilda. Squeezing her tight. I could hear his laughter, and her squeals of delight. The two of them together, as full of life as two people could be. I looked at my Nathan on the bed in front of me, unable to see me, unable to hear me, unable to breath, or to even make his own heart beat. He was larger than life, and I couldn't imagine condemning him to a life of less than nothing. If it worked now, I'd be doing just that. Sentencing him to a mere existence. Forcing his kids to watch him die a long, slow, lonely death instead of the one that had come for him now.

If it even worked.

No. I couldn't do it.

"Make them stop," I decided.

The doctor looked at me again. "You're sure."

"Yes. Make them stop."

Without another word, the room quieted. The people faded from view. And I stood looking at the body that I had loved, and laughed at, cuddled, and cared for. I looked at the hands that had held mine and touched me and helped me. The face that had smiled at me, talked to me, comforted me, encouraged me.

Stilled.

Abandoned.

Discarded.

Two hours before, he'd left for work, laughing and joking. Now he was gone. How is that even possible??

And what do I do now?

Oh my God.

What do I do now? How do I do anything? How am I supposed to look after everything – everyone – all by myself? I don't know what I'm supposed to do. I don't know who I'm supposed to be. I don't know anything. I don't know anything anymore.

I moved from Purgatory into My Own Personal Hell.

And three years later, there I stood in the middle of nowhere, a million miles away, still asking myself the same questions. Still as lost as I was the day it happened. Still standing, wondering why I couldn't just fall down.

Looking at some stranger's license plate, hoping they were still seven.

Because we are six.

And I wouldn't wish that on anybody.

Making A Plan

All conscious, rational thought drained from my mind. I don't remember deciding to leave, choosing a direction, or even doing so. But I spent the next two days driving along the chaotic pathway carved through endless hectares of mountainous woodlands. Except that where forest, thick with leaves and life, once stood, the mountainsides were spiked with the stark, sharp skeletons of trees burnt to charcoal by fire. Every turn in the road brought yet another layer of death and destruction into view. The blackness of the landscape seemed to absorb any light that touched it. It might have been a beautiful sunny day, but the matte scars left here by the ruthless fate that raped the world with its fury were a black hole consuming all things good. I wallowed in my despair along with the souls of the tiny and insignificant lives lost here. Somewhere in the back of my mind, a decision was made. A choice. One over which I could have some kind of say. The only thing I had left that I could control. Sometimes God *does* give you too much. This was too much. It was too hard.

Everything was too hard.

Waking up was the worst part of my day.

I had spent twenty-some years being awakened by the cheery Attack Of The Day of a man who came to consciousness every morning with a song in his heart.

"Good morning, Good Mooooooorrrrning!!" he would sing loudly, dancing his way to the bathroom, usually stopping on the way to try to hug me enthusiastically as I tried to be One With The Bed. I was never sure if he was genuinely happy to be awake or just loved to get me going in the morning with a burst of Fuck Off. He'd settle for slapping my butt through the covers, "Come on Lazybones! You can sleep when you're dead!"

But the radio would be blaring, he'd be singing along, knocking on bedroom doors, bustling through the house with an energy that never reached me before eleven, if at all.

As they got older, the boys began to resist, realizing the comfort of a warm duvet was infinitely more enjoyable than being tossed in the air by Dad's exuberance.

Gilda, on the other hand, would be awake the moment she heard him and be waiting in her bed, fists clenched tightly to her chest, cheeks bursting with excitement, giggles squeaking out of her belly like the birds chirping at 4am, waiting for Daddy to come wake her up. He would bust into her room with a hearty, 'And where is my Gilda Bear?!! I can't start my day without my hug!!' Her squeals of delight pierced through my fog without fail, forcing a grin no matter how much I wanted to go back to sleep. Eventually, Gilda and Daddy would be sitting down to breakfast, up, washed, and dressed, ready for their day, while me and the boys would straggle on in to join them. There was never a day that didn't bring a new adventure for Nathan.

Waking up now was excruciating. The list of chores to be done scrolled through my mind before my eyes were even open. The constant badgering of trying to convince teenagers to get out of bed and get to school wore me down. I was forever tripping over dirty laundry, running out of toilet paper, cursing crusty dishes from the night before in the sink. Making breakfast for kids who didn't want to eat. Arguing about what was and was not appropriate to wear to school. Signing the never-ending stack of notes and agendas. Trying to get all the bodies in one place and paying attention for half a second to be able to plan out the rest of the day so that everyone got picked up and dropped off and brought back home again at something remotely resembling the right time.

It's not that I didn't do all of this before he died. But now, it was just all so much harder. I have never been able to figure out why things that came so easily before, things that were so routine and organized before, things that I was really good at before, were now so bloody hard to do. I couldn't keep up anymore. There was never a moment when the list could even take a break. I went to bed exhausted. I woke up exhausted. The fact that I had no idea when I'd last washed my sheets didn't even register.

I tried to remember the last time I'd used the stove. I know I ordered Chinese Food for Christmas dinner last year.

I hadn't had a cold in the last three years. There was no time to go down. I couldn't take a day off. I couldn't just spontaneously decide to go out for dinner or a movie without reminding everyone to put on a clean shirt and brush their teeth. I couldn't go out anywhere without having to pay for all of us.

I couldn't just decide to paint a room, take a course, or buy a new computer. Everything that would have previously come as the result of conversations, opinions, input, not only from Nathan, but from my day to day interactions with everyone I knew had now become impossible undertakings while I researched and questioned and second-guessed each and every detail of every decision. From the kids to the groceries, from changing to a new dog food to whether I should dye my hair. Every moment of every day was now filled with indecision and fear. Fear, not so much of making the wrong choice, but of having to do double duty when the time came to repair the damage. Without help. Without encouragement. Without the energy that comes naturally from other people.

Because I lost them, too. The people were all gone.

The first weeks, even months after he died, there was always someone else in the house. Twenty-four hours a day, for months. People stopped by to visit. They brought food. They came by to help with some of the gardening and heavy work of the house. They called. My mom and the kids' friends and cousins were regular overnight guests.

But eventually, they all had to go back to living their own lives.

The first day the house was empty was jarringly apparent. It was just before lunch when the twins noticed it. And when the six of us sat down to a pizza dinner in silence, twelve eyes staring at the center of the table, I remember wondering if this was what it was going to be like from now on: all of us existing together, lost in our own thoughts. Disconnected from each other, from the rest of the world.

I was able to keep the house, so the kids kept their schools and friends and jobs. For the most part, their days went on very much the same as before. Until they got home and nothing was as it should be. Nor would it ever be.

Gilda rarely smiles anymore.

Nathan's family, my family, his friends, all miss him terribly.

When they think of him.

But the fact is, they can go for long stretches where he doesn't come to mind, and their lives go on as they did before. I see their posts and hear from them on the days when they think of him most: birthdays, the Death Day, holidays. Then they all assure me we're in their thoughts and prayers.

The other 350 or so days a year, I am alone.

I lost my friends. I didn't realize it at the time, but it seems that all of the friends *we* had were friends that either he or we had. I am more the introvert, and any friends I did have I either lost touch with or outgrew. Everybody else in our lives only connected me with Nathan. Without him, I don't fit in with the couples anymore. There are even two wives who have decided that because I'm now 'available,' their husbands are not!

Okay, gimme a sec. Because that shit's funny.

As for all of the friends in general, there are three. Three people, outside of my own immediate family, that I still see regularly from our life before. Three.

I have been invited to eight events since he died. Two birthday parties, one Girls Night Out, one New Years' Eve gathering, two celebratory barbecues, one dinner, and one visit where I was the sole visitor. I attended every one of these, because mostly, I figure I can't feel shitty about not getting invited out anywhere if I don't go, so I go. It's hard, but I go.

Other than that, I sit home night after night, doing my best to avoid the To-Do List with Netflix binges. The kids are my sole source of social interaction. And more and more now, it's just Gilda and my mom. I love them dearly, but as my primary go-to's for conversation, I wouldn't call them stimulating.

I've never been good at making new friends, but I do know that to make a friend, you have to be one. And that's not really working for me.

In some ways, though, the absence of the people is easier to accept than the absence of the souls closest to me.

When it comes right down to it, I lost my family, too. My kids are detached from each other, and from me. They see each other, they talk, they interact. But they don't go out of their way to spend time together. They don't seek each other out the way they used to.

I remember taking them out one day to give Nathan some extra sleep time after a late night. I watched the five of them lying, bellies down, in a park wading pool, fully clothed after I'd warned them not to get their shoes wet, head to head, yelling words at each other under water and trying to guess what they were saying. From where I sat, mesmerized by them, it looked like great fun. It also looked like great fun for many of the other kids playing in the pool at the time. More than once a strange child would try to join my crew, wedging themselves slowly into the circle of heads. And every time, without malice, intent, or plan, my children gently worked together to tighten the circle and prevent others from joining. I was fascinated by their display of allegiance; not everything needs to be shared with everyone.

Often over the years, I was witness to moments like this, where my children showed the commitment to family that I feel defines the word. But I haven't seen any lately. They've lost each other, too.

Yet the routine and the busy schedule of my family are all that keep me going. I trudge through my To-Do List, very much aware that it will never be done. It is at once a bottomless pit of drudgery and the most intense relationship I have.

I haven't touched another living person, save my children, in three years. I have not been touched. As much as I enjoyed an incredible private life with my husband, I don't seem to be able to even make eye contact with a stranger. The mere thought of being intimate with anyone terrifies me. Still, I can't stop thinking that it's what I want more than anything. I am consumed by the desire to simply be *with* someone. Someone who looks at me and sees *me*, and is okay with me being broken, and doesn't expect too much, but who just wants to make me feel like I matter again. I want someone to look at *me*. Not Nathan's widow. Not the kids' mom. Not the pathetic, shattered woman who likely hasn't showered in days and is still wearing her dead husband's sweat pants. But *me*. The woman who still has so much love to give. The woman who has learned so much about caring and giving and losing. About devotion and support and empathy. The woman who, despite how aloof and strong and solitary she seems, wants more than anything to connect on some kind of personal level with a living breathing human being.

But for so many reasons, I can't.

I can't imagine sitting across a table from a man whose attention is focused on me. I can't fathom revealing my *self* to him. I can't even entertain the idea of being physical with him in my most private thoughts.

And who would he be?

He'd have to be someone who is larger than life *and* Nathan. There would always be three people in that relationship, and he'd have to be okay with that. He'd have to be fabulous with my kids and my family. He'd have to be acceptable to the public who worshipped Nathan. He'd have to be everything I want and more. I can't imagine that this man exists. I am all by myself.

But that's lost, too. I have no idea who my *self* is anymore.

Everything I did, everything I was, everything I was going to do and be are gone. Every plan, every idea, gone.

Moving forward, every single day is different from what I had expected it to be.

For me, like everyone else, it's about missing him whenever I think of him.

But that's pretty much every minute of every day.

His clothes are still in the closet. Not so much because I'm overly attached to them, though there are a few things I'd like to keep. But because I haven't had time to gather them all together, wash them, dry them, pack them up, figure out where to take them, and take them there. So, he's in my mind every time I get dressed, undressed, do laundry, buy laundry detergent, see someone wearing a stained shirt...

My house is our house. We bought the sofa together. We installed the kitchen counter. We won the television. We slept together in the bedroom. The kids would die if they ever knew we'd had sex in the van. I could replace everything in the house, but it would still be his.

I could move, but then I'd have to do all that laundry, so that's not happening.

I watch the kids and I'm constantly distracted wondering what Nathan would think, how he would handle this problem, or what he'd say about one of their latest ideas.

Every moment now is an experience he's missing. Every song on the radio. Every new movie. Every election. Every game.

It's like we all got on a ship and sailed away, leaving him on the shore. Only we can't ever go back, and he can never join us. But every minute, every day takes us farther and farther away from him, and I have no idea where I'm going.

The kids' futures are mapped out fairly well. They'll get off at their various stops: go to school, move out, get married. Whatever. It's all variations of the same expectations.

But *my* future is gone; I'm looking across a dark sea and no matter how much I try to squint and focus, I see nothing.

I have no idea what I want to do. I don't even know who I am if I'm not moving forward with him. My ship has no map, no direction, no plan, no purpose. The captain's not listening. The crew is ignoring me. It's been so many days, months, now years, of sailing an ocean that holds no sign of hope for me. I try to think of things that matter to me, but what matters most is beyond my reach.

There is a part of me that breaks every time I realize that I will never have love again. There is another part of me that is more shocked than I would have expected to realize that I will never have sex again. It's been three years since I've been kissed. And the thought of that never happening again is one more drop of despair in an ocean of grief.

The sense of solitude, of aloneness, isn't about being lonely. You can be sitting in the middle of a room full of people and feel lonely; I've felt that before. This is different. This is more a feeling of isolation, of having been forgotten, left behind. Felt on a level that often finds you wondering if you ever really existed. A ghost in the living world. Unseen. Unheard. Untouched.

Invisible.

Or anonymous.

Or, worse, both.

But not by choice.

It's a bubble from which you watch the world around you. You witness the passing of time, not through the spherical window that surrounds you, but through the black curtain that envelopes you, leaving only tiny cracks through which to peek, cracks that seem to close the moment you focus on them. You are aware of the world around you, but have no way to interact with it, no way to reach it. It goes on and on without you.

Eventually, you stop trying to catch a glimpse.

Eventually, you stop noticing the enticing cracks of light.

Eventually, you don't even care anymore.

The solitude has found its way into the corners of my mind where it has planted seeds of surrender that feed on the dreams for the future that once lived there. Where there is no hope, the cold, dark depths of the despair beckon, like Sirens, calling my soul to its destruction. The emptiness left behind lets the song echo until I can hear nothing else.

Many times over the past three years, I had made a plan to give in to the call of despair. But never had I felt so captivated by the idea.

Two days of driving through Nature's burial ground, my mind filled with the stale, wet scent of seared life, with the memories of life lost, with the fatigue of having to fight through every single day for the merest existence, brought acceptance. Acceptance of surrender. Knowing I would forfeit every chance I might have of change, of a new but unimaginable hope. Knowing the finality of my decision, the irrevocable inevitability, the absolute omnipotence of it. Knowing I would never see my kids grow up. Believing to my very core, that they were strong: strong enough to overcome. And convinced that somehow, they would be able to find the hope that I couldn't, so that they could move forward, stronger and faster without my holding them back like the anchor I had become.

I pictured the date in my calendar. Though I had postponed it several times, I had been labeling it 'First Date.' If anyone saw it and asked, I was prepared to say that it was the anniversary of my first date with Nathan. But in my mind, it would be our first date together since he left. I'd been planning it since that day.

I was in British Columbia now. There were mountains that reached to the sky, and I could see the snow, even in July. That had always been my plan: to back the van right up into a snow bank, forcing its exhaust to back up inside, and just go to sleep. It would look like an accident. The kids would see it that way. All my affairs were in order; while I was attending to all of Nathan's final arrangements, I made my own. My will, my funeral, letters to the kids, were all done and in place. There would be very little work for them, and they'd be able to move on fairly quickly.

My 'First Date' was scheduled for about a week away. I planned to drive through the mountains and enjoy the scenery until I could find a good place. I'd know it when I saw it.

The van drove on, seemingly picking out its own path wending through the mountain roads, while my mind quieted, slowed. Acceptance filled me. Acceptance of my end. Of my surrender. Of my fate. I had no fight left and nothing to fight for. If I ate, if I slept, I did so without purpose or decision. But while I journeyed on to the inevitable, the memories yielded, the regret faded, and the sense of loss melted away.

I allowed the solitude to take me, to control me. I gave myself over to the emptiness, beyond sadness, beyond caring. The miles passed, and with each one, the determination I thought I would need in the end was replaced with concession. Resistance gave way to permission, repulsion to reception.

I was done. Not my choice, but at the same time, my choice. I didn't need anyone's approval or opinion. I didn't have to explain myself, justify my decision, or defend my weakness. In that moment, I was truly doomed.

And in my whole life, I have never felt more free.

Making It Up As I Go

With a little more sleuthing than I'd expected, after I don't know how many days of aimless driving, I discovered I'd reached Cache Creek and a fork in the TransCanada highway. South to Vancouver and more sightseeing. Or east through Kamloops and back over the mountains to the Ice Fields and my inevitable fate.

I stayed left.

It was still early morning when I rolled into Kamloops. And by rolled, I mean that quite literally. How anyone could have ever imagined settling here was beyond my level of understanding. Just getting in and out of the damn gas station required maneuvering skills I was now thankful to have gained after weeks of driving through the mountains. You couldn't level a table here!

I left with the hope that my gas tank was actually full and not just tipped enough to hit the thingy that said so.

I had a destination and a week to find it. The last thing I wanted was some fender bender with a local that would knock me off my schedule. As it was, it wasn't actually a conscious decision to turn north on the 5 leaving town as much as it was more a steering and traffic issue; the van more or less just kind of leaned that way.

It was just as well. The road less traveled would be less travelled, which suited my state of mind and heart.

The highway followed the North Thompson River north, snaking its way through the natural valley the water had found. The scenery was spectacular. I'd seen pictures, good ones, professional shots of places like this, but no photo had ever captured the sheer magnificence of the land. As I moved along, every moment created a new vista. Every time I blinked my eyes, I was met with a new and different view, unique and more beautiful than the last. I'd experienced the feeling of smallness looking at the stars at night around a campfire. But the stars were too far away to be real; the comparison was never a fair one. The mountains, however, were right here, in front of me, under me, around me. I was looking at places on which, I realized, I would never be able to stand. No matter how much I might want to go there, or how fit I was, or how young or how rich, there was no physical way to *get* there. Plateaus and outcroppings that quite probably had never been visited by a human being. In all the history of human beings.

The majesty of what I was seeing had me tearing up. I don't know what emotion was washing over me as I went. I just know that it was so much bigger than me that it filled me. It overflowed my mind and my body and my heart. I pulled over to gather my wits a bit. As I put the gearshift in Park, the tears flowed freely. Yet I wasn't actually crying. I felt no despair, no pain, no weight. Just a steady flow of tears, soaking my cheeks, dripping onto my shirt.

I closed my eyes, surprised to see not the blackness that comes from blocking the world from sight, but a flash of light, straight ahead, burning brightly, moving just enough to let me focus on it, growing brighter, bigger.

Great, they're gonna find me dead here from a freakin' stroke!

I peeked carefully out, expecting to see that the sun had broken through the clouds, but it was still overcast and drizzling lightly. I decided to walk for a bit.

I'd passed few cars in the last couple of hours and didn't expect to see many more. I strolled slowly along what little shoulder there was, kicking stones as I went. *BC really likes to gravel their roads.* I was comfortable in shorts and a hoodie, and my new hiking boots were solid enough that I figured I could chance a little detour into the bush for a pee. Within ten steps, I couldn't see the road behind me.

But I'd left some muddy footprints, so I wasn't worried about finding my way back out. I'd heard stories of hikers who'd got lost just yards from civilization; I didn't want to be one of them.

I found a small area with no small cheek-impaling seedlings to threaten my task, conveniently tucked between two beach ball-sized rocks for balance, and popped a squat. Shorts wedged handily behind my knees, feet spread as far as possible to avoid the splash, I released my bladder as Nature intended.

I think it was the smell that caught my attention first. Though the grunt that came with it could have actually preceded it. But the stink was real.

My nose crinkled instantly against the dank, musky stench that seemed to wrap itself around my head with a physical weight to it, at once both a repulsive and an oddly pleasant odour. My mind filled with thoughts that were quite alien to me. Ideas and feelings that I couldn't put words or images to. There was in insane fear, deep in my gut, one that froze my legs in place, glued my arms around my knees, and refused to let me lift my head. But there was a curiosity there, too. An overwhelming need to know what was happening: what is this sensation, this experience that I have never in my life felt before? Yet I knew what to do like I knew how to breathe. Time vanished from existence. Rational thought evaporated with each heartbeat. My body turned to stone while my mind reached out around me in a quest to answer questions I couldn't form.

I felt the heat of him in waves. The air around the back of my neck and ears warmed and cooled. The sound of him was so close in front of me I could feel the burr of his voice as the air passed in and out of him like waves lapping my feet on the beach. He moved suddenly, from side to side and I felt the ground through my feet, protesting his weight. Still I couldn't move. My own breath was slow and shallow, a complete contrast to his. As the air between us thinned and thickened with his movements, I was able to track his position in my mind. He was curious, too.

He sniffed some more, raking the ground between us. He wanted my attention. He wanted to see my face.

I wanted to slither under a rock.

He let out a grunt, aimed directly at me. A bark almost. But it blew my hair down over my forehead.

I felt him back away from me, just enough to tease me into believing he was going to leave. My eyes searched up past my eyebrows, through my hair, but he was just out of my sightline.

Without warning or preamble, he exploded in both size and sound, forcing my gaze up, and up – and up – as he towered over me, reared onto his hind legs, with a roar that filled the mountains around us.

He – and I was now suddenly left with no doubt as to his being a he – stood before me, filling my field of vision, overloading my sense of smell, deafening me with his declaration of strength. He was as commanding as he was terrifying. And I was completely at his mercy.

He waved his, his paws? *Christ, the dog's got paws, what the hell are those things?!!* He waved his paws through the air at me, gesturing wildly, yelling at me, posturing as only an eight-hundred-pound grizzly bear can, mud and wet spraying over me from the filthy fur of his belly.

I would have expected him to be as clumsy as he was big. But he moved with a kind of giant grace that had me entranced. He dropped to all fours and reared back up two more times, as I watched, waiting for him to decide to end me. The third time he fell to his feet, he was close enough that I heard the scraping of the rock to my left. His claws were like knives, hooks that could impale my torso like grappling a side of beef at the butcher's.

As suddenly as he'd started, he stopped and quieted, his breathing slowed, and he stood looking at me with one eye, his head tilted at an odd angle. His enormous brown eye bore into mine, and for a moment, I thought he was asking me a question.

I looked back at him, confused at the thought.

He grunted once more, turned, and disappeared into the brush.

How long I sat there, still squatting with my bare ass hanging out, I'll never know. I do know it took some doing to be able to stand up again. I fell forward onto my knees and elbows, willing the blood to return to my head. I planted my hands in the mud and pushed against the pain and protests in my knees to straighten them, but still couldn't stand upright. Bent over like that, hands and feet solid piers in the ground with my still-bare ass up in the air, I saw it. Just a few inches from my left boot that was now covered in mud and a little stuck, the satiny black stood out against the dark green of the foliage around the bottom of the rock. I reached back to pick up the bear's claw – he must have broken it off against the rock. I could see the scratches left behind by the powerful stroke and ran a hand across the cold rough surface. The dogs had lost claws like this before; like fingernails, they'll break off and I'll find them on the floor. This claw, though, was the size of my finger. In fact, it was hollow, and I could fit my fingertip inside of it, doubling the length of my digit. The curl to the point at the end of it, seen clearly against my own hand, left a hole in the pit of my stomach as imaginary as it could have been real.

I stood slowly, replacing clothing as I went, and numbly retraced my steps back to the van. I sat with the engine running, trying to get warm, trying to stop shaking, staring at the bear's claw sitting on the dashboard.

I was supposed to know something. A thought was forming, but I couldn't grasp it. It was like trying to run into the fog, but when you got there, it had moved. I was supposed to know something.

But the only thing I knew for sure, was in that moment, I, and anyone else on the planet, would never be more fully and completely prepped for a colonoscopy.

A knocking on the window next to my head pulled me abruptly back to the reality of my situation. A torso, clad in an official looking uniform, stood stubbornly on the other side of the glass, waiting. The window rolled itself down faster than I was able to collect my wits.

"Ma'am," he leaned in to look at me, all young and concerned. "I drove by a couple hours ago. You're still here. Are you okay?"

I mumbled something that sounded to me like, "I don't know."

The officer evidently heard, "I'm drunk."

He asked me to hand over my ID, and to get out of the van to speak to him. I poked around in the glove box for the van's papers, but my backpack with my wallet in it was in the back. He reached in and turned the engine off while I opened the hatch to get it.

A lifetime or two later, we were still there at the back of my van, him standing tall, reading my papers, me leaning wearily on the tailgate. He told me to wait there while he went and sat in his cruiser for a while. When he came back, he looked genuinely worried about me.

"What are you doing here?"

"I'm um, I'm just still, um, kinda thinking. I guess?"

"And what are you thinking about?"

I thought about that. "I think, I'm wondering why I'm not dead." I laughed, though I have no idea why.

His eyebrows disappeared up under his hat. "And why would you think you were supposed to be dead?"

Reasonable question. "Um. Because of the bear?" Hearing the words out loud startled me a little. "Yeah. Because of the bear." I was nodding with a certainty that I didn't feel.

"You saw a bear?" he asked doubtfully.

"Yeah. I saw a bear. I was peeing. And he, um…" I had to think hard about what the bear had actually done. "He, um, he came up to me while I was peeing and yelled at me."

"He yelled at you?"

"Yes."

"Ma'am, have you been drinking?"

I smiled at that. "No. Not lately, anyway."

"Drugs?"

"No," I shook my head, holding in a grin at the absurdity of the question.

"Where did you see the bear?"

I hitched a thumb over my shoulder. "Just in there."

"Can you show me?"

I shrugged. "I guess so."

He walked calmly and slowly with me as I picked my way back to the spot where I'd been earlier. We both stood looking down at the ground, peering around for clues: him for some idea of what had happened to me, and me, suddenly looking for proof that I hadn't imagined the whole thing.

He tiptoed around a bit, shining his flashlight on the exact spot where I'd peed. My footprints were appropriately askance between the two rocks. I saw him nod absently and was relieved that he had the discretion not point out the obviously human turd in the middle of it all. But his mouth dropped open most unflatteringly as he shone the light horizontally across the small clearing that had very obviously and very recently been tamped down and trodden by paw prints that almost equalled the length of the man's boot.

"What the hell?"

I didn't have an answer for that.

He aimed his light at me, head to toe and back, I guess realizing that I might have been injured.

"Are you okay?"

I nodded absently. *Okay as a person can be who was just yelled at by a giant bear.*

"You're still pretty shook up. And I don't blame you!"

Somewhere in my mind, I accepted that what had happened had *actually* happened.

"Where are you heading now? I'm thinking you might want to be with someone? Are you alone?"

"Yeah." Utterly and completely.

He pulled out his phone and took some pictures of the ground. When he was done, he took me by the arm and led me back to the van.

"I think I'd just like to find a spot to camp for the night. In here with the doors locked."

"There's a campground about a half hour ahead. Are you okay to drive?"

I looked at him directly. He had kind eyes. "Yes. I am."

"Are you sure?"

I wanted to say, 'Yes, if I was going to die today, I think it would have already happened.' But I didn't.

"Yeah. I'm good. I think I just needed someone to give my head a bit of a shake."

"How are you for gas? You were sitting here quite a while."

I got into the driver's seat and started the engine. "I still have a half tank," I assured him.

"Good, that'll get you to the next gas station easily. But stop in at the campground for the night. I'm heading back along your way. I'll follow you and make sure you get settled in okay."

I was glad of his offer.

True to his word, he pulled into the campsite, found me a good spot, and made sure I was equipped to bunk in until morning. I thanked him, wondering at his age, thinking he couldn't be much older than Dan. I would look back at that moment later and realize it was the first time I'd thought of one of my kids as an adult. But for now, I was happy to be able to fall back into the routine I'd created for myself on the road, making something to eat, tidying up my space, getting ready for bed. As much as I was looking forward to a good night's sleep, realizing how drained I felt, I wasn't surprised to find myself lying awake with my thoughts well into the night.

I stuck my finger into the bear's claw for the thousandth time, peering at its silhouette against the backdrop of the van window, lit dimly by the night sky. And not for the first time I wondered at the power of an animal who could have ripped me to ribbons before I'd had a chance to scream. I flashed back to the vision of him standing, at full height, on his hind legs, his front paws black against the gray sky above, two enormous clubs each with five blades that held my life in the balance. And yet, I was beginning to understand that I hadn't actually been afraid of him. Nor afraid of dying. Or of him hurting me. I'd been afraid, yes. But of what, if not death or pain?

What exactly was I afraid of?

Well, for one thing, no one was ever going to believe me. The cop had, but nobody else would be able to see the evidence, and he hadn't until he'd seen it himself.

But no, that wasn't it.

I'd felt the fear, deep in my bones. It had stopped my breath, slowed my heart. But it had also sharpened my senses, I could hear and feel and sense what was happening around me on a level I'd never experienced before. I could feel his movements. Follow him as he paced in front of me. I could smell his intentions. I could hear his thoughts. Somehow, I had known that he wasn't going to hurt me. He wasn't there to kill me or eat me. And thinking back now, I had known that at the time.

And yet, I was still terrified. The fear was real.

But if I wasn't afraid of the bear...

It wasn't of dying. Or of pain. At this point I was sure I was *ready* to die, and there couldn't possibly be a pain as intense as what I'd already been carrying these last three years.

So, what could be worse than what I already had?

Except more of what I already had?

Living was where the pain was. Life hurt. Dying would be easy. It was living that killed you.

The thought of going on, of moving forward suddenly fell on my body with a smothering weight that the bear could not have matched had he mauled me to my end. The unbearable weight of moving forward pulled me down to the ground with it, pulling me under, until I coughed at the thought of the muck and rotting leaves and opaque brown water filling my mouth and lungs.

Yes, the living was terrifying.

And the bear left me to live.

He left me, half naked, exposed, and vulnerable; he left me alone, afraid, and alive.

He left me exactly the way Nathan had left me: to fend for myself, without help, without strength. Confused and lost. Empty. With no idea what to do next. Sitting. Staring off into space, with nothing but my thoughts.

It was paralyzing.

Having to go on without direction, without confidence, without purpose, without help or hope. Part of me knew I couldn't stay there. But the part that knew I had to move had no idea what to do next. I'd sat for hours trying get my mind to think, to work, to plan.

But I'd been stuck, stuck in my fear. Trapped in my despair. Caged in my own mind with a heart that wasn't strong enough to overcome.

The fear had been real. But it was a fear of what happens now. Does the bear come back? Do they find me dead here one day, because I couldn't save myself? I can't protect myself. I can't look after myself. I can't. *I can't.*

And yet…

I did.

I did pull myself together. I did get myself safe. Help did come. And when it came, I took it.

And here I was, snuggled into my sleeping bag, safe, warm, looking at my own hand in the pale light of the night. A hand that wore the claw of a fierce beast: a powerful and fearful predator who had spared me. A threat that could have erased me from existence had chosen instead to show me mercy, to gift me with a piece of his strength, and to send me off into the world to make my own way.

He took nothing from me. I came away from our encounter with what I came into it. *Mostly*, I snorted. I am the same person now that I was before.

Yet, not quite.

I was changed somehow.

I was changed because this thing happened to me. I was changed because what had happened to me, now, had me thinking thoughts and ideas that weren't there before. I was not the same, nor could I ever again be the same, because my perspective had somehow shifted.

But what, exactly, had changed?

I was still a widow. I still had five kids. I still had the same responsibilities and chores and stress and crap in my life that were there before. I still had, well, me.

The bear was gone. The event was over. And I was okay.

The fear had subsided. It had melted away. But when had that happened? I was terrified still when the cop had shown up. I was still out of sorts when we'd gone back into the trees. I was happy to have his help afterward.

I was happy to have his help.

Not that I'd truly needed his help. But I was happy to have it. And he'd seemed happy to give it. Again, I was reminded of Dan. My first born. My son. The one of the five most like me.

My nose burned suddenly at the thought of him, tears threatening. I thought of him smiling, his bright eyes lit with the effort. Him horsing around with his brothers. Him sitting on the floor with Gilda showing her how to brush the dog with the vacuum. I felt the happiness spread through me again as I thought about him. Thought about all of them. About my mom. And my sister. And her kids. And the bloody dog.

It occurred to me that *that* was when the fear had left me. The fear of living had faded to a dull hum in the distance when I'd thought more about what I still had left.

But I had lost so much. The fear made it clear exactly what was gone. All of my strength and confidence and hope had been taken from me. I had nothing, no tools with which to forge my future. I had no reason to believe that I would be able to make it, no matter what *it* entailed. I had given up, been defeated, and decided to be done. I'd lost my hope, my future, me.

Yet, when I'd thought about my family – my people, my memories of them, my love for them – the fear had gone.

Only, none of my hope or will or perseverance had returned. I was still lost.

I thought again of the kids, helping me make Christmas cookies when they were little, eating more than they helped, the boys blaming Gilda, John inevitably throwing up. I remembered them working together to sing a song for me, with Gilda in tow adding a modicum of challenge for the listener. I recalled the last time we cleaned out the garage, an event that basically turned into a heated game of basketball using two garbage cans and head-sized ball of tape.

The happiness returned.

I tapped on the window with the bear claw.

How is it possible to feel such despair alongside such happiness? How can one person feel completely opposite emotions at the same time?

How do you get to a point where the thought of living is more terrifying than dying?

The bear left me alive.

Nathan left me alive.

Nathan left.

I thought back to that day, anger welling up instantly. My mom is always reminding me that he didn't leave by choice. I know this. It doesn't help worth shit to hear it, but I know it.

I know it, because he never would have left Gilda.

Never.

There had to have been one hell of a deal on the table for him to go. There had to have been something that told him we would be okay, for him to give in. I know my husband. If there hadn't been something amazing coming for Gilda, for us, he'd still be lying in a hospital bed somewhere in a coma, fighting for his life, fighting for us. There had to have been a guarantee for us.

I thought about that for a bit.

What if he had?

What if he'd made a deal for us that said, I'll come along, but my family needs more?

That actually sounded like something Nathan would do.

And if he had… If he had struck a deal for us, something that said we would go on to live amazingly long and happy lives… All of us… If we had that kind of guarantee…

The impact of that idea hit me hard.

What would life look like if I had a guarantee?

How would my life play out if I could live it without fear?

I was wide awake, lying in the Rocky Mountains, all by myself, tapping on a window with a bear claw, from a real live bear that could have killed me that very afternoon.

I saw myself, suddenly, as the bear would have seen me. Small and insignificant. But standing my ground. Meeting his eye.

Braving his assault. Showing no weakness. Showing no fear of him. Proving my worth.

The bear was a predator who was likely used to having his way with his prey. His expectation would have been infinitely more than the caution and calm that I'd somehow mustered. Panic, resistance, violence, all would have made sense to him. But instinctual, rational, control, as unintentional as they may have been, would have surprised him.

I found myself wondering how much of the outcome of our encounter was my own doing.

I stopped tapping and looked at his claw.

What if I could face everything in my life like I faced the bear? What if it didn't matter, really, about all the reactions and emotions and bullshit? What if I could just feel all of that and go ahead anyway? Without fear?

What would I be able to do? To accomplish? To change? To become?

What if the bear was trying to show me that fear is fully and completely irrelevant?

Because a woman who can sit there calmly shitting herself in the face of a creature who is under no delusion of grandeur, has got a pair of Lady Balls made of titanium.

I finally drifted off thinking, *A woman like that? I like her.*

Making A Big Deal Out Of Nothing

I woke later than I'd expected and was moving again by noon. Still in a bit of a daze after the events of the day before, I'd coasted through my morning habits and was driving along lost in thought. At some point I remember seeing signs for Blue River and Valemount before latching on to some ancient French lesson that helped me make the connection between Tête Jaune Cache and the Yellowhead Highway. I turned right onto the Yellowhead, in the direction of Mount Robson and beyond.

The driving had lulled me into a serene but alert meditative state, one where I could follow random thoughts, or not, while still enjoying every new view with every new turn in the road. It was as if I had somehow split into two separate people, on the same path, but sitting side by side having completely different experiences.

One was enthralled with the landscape, its beauty, its majesty, and its kaleidoscopic vistas. The other was free to explore the thoughts, ideas, and emotions the visions provoked.

And provoke they did!

My thoughts kept turning back to my encounter with the bear. Now that the initial adrenaline rush had completely waned, I was able to remember details and moments with absolute clarity and focus. The bear's eye was brown. A deep rich ochre that shone from within in the dim damp shade of the forest. Like glass, an orb he used to view me, and through which I could see him. We'd been connected on some level, he and I. The two of us in the same place at the same time, interacting, communicating. It was easy to tap into the emotions of the moment; they were fresh and strong, hard to ignore in fact, like a pot of coffee brewing before you've fully awakened. The fear was there, but recognizing it for what it was, irrelevant and bothersome, I was able to push it aside and concentrate instead on the curiosity. I had tapped into instincts that humanity had buried ages ago, reactions that moved me to my core. I was thinking and feeling things that had no rational logic, no intent, no direction. It was nothing more than cause and effect. The bear acted, and I reacted. I acted, or didn't act, and the bear reacted. Like a dance. We were intertwined and one, sharing a moment, both of us in the same time and space, but having completely different experiences. I realized that we were both acting on the same level of awareness. I had transformed into an animal who, like him, was keenly curious, with a sole purpose, and a distinct plan of action, even if I didn't know what that plan was. I had reached out to him on his level, challenged him, and walked away.

The walking away part still had me confused. I'm sure it was more that he just wasn't hungry at the time, although maybe something about me just didn't strike him as tasty. And I was certainly no threat. But I was pretty sure that not many people who had ever come face to face with a wild grizzly bear were around to talk about it.

And that brought me back to the fear.

There had to be some part of me that had been afraid of the bear. If for no other reason than because, *it was a bear*!

So, if I assumed that I had actually been afraid of the bear, I had still had the wherewithal to give in to my instinctual nature and let it guide me through the encounter. I hadn't even gone through a list of possible reactions in my mind; I'd just let my gut take over.

Despite any fear I was feeling, regardless of anything that made any kind of sense to me, with no loyalty to any evolution of human intelligence, I moved through the moment and survived.

It struck me then that it was possible to actually do something that was completely contrary to what I was feeling at the time.

It was possible to feel one thing yet do something else.

I could feel happy and cry at the same time.

I could feel sad and laugh.

I could feel fear and act.

It was the last thought that had my mind going in circles until I finally had to pull over and give up the driving side of my journey so I could figure it all out. I pulled into a rest stop at the end of the lake I'd been skirting for the last little while. I could park the van and walk easily to the water's edge, where the merest hint of a breeze gave the surface just a suggestion of movement. I sat cross-legged on the gravely bit of beach, just out of reach of the wet lapping of waves too lazy to try.

The lakes I'd passed had all had a weird green colour to them: a pale, opaque, minty colour, like the Jello fad of my childhood when someone thought it was a good idea to add milk instead of cold water to the stuff. This lake was no different, but I was surprised by the clarity of the water within reach. I patted the surface gently with both hands, sending rings of ripples out, watching them until they were at last swallowed by the depths of the hole beneath.

There is something so very hypnotic about water. As I played quietly, softly moving my hands through the icy chill, I felt the lake reaching back to me, tickling my palms, swimming through my fingers, touching me as I was touching back. My hands looked distorted through the clear fluid, and I wondered if the lake saw me in the same wavy, hallucinatory haze. I lifted my hands from the water, slowly, trying not to disrupt the surface tension, trying to sneak away unnoticed, but the drops that came with me were eager to return home, and fell back into the lake, melting into the whole as if they'd never existed. I followed the rings of their travels as far as I could, until they, too, were one with the lake. I escaped into my trance with the water until a chill passed through me with a violent shiver. The sky was as gloomy as it had been for days, but it had dimmed considerably marking the late afternoon. I stretched my legs out to begin what was sure to be a long and tortuous struggle back to vertical. The cold round stones beneath me protested noisily, taking revenge on my bare legs with a chill that ran through me. I hugged myself tightly, tucking my chin and nose into the neck of my hoodie, eyes shut tight, in an effort to fend off the cold.

A light fluttering on my left shin could have been the wind teasing the hairs on my unshaven legs, but, as I didn't feel the same sensation on my right shin, my lip curled up in disgust at the realization that I was going to have to at least take peek at whatever had just landed on my leg. It wasn't walking around, but it was moving enough to catch my attention.

Hoping it would go away, I waited. I'm not a bug person. I don't even know how I'd made it this far without being totally overwhelmed with the bugs I'd encountered. I think I enjoyed a grim satisfaction in the mass extermination I'd been inflicting across the country. The front of the van had a layer of dead bugs a quarter inch thick smeared across it. Until I'd got to Alberta, where the buildup of corpses had just started drying up and falling off in chunks. Disgusting, yes. But oddly acceptable for a bug-phobe like myself.

Although, on further reflection, perhaps I had improved some in my paranoia.

I no longer had random shoes lying around the house where I'd managed to smash the life out of some tiny unfortunate soul who happened to find its way across my floor while screaming and dancing like I'd discovered fire ants. I was now able to move a shoe from its Place Of Execution after only a few days and vacuum up the dried remains of the critter all by myself. Nathan used to do that for me. He'd come home, find a shoe in the middle of the kitchen, and deal with it. But now, I'd had to find a way to cope with bugs in the house on my own. So, there's that.

And now, I was sitting calmly, at the edge of a lake in the middle of British Columbia, knowing there was some kind of crawly thing on my leg, steeling myself to look and see what it was. This, I decided, was Personal Growth!

I squinted through the protection of a curtain of eyelashes only to come eye to eye with the biggest friggin' dragonfly I'd ever seen.

This thing had to be the size of my hand, sitting like a king, right there on my bare leg, looking straight at me. Like he was waiting.

His wings were flapping, quickly, but not enough to fly away. I guessed that's why he didn't feel as heavy as he looked he should, and explained the fluttering. I took a deep breath and tried hard not to panic.

This was not the kind of bug one squashed with a shoe. This was the kind of bug one shot. With an arrow.

I didn't dare swat at him for fear he'd take a chunk out of my leg. I didn't want to shake him loose; what if he came at me? I pulled my hood up over my head, just in case.

Well, I thought, he couldn't stay there all day. I resigned myself to stay calm while I waited for him to move on.

After quite some time, I started to realize, he may have been waiting for me to move on. It was a stalemate.

I glanced carefully around for something to encourage his departure. A stick or a leaf, maybe. But there was nothing but small stones within reach. That would have to do.

With stealth and focus, I reached carefully and slowly to my side, and picked up one small stone. With a cough, I tossed it quickly in a small arc, hoping to land it next to my leg, close enough to make a noise to startle my visitor away, but far enough so as not to hit him.

The stone landed with an audible click, and the dragonfly lifted himself quickly off my leg, to my immense, though short-lived, relief.

He hovered in midair, right in front of me, and I shut my eyes tightly again.

He buzzed by my face, close enough to feel the wind from his wings, and left.

I let out a breath and opened my eyes, glad to be rid of him. It was time to go. As I leaned onto my hip to start the process of righting myself, I discovered my little nemesis sitting solidly on a tiny rock to my right, within arm's reach, facing the water in front of us.

Seeing him from the side, I was struck by the colour of him. His entire body, the size of my middle finger, shimmered in shades of the most splendid iridescent blues I'd never seen. Waves of colour flowed from his head to his tail, as if he was breathing in time with me. His wings were all but transparent, save for a blue and purple dot on each side. I imagined that the Lady Dragonflies likely thought him quite handsome.

Without warning, he jumped from his stone into the air and promptly landed on my left knee, which was bent and quite close to my face, seeing as I was trying to get up at the time. I froze.

Get off me. Get off me. Get off me, my mind screamed at him. Or maybe I squeaked it aloud.

I hazarded a glance sideways at him; he was looking right at me with his giant buggy eyes. He didn't look so pretty this close and from the front.

As suddenly as he'd landed, he jumped off and landed back onto the beach beside me. I tried to scramble up to my feet, but I'm not twenty anymore, so it was more of a grunt, a curse, and a process. On my hands and knees, I found myself face to face with the bugger sitting right on my hand.

What the hell??? Please get off me. Please get off me!

He fluttered a bit more, and took off again, landing in the same spot in the stones. I managed to stand up, teetering awkwardly, having to take a full minute to wait for the blood to return to my head and clear the black screen from my field of vision. I felt my hair move, ever so slightly.

So help me, if you're on my head!!!

He was on my head.

He walked around a little and jumped back off, landing once more in the same spot on the beach. I took a step in the other direction, which was not the way I wanted to go, but away from him was a plus.

Once more, he flew up, hovered inches from my face, and landed again on the same tiny stone.

It struck me suddenly, that maybe he was a she and maybe she was protecting a nest. As a mom, I was doused with a wave of familiarity, compassion, and respect. I moved to make as big a circle around the spot she was protecting as I could. And she stayed in place.

A few more steps toward the side and I turned to look back at her, still watching me, still holding her ground. The clear path I'd come down along to the water was between her and the van. I eyed the three-foot cliff I was going to have to climb to make my escape and looked back at the dragonfly.

Great.

Well, wanting to escape weighed heavier than the easy path, so hands up on the ledge like a kitchen counter, I hiked one knee onto the solid earth at hip level and heaved myself up and onto all fours, pulling something in my groin in the process. I rolled onto my side, hating dragonflies.

When the initial stab of pain subsided, I sat up carefully, hands in the dirt and grass to either side of my butt, feet dangling over the edge like a kid on a chair. My dragonfly was still sitting there, watching me. Much as I was watching her, I suppose.

Absent-mindedly, my hand rested on something smooth and round, and it was comforting to circle it gently with my fingertip while I summoned the umph to get up again. Still staring at my friend, I plucked the marble sized pebble from its bed in the ground beside me and was rolling it around in my hand when she rose from her roost and hovered at eye level with me, without coming closer. She watched me again, eventually settling back down in her spot.

I wanted to get going. I'd been sitting here having it out with a dragonfly for the better part of an hour, I guessed. I wound up to toss the pebble from my hand when the colour of it caught my eye.

Wiping it clean, and taking a good look at it, I didn't think it was a pebble at all. Maybe a piece of glass, weathered by Nature into a fairly smooth ball. It was green, opaque, almost identical to the colour of the lake itself. I wondered if maybe it was a rock coloured by the water over time.

Either way, it was pretty, and I liked it, so I tucked it in my pocket.

When I looked up again, the dragonfly was gone.

A little insulted, and more than a little hurt that she'd just left, without so much as a fly-by, I hauled myself back up to my feet and made my way back to the van.

I had thought I might spend the night in Jasper, but a quick drive through the middle of town changed my mind quickly. I had imagined Jasper to be a quaint, small town in the mountains, not the overcrowded, bustling mecca it looked like through my windshield. I was looking for solitude and tranquility. The energy in town was deafening.

My travel options were few as Jasper is a bit of a remote hub. I opted for south along the 93 to the Columbia Ice Fields. I felt like I wanted to see some glaciers and snow, though I couldn't imagine why. Even in July, that was going to be cold.

I drove for a bit longer before finding myself pushing the van through a series of steep hairpin dirt roads, climbing the side of a mountain to a tidy little campsite perched precariously on the edge of a ridiculously sharp slope. I locked the passenger side doors and pushed all of my supplies up against them, so I'd have to get out the driver's side. That first step out the other side in the middle of the night could be my last!

It felt like bedtime after a long day, even though I'd only travelled a few hours. So, I hunkered in, got warm and cozy with sweats and sleeping bag and closed windows, ate a sandwich that tasted far better than it should have, and settled in to reflect on my day. Once again, I found myself playing around with my bear claw.

Reaching up, tapping it against the window, I was thinking about fear again, and how I'd stood up to the bear. I smiled, allowing myself a little pride. Yes. I could be proud of myself for yesterday. I'd survived an encounter with a full-sized male grizzly.

Pride turned quickly to embarrassment as I vividly recalled my humiliation at allowing myself to be bullied in spectacular fashion, injuring myself in the process, by a dragonfly.

I couldn't help but laugh.

I imagined how I must have looked to the dragonfly. Huge and threatening. Until it tried to be friends. And then I cowered like the Lion in Oz.

I am pathetic, I told myself. But in my defence, it was a big-ass dragonfly.

I thought about her. I don't know jack about dragonflies, but I liked thinking of her as a mom protecting her nest. In fact, that had changed my whole perception of her. Suddenly she was no threat; she was an ally. She was strong, she was capable, she was friend.

She fought me, a giant foe, with everything she had, and she had very little. She was persistent. I wondered suddenly if she'd been afraid and guilt welled up inside me like a pot of pasta left on the stove. I hadn't meant to scare her.

But still she'd held her ground, even though she didn't stand a chance. Even though she might have been terrified. She'd protected her own.

Once I was out of the way, once she'd managed to get me a comfortable distance from her, she'd sat quietly watching me. Probably curious. Probably relieved.

She would have been grateful to still have whatever it was she was protecting. I wondered if a dragonfly could feel gratitude.

I could.

Couldn't I?

I thought about my kids. Yes, I was grateful for them. When I wasn't resenting them for anchoring me to this life. I was certainly glad I had them.

I was grateful for my house. More for the forethought that had us make sure we always had insurance and wills and a plan in case the worst happened. Which it had. I was able to keep the house. And the van. And everything that went with them. I had the right to inherit all of it. Even the copyright on Nathan's books, which meant that, because I was careful with my money, I hadn't had to get a job yet.

I thought about that, wending my way to the conclusion that I was even grateful that I lived in Canada, where I, a woman, could legally inherit and own all of our property. And I could do so without having to marry again. Without having to marry one of his brothers. Because, as it occurred to me, there are many countries in the world where women aren't that lucky.

I was pretty lucky at that.

If things had to be the way they were – and by then, that was a fact of which I was beyond certain, because I had unsuccessfully begged and bargained and offered my very soul to the devil himself to have my husband back, repeatedly – then yes, I was pretty damned lucky.

Clinging to the bear's claw, I rummaged through my clothes until I found the little green pebble.

Even in the blanched dim of twilight, it still had a green glow to it. It wasn't perfectly round, but it was smooth and comforting to roll across my fingertips. It reminded me of the emerald earrings Nathan had given me for our tenth anniversary.

I hadn't wanted them. But it mattered to him.

When we'd married, we were young and broke. He'd wanted to buy me a big diamond engagement ring, but we both knew that the money would be better spent elsewhere. The fact is, I never actually *liked* diamond rings, and it took some doing to convince him of that. Same as I don't *like* roses. I'm an emeralds and carnations kind of girl. But trying to persuade a compassionate romantic like my husband that that's even possible takes some time and finesse.

To my surprise, though, when we finally did go shopping for an engagement ring, emeralds that looked like what I thought they should look like can finance diamond mines. I couldn't hide my disappointment. Until a conversation with a jeweller, who ended up making us a ring with a full carat green garnet set in it like a diamond solitaire, changed my mind. Nathan proposed to me with that ring, and while I was thrilled with it, he couldn't hide his disappointment. There was no amount of convincing that could make that ring an acceptable substitute for what he wanted to give me. As we became more stable, he tried, year after year, to get me to give up the ring so he could replace it, but I would have none of it. And while I managed to prevent him from wasting money on a diamond I would never wear, I couldn't say no to the earrings.

The stone in my hand had warmed with my touch, and I held it to my lips. Yes. I was lucky.

Lucky to have married a man who loved me every moment as if I were more important than he was. Lucky to have been able to create a history together, a family, memories. Lucky to have had him as long as I did.

I was lucky to be able to keep what I had.

I was lucky to be capable of managing it all.

The tears were flowing freely, from my eyes past my temples, pooling uncomfortably into my ears, until they overflowed and began to soak my hair. But not for the first time, I realized that I wasn't crying. I wasn't sobbing, there was no begging, it didn't hurt.

Quite the opposite, actually. I felt good.

More than good. More than really good.

The tears flowed and I felt wonderful.

Not happy, really. No, not happy at all.

But good.

And lucky.

But lucky's not a feeling. It's an adjective.

Lucky is when you win. When you win the lottery or catch the bus on time or have a good day. When things go your way, that's luck.

I suppose, things had actually gone my way. I was back to '…if things had to be the way they were, and I couldn't go back, then I was lucky.'

So, what was the feeling that goes along with accepting that one is lucky?

The stone on my lips brought to mind the dragonfly, and how lucky she must have felt to have me gone. My fingers wrapped around the claw, and I thought of how lucky I'd been to escape his threat.

I wondered if Nathan had been watching. I thanked him for keeping me safe.

My next thought was that that was silly. Unless he did make a deal. Unless I do have a guarantee.

But don't I?

I have an income and a roof over my head and my kids. I have my wits about me, I've managed so far, I'm still here.

But if that *was* even possible, then nobody would ever die without making sure their loved ones had the friggin' lottery numbers. *Bunk.*

But I did come out lucky.

Why me? What made me so special that I got so lucky?

And who do I have to thank for that?

With the next breath, I felt like my bones had suddenly dissolved like warm wax. I slumped into a pile of tears and cried with absolute abandon. I gave myself over to the mercy of whatever had conspired to leave me with a life that could not be better had I designed it myself. I cried without grief, without sadness, without malice or threat or hate or despair. I cried with a purity that cleansed my soul. I felt my spirit soar with the freedom of having been released from whatever it was that was weighing me down. I welcomed into my heart a force that has lifted me from the depths of agony and futility. An enigma that brought with it hope. And something more that I couldn't yet recognize. An energy that would change my life and everything in it. A force that had the power to change me.

A mystery that I came to realize was nothing short of Overwhelming Gratitude.

Making A Good Target

I might have been shedding tears of good luck and gratitude, but there was no escaping the swollen eyes and sore face I awoke with in the morning. I rolled over to bury myself back into my blankets for the duration, only to be forced against my will into a day that could really only get better, by a piercing pain that shot through my groin like I'd just been tased up the coochacha! When I regained consciousness, I lay on my back trying to figure out exactly which moves my body was going to permit, hoping I didn't end up peeing myself before being able to haul my ass into the great unknown to find an outhouse.

As it turns out, the muscles that seize during a dragonfly-induced spasm that is re-enacted within hours are the same muscles that one must manipulate in order to release the hold on one's bladder. Not only did I make it to the outhouse, but I was able to partake in an entire conversation through the crack in the old wooden door with an elderly gentleman from Washington who had a prostate issue and understood completely the concept of urinary difficulties. Finally digging deep for my rusty Mom Skills, the ones that encourage Number One Relief Under Pressure, I managed my business and did my best not to make eye contact on the way out.

The further I got from the outhouse, the more I recognized the intoxicating scent of melting snow. I hadn't noticed it the day before, what with being distracted and all, but I was sitting in the middle the Columbia Ice Fields where glaciers and melting snow in July were the order of the day.

The memories triggered by the impending arrival of Spring as heralded by increasing stretches of blinding sunshine and the incessant dripping of ice and snow as it dissolved over days and weeks under the promise of warmth and renewal, came to me from corners of my mind far more obscure than time should have accounted for. Connections that should have been but a few months old felt as if they'd been unearthed for the first time since the Beginning Of Man. Spring had once been my favourite time of year. I took the heat of the sun and the light of the day and converted it all to a power that saw rooms cleaned, flowers planted, walls painted, repairs made, and renovations completed. There's a reason all five of my kids have winter birthdays. I was prone to a fever that boosted my mood, taking everyone I knew with me. A fever that brought enough energy to get me through past Christmas.

I was like a shark smelling blood. Every year, it started with the first day, the moment I would walk out the front door only to be overcome with the smell of the snow melting. By the end of the day, I had boxes out for winter coats and boots, opened windows, and summer sheets at the ready. Even our typical March Break Blizzard was a minor waist-deep inconvenience if Spring was just around the corner. Oh yes, the scent of it was invigorating.

It was probably the third or fourth "Excuse me," that finally broke my trance and found me standing in the middle of the roadway on the side of a mountain with a thirty-foot RV in my face. The occupants must have thought me daft. But as Canadians do, I apologized for being in their way while they apologized for bothering me. I moved and they continued on, but not without considerable respect and awe on my part for the driving skills that saw them crawling along like a mountain sheep on steroids. Still shaking my head at the wonder of not having heard them crash to the highway below, I got back to my van and set about getting me back on the road. I bundled up against the morning cold and left in search of a sliver of sunlight in which to warm my spirit and eat my breakfast.

As luck would have it, it was likely going to be noon before dawn came over the mountains between me and The East. But the glare of the reflection off the glacier coming down the mountain to the west was an adequate substitute. I pulled into a rather large rest stop area mere minutes down the highway from the entrance to the campground. It was quite empty, so I pulled the van up to the guardrail, facing the jagged and complicated valley that sat between the mountains in the distance and the cliff directly in front of me. My entire windshield was transformed into a painting of one of Nature's most breathtaking scenes.

I think, because of the kids, I had learned how to stop. As much as I hate being around people, when I find myself forced to do so, I like to sit back and watch them. It's infinitely more entertaining than interacting with them. Especially on the casual impersonal surface level that we tend to inflict on each other. I could sit in the van, across the street from the school, waiting for the kids, and watch all of the other families going through the same routine as I was. Some would stop and talk to each other. Others would trudge on by, head down, absorbed in their own troubles. Most parents' faces would glaze over as they tried to listen attentively to their children's reports of the events of the school day. I knew that feeling too well: the repetition from day to day and child to child could be painful. Other parents just flat out ignored their kids, walking ahead of them, forcing little legs to skip to keep up, all the while the child's mouth would be chattering away. My heart would break a little for them. Nowadays, I could drive by a school and just cringe and the majority of the parents, picking up their kids, who didn't even look up from their phones to say hello. Lyrics of another era sprang to mind: sad words of warning for parents whose kids grow up to be just like them. For me, though, it was fascinating to pay attention. I never failed, when I took the time to just sit, and watch, to learn something I hadn't known before.

So it was, this day. I sat munching on some fruit and cheese looking out my window, straight ahead, with my expectation of seeing Anything Interesting Happen at a relative zero.

The mountainsides were scraped with shades of grey, from the palest whites to the darkest blacks. They wore skirts made of trees, but were topless, their ragged peaks reaching for the sky with sheer and absolute confidence. Streaking down the middle was the glaring white of the snow atop a glacier, a miles-long sheet of ice that I'd somehow expected to be more impressive. It was sliding down the mountain at a speed impossible to discern in its sloth, until coming to an end as an abrupt cliff at about the mountain's rib height, where it had broken off into a shear wall of blue, reminiscent of a roughly cut topaz in its clarity and intensity set off by the full sunlight from over the wall of rock behind me. Though nothing was moving, every few minutes or so, I would be hit with a piercing stab of light that had somehow aligned itself to travel perfectly from a hundred million miles away, to target in on a piece of ice that was likely five miles past me, only to reflect directly back into my eye. I found myself watching and waiting for these flashes of brilliance, as if they were a message that I dared not miss.

Having eaten, I was beginning to warm up a bit and opened the window to take in the fragrant and fresh air. My mind began to empty comfortably as I watched, observed, breathed, feeling no obligation to do more than that. It was as much a gift to behold such a view as it was to have the time to enjoy it. As my mind cleared, I was able to absorb my surroundings with all of my senses. The chill in the air tickled the skin on my arms and face while the silence sharpened my hearing until I was sure I could make out my own heartbeat. My nose reveled in the scent of a million different trees mixed with snow and, I was pretty sure, a hint of fish? My mouth watered as every breath I took reminded me of the perfect apple I'd just finished for breakfast, the extraordinary taste of which still lingered on my lips. I did my best to memorize every detail of where and when I was, so that I could take it with me when I left. Nothing I'd ever seen, including pictures of places just like this, had ever come close to the real experience. I was at once sad that I would never be able to fully share the reality of being here with anyone, and almost jealous of the luxury of being able to have and keep it all to myself. Not everything needs to be shared with everyone.

A cloud suddenly appeared, and expanded down the mountain in the distance, a little to the right. At first, I thought it odd that a cloud could just pop into existence, especially so low. But as I watched, I came to realize that it wasn't a cloud at all. It was snow. A good chunk of snow must have just let go and was sliding to the bottom.

It sure was taking its time, falling slowly, almost gently.

Until it reached the tree line, which is when the idea of scale hit me, and I realized what I was watching was an actual avalanche. An entire patch of trees was mostly buried, the odd trunk stripped of its shape and sticking up awkwardly out of the now settling wave. I couldn't begin to hazard a guess as to the size and magnitude of what I'd just seen, but I do know that it wiped out, quite literally, thousands of trees!

I stepped out of the van to get a better look. I thought I might hear something, but it was too far away. For a moment I had a little panic that someone might have been caught in the slide, but I couldn't see how anyone could have even been there in the first place.

I stood watching for the many minutes it took for the cloud to lighten and finally settle. In the grand scheme of things, I would be hard-pressed to point out to anyone exactly what had happened and where. But my gaze was locked on the spot, fascinated. In the middle of the white patch that was about the size of my thumb as I held it up in front of me, a white smear that had just replaced what had been, a few minutes before, a lot of dark rock and trees, my eyes narrowed in on a tiny speck of black until they crossed uncomfortably. I focused on the speck, trying to figure out what it was. Would a bear look that tiny from here?

The dot didn't move, but it did seem to be easier to see. As I watched it with a curiosity I'd come to welcome, I could have sworn it was getting bigger. In fact, it didn't take much longer for me to be convinced that, yes, it was getting bigger. Whatever it was, it was moving. And it was coming straight at me.

I squinted tightly, trying to get a better idea of what it could be, and thought I could just make out the wings of a bird. At the rate it was growing, coming closer, it would fly right over me within another minute.

It would have been nice, I think, if it *had* actually flown right over me. But that's not quite what it did. It rather flew *at* me.

It was a big bird. And it was flying hard and fast. His wings were pumping, alternating a rich deep brown and a bright white as they pulled his body through the air. I could see his head jerk from side to side, as if he were spying me with one eye and then the other. His belly was white, and his feet were tucked up inside the fluff of it. I waited for him to alter his course away from me.

He, apparently, was of a different mind. He kept coming.

It might have made sense for me to duck. No pun intended. Or to have hopped back in or behind the van, had I been thinking of course. But seeing as I wasn't thinking, clearly, I began waving my arms in the air and yelling at him, "Hey! Stupid bird! Don't hit me!!"

English was not his first language.

My last glimpse of him in front of me was through panicked fingers covering my eyes. I saw his head and face as if they were a series of photos in a flip-book that I could stop at will. The size of him, the weight of him, would be able to knock me flat. I watched him reach for me with talons as sharp as needles, the fluffy feathers around his ankles ruffling against the air through which he was cutting. I held my breath and stood my ground as the powerful beat of his wings sent my hair in every direction; I wasn't sure I hadn't been slapped in the face by his wing. I turned instantly, following his flight as he skimmed over the top of my van, his wings easily spanning its width, across the parking lot and skated across the roof of the shed on the other side, plucking an unfortunate and very surprised chipmunk from the eaves. The bird banked back around toward me with a skill I couldn't have guessed, pumping his wings once more as he passed me, proudly showing off his prey and disappearing into the distance.

I'd thought it was an eagle, but he was a red-tailed hawk. As I stood watching him go, I ran my hands through my hair trying to put it back into place, and maybe making sure the smart ass hadn't pooped on me. But what I found was a feather. As long as my hand from wrist to fingertip, and three fingers wide, it was a deep rich russet, tapering to a black and a white stripe at the end. It was waxy to the touch, rigid and strong. I worried that he might be hurt or in danger without it - it was definitely more red than brown, marking it as a tail feather - but he'd caught a chipmunk and made a good fast getaway, so I didn't worry for long.

I scanned the sky for him, somehow feeling as though I should thank him for the gift, but he'd vanished into the ether.

I looked back in the direction where I'd seen the avalanche, wondering if maybe the hawk had been forced into a sudden evacuation. But I couldn't be sure if I was looking in the right spot or not. Both hawk and avalanche were gone. And if it weren't for the feather in my hand, I would doubt I'd ever seen either.

I'd been on the odd end of Nature these past few days. I'd collected some very unique and memorable souvenirs. I reached into my pocket, pulling out the other two. A claw, a pebble, and a feather. Gilda was going to go out of her mind when I gave them to her and told her all about the adventures I'd had getting them.

I shuffled through my mementos, admiring the colours, the black, the green, and the russet. Separately, they were what they were. But together, each one seemed to somehow take on the hues of the other two. Each one was hard and solid and strong. Yet fragile. And temporary. Each had been a gift, a surprise. And somehow, I was glad to have each one of them. Nature had seen fit to give these to me. Here in this place. Now in this time.

With the tears I was now beginning to recognize as a welcome reaction, I gave myself over to the wave of emotion that melted me to my bones, and brought me to my knees, right there in the parking lot next to my van. I allowed the gratitude to fill me, overflowing my soul once more as I surrendered to it, only trying to understand what it was I was supposed to do with it.

Because it occurred to me, that, as grateful as I was, I had no one to thank.

I knelt peering through tears at my hands splayed out before me, palms up, a makeshift table beneath a bear claw, a glass pebble, and a tail feather, weakened by the power of such Overwhelming Gratitude, while I tried to wrap my mind around something I was supposed to know. Something deeper that was trying to get my attention. A light on the other side of a lake that was shining in my eye, coming closer, getting brighter. Something important. Something profound. Something just out of my reach. It was like trying to remember a dream: the details slipped away while the emotion stayed, leaving residual feelings in the wake of an unseen memory. I was completely crippled by a staggering sense of appreciation. Brought to my knees by a powerful and pure feeling of gratitude.

For what?

What could I possibly have to be grateful for? What did I have that was so great that I should be brought to my knees in appreciation? What was left that could make me feel so good?

And there it was.

The answer was, Nothing.

I had nothing. No future, no hope, no sense of direction or belonging or purpose. Nothing to look forward to. Nothing to make me think that life was worth all the trouble and the work and the stress and the worry. Nothing to make me want to get up in the morning. Nothing worth fighting for.

I had nothing to contribute. Nothing left to give. Nothing I did or was or wanted or would be counted for shit. I just didn't matter anymore.

There was not a single thing that I could think of that made the whole fucking process of life *worth* the cost of living it.

The anger welled up again, growing in the pit of my stomach, expanding up into my chest, filling my ribcage, forcing itself painfully into my throat as I tried to push it back down. But it was too late. The ugly monster that had taken over my life, that had turned me into the bitter, self-loathing creature I had come to hate with every heartbeat, reared its head again and took over. I held my breath, forcing it down, pushing with all the might I could muster, but it was a lost cause. Once the anger settled in, I was helpless against it. The frustration in losing myself again to the evil that consumed me, only fuelled it.

With no thought to the searing agony in my knees, I reached into myself with the strength that only pure hatred can create and pushed back with a ferocity that echoed back from the mountains that surrounded me. I unleashed a tidal wave of sound from my crushed and tortured heart, aimed it at God Himself, willing it to hurt Him on some level I couldn't envision. To punish Him for taking away everything that mattered to me, leaving me broken and ruined, and then making me feel like I had to fucking thank Him for it?

"FFFFFuuuuuuuucccccckkkkkk YYYYYooooooouuuuu!!!!!"

The words exploded from my mouth, tearing at my throat, over and over, echoing back off the mountains, through my head, through my soul.

"FUCK YOU!!! I WILL NOT THANK YOU YOU MOTHER FUCKER!!! I WON'T DO IT!!! YOU CAN'T MAKE ME!!!"

I clenched my fist tightly around my trinkets, wound my hand back and threw them with everything my middle-aged muscles could muster.

Like insult to injury, I realized in a half second that my throwing arm was not what it used to be. The pfft-pfft of the claw and pebble hitting the gravel six feet in front of me was only bearable in comparison to the complete and utter ineffectiveness of throwing a fucking feather in a shear rage.

I watched as the stupid thing fluttered gently to the ground, landing softly and silently in absolute contrast to what I felt. I kicked the gravel violently with my boot, with the intention of ripping the damn thing to shreds with my venom, only to jam the shit out my arthritic right knee, the jarring jolt of pain shooting up into my leg and landing square in my already-wrecked groin.

I limped feebly back to the van, managed to get in and get it started, manhandled the transmission into reverse and backed out spewing stones with the satisfaction I'd been denied by boot alone. Peeling out onto the paved highway, I put the windows up while I tried to vent the anger that consumed me. I screamed. I beat the dashboard. I pushed the gas pedal until the van began to shake, careening wildly, dangerously, down the road. My grip on the steering wheel made my hands numb, and I waited for them to just let go and send me soaring over the road's shoulder to my death in the abyss below.

My knee cramped unbearably, my shin seized, pulling my foot back with it, easing it off the pedal. I wallowed in defeat, unable to even throw a fulfilling temper tantrum. My impotence threatened to swallow me whole as I watched the speedometer slow to the speed limit. I drove in silent tears, willing my mind to stay quiet, to shut up, to stop inviting conversation with anything or anyone outside of my head. I refused to feel beaten. I denied the gratitude. I rejected the humiliation.

I tried to focus on control. The only thing I had left: the ability to think what I bloody-well wanted to think. And I couldn't even do that.

The kilometres ticked off, one after another, marking the time and distance between me and whatever forces had conspired to ruin me. The anger began to calm, and as it did, the gratitude began to return. I resisted both. I would not give into the manipulation of my mind. It was my mind to control, mine to use, mine to enjoy or ignore as I saw fit. Thoughts and ideas that came and went were mine and mine alone. No god or nature or force or energy could make me feel anything I didn't want to feel.

I drove on enjoying the enforced silence I'd claimed until the warning beep alerted me to the van's need for gas. It was another half hour before I found a gas station in Banff where I filled up and then ducked inside for a quick pit stop.

Back in the van, I sat munching on a bite of my Oh Henry! carefully sucking off the chocolate, then plucking the peanuts out of the caramelly goo that stuck them to the fudge middle before rolling that around my tongue and cheek until it melted. Mindlessly, I only had one big, maybe two small bites left, when I was overcome with guilt.

Stunned that a pile of natural garbage could spark such fierce emotion, I realized in a panic that I'd abandoned my trio of trinkets in the most callous and unforgiving paroxysm of anger the mountains had witnessed since their creation. I shoved that last piece of chocolate bar – yes, it was definitely *two* bites – in my cheek and pulled back onto the highway, turning right, back to the rest stop, in hopes of rescuing my belongings.

Making Amends

I raced back the hour and a half to the parking lot where I'd seen the hawk, oddly not surprised that I'd passed not a single car on the way. As I drove, there was a panic swarming around my head, dense as gnats on a warm summer evening: a dread that someone might have found my things and made off with them. I would never forgive myself, I thought, wishing I could find the fury that had charged my departure from them in the first place to get me back there faster. When I finally pulled in, the results of my outburst were immediately apparent. Half of the parking lot looked like it'd been set upon by a group of hormonal teenaged boys who'd just been given the keys to new souped-up coupes with black windows and purple LED under-lighting.

Or one crazy ass mom in a minivan…

I sifted through dirt and stones, finding the bear claw, unscathed, quite easily. The pebble, smudged with tears and coated with dirt, blended in well with the other million or so stones in the vicinity, and took a bit more effort to locate. But I'd lost the feather.

There may not have been any people through the lot since I'd left, but the wind must have reclaimed the third of my three gifts, and I felt the loss in my bones.

"I'm sorry," I whispered, to the feather, I think. "I'm sorry I'm such a fuck-up."

Tears from some bottomless well in my heart leaked from my eyes. I climbed back into the van, exhausted, defeated. I was so tired of losing things that mattered to me.

Although, to be honest, this one was my own doing.

My fingers deftly played across the surfaces of the two objects in my hands. The parallel ridges that ran the length of the flat underside of a claw that I would have thought to be smooth felt rough against my own fingerprints, while the smooth curves of the pebble, pocked here and there where its original face still showed despite the exploits of time, felt foreign and discordant. I had spent so much time with them, examined them with such scrutiny, I felt I had a deep and personal connection with each. But the feather had been so new, and the guilt of my betrayal weighed heavy on me.

I thought of the hawk who'd gifted it to me and wondered if he'd be angry with me. It had been a part of him, he'd entrusted me with it, and I'd failed him. I accepted that he'd chosen me. From across the miles he'd spied me, sought me out, and given me one of his most valuable possessions. He could have dropped it anywhere, but he hadn't. The feather's worth expanded in my esteem, and I felt the loss doubly.

"I'm sorry," I whispered again. "Please forgive me. I didn't even get to thank you."

I looked at my hands, outstretched, still holding the claw and the pebble, and stared until my vision split making it look like there were two of each set upon three hands. The sight was unsettling; I had neither need nor want of the extras but lacked the will to focus my eyes back to their shared image. No matter how I perceived the confusion before me, one of the three hands was conspicuously empty, and I understood that the price I would pay for my outburst would haunt me. Closing my fists tightly around what remained, I made my way back to the van, giving up, once more, surrendering something that mattered to me, turning my back and walking away.

A sense of defeat washed over me like a weighted, hooded cloak, pressing down on my shoulders, obscuring my vision, limiting my view to only that at which I was looking directly. The van rolled slowly through the parking lot, coming to a rather loud and abrupt stop without my having to brake. Somewhere in the depths of my mind, a rogue thought registered the realization that I'd hit something. Numbly, I shifted the gear into Park and sat dazed, falling into the comfort that comes with staring blankly into the space directly in front of my face.

I've always wondered at the body's ability to do that. How you can sit for minutes that feel like hours, in a trance-like state, without blinking. It feels a little euphoric, actually. Not unlike a wakeful sleep. Given the luxury of having no one around to interrupt, I indulged myself in the refreshing escape of just being. My body stilled, needing no direction or impulse from my consciousness. My mind emptied, cleared, refreshed. Slowly, I began to waken, but without losing the serenity of the hypnotic state, I could discern the images in the side view mirror on which my gaze had locked, without noticing their detail. Yet my peripheral vision, along with my hearing and the sensation of the air moving around me sharpened. I could interpret the colours and shapes of the mountains, the snow, the trees, the guardrail, the surface of the parking lot, without moving my eyes from the vanishing point in the mirror. My perception of the world reversed, with the edges of my mental view screen sharpening while my focus in the middle blurred. I was at once both aware and curious of the switch and played with the challenge of noticing details of the world around me without looking at them. Without looking, I could see the tree line, a cloud, a sign. I hadn't noticed the sign before, only that its post was one of many that held the guardrail in place. My attention followed the post to the ground, where it was perfectly spaced amongst all of the other posts, standing at attention, each one a shorter version of the last as their distance from me increased. A tiny flicker of movement at the bottom of the sign-post brought my awareness back to it. A muted change of colour blinked slowly in time to the breeze, like a single blade of grass bowing to the wind. Except this grass was red, not green.

I forced myself awkwardly from the van, dragging my mind painfully from its stupor to confirm what I had already concluded, and squinted hard at the bottom of the sign post, impatiently trying to focus through watering eyes, only to spy my feather, pressed up against the thick wooden block, quivering precariously, threatening to make a break for it against the predatory threat that was me. I stopped, fixed my attention on my goal, and willed my flimsy prey to be still, to wait there, to trust that, this time, I would take care of it. I promised to protect it, to respect the gift of it, to value it for the message it brought and the sacrifice that gave it to me. I breathed deeply, bending the wind to my will, forcing it to back off and return my favour. I stepped slowly, deliberately holding my breath as I crouched to take back what was mine. I had been entrusted with its care, and I intended to live up to my responsibility. As I reached out, the feather fluttered in the stilled air, as if reaching back to me, accepting me, and forgiving me for the horrors and abuses I'd inflicted on it. I took it gently in my hand turning it over, a gasp hitching in my throat as I saw that I had damaged it terribly: there was a tear along the rachis about one-third of the way from the top, creating a vee in the vane, the barbs split violently away from the quill. I held it tenderly in my hands, examining it quickly. It was holding together, but I didn't think it could last much longer in the wind. Carefully, as if holding a newborn babe for the first time, I carried it back to the van, cradling its tip, willing it to live. I climbed into the back of the van with it, laying it gently on the cooler, trying to come up with a way to repair it.

I peered at it closely. At first glance I'd thought I'd peeled the soft barbs from the hard quill, leaving them vulnerable, each barb precariously holding on to its neighbour, a chain filled with weak links. But somehow, I'd managed to actually split the rachis itself, cleanly, straight up the middle: the russet fingers were still firmly attached to the hand. I blew a heavy sigh of relief down my chin into my shirt. The feather would live, but it would be forever changed. It would never again be able to fulfill its original purpose. But it would go on to have a deep and indelible impact on me. I picked it up, caressing it tenderly with a fingertip, the lines of its form guiding the lines of my skin, up and out to its edge. It was soft and so very fragile yet had provided the hawk with the ability to soar through the sky with ease and grace, speed and focus, agility and threat. Alone, it was harmless, useless even, pretty, but not overly remarkable. But when gathered with others like it, bent to the function for which it was created, it became part of an efficient and fascinating predator. As part of a hawk, it was a force of considerable prowess. By itself, it was just a feather. But a feather that carried with it the memories of a lifetime and the expertise of a master. This feather had seen the world in ways that I never would. It had soared to heights that I couldn't reach, touching the wind, touched by the cold, cutting its way through the air, basking in the heat of the sun. It had travelled with a freedom and innocence that no human being would ever know. It had escaped the weight of the world and witnessed it in its most pure form, from a distance, separated from it, released from all danger, all harm, all worry. It had viewed life from a perspective that allowed for clarity, peace, and understanding. I held the soft ridges to my lips, my eyes closed at the sensation, and for a moment, I was there, high above the mountains, apart from them, circling, lazing in an effortless glide, warmed by the sun, cooled by the breeze. There was no room here for worry or fear or anger. My mind emptied of all darkness, revelling in the peace of the space around me. Duty melted away like raindrops trickling down a pane of glass, melding together, gaining speed, falling. The pressure of responsibility lessened until

I felt as if I could float, raised by the strength of the wind; the tethers that tied me to my world and my life unraveled, snaking away, letting me go. I was aloft, free of my burden, summoned to a life of ease and calm. Without the anchor of my obligations, my mind recognised a tiny light in the distance. I knew this light now, and with a sense of cleansing, I welcomed it to me, watching it grow as it came closer. It approached, growing in intensity, filling my field of vision, surrounding me in the glowing warmth of it.

My throat tightened reflexively around the part of me that swelled to greet it. My insides were expanding, reaching out, receiving the light into myself. The tears sprang forth with complete abandon as my voice found its way through, winning its way past the muscles that ached with the effort of holding back an energy that refused to be thwarted. I gave up the fight and allowed the light to take over my body, heart, and soul, crying tears and sobs of pure gratitude. I fell over onto my bed of messed blankets and discarded clothes, curled my knees into my chest and surrendered to the light.

Crying is funny thing we do. We hate doing it, because it hurts. And it leaves us looking pretty ugly. But I've always found the *language* of crying to be one of the most ridiculous undertakings of human life. Children don't put words to their tears. But by the time we're adults, we're saying some really whack shit. It starts with some generic waling, the kind of wah-wahing that can go on for some time. But eventually, we start to vocalize what we think the problem is.

I can't do this... I can't do this... It's too much... Too much... I hate this... I can't do it... Can't do it... Why is this happening?... I can't do this... And we cycle back through the mantra of our despair.

Until, at some point, the actual crying has eased, and we're left there, lying on the bed like a drivelling idiot, whining on and on about how *I can't do this... I can't do this... I can't do this.*

And that's when we start to tune in and hear ourselves. We clue in to the crap that's coming out of our mouths, register the meaning of the words, and actually start to feel silly. We're embarrassed at what we're saying, at how weak we are, at how pathetic we can be. I think this is the real reason no one wants to cry in front of anyone. And it certainly has to be the reason no one wants to see someone else cry. The universal response to someone crying is, "Don't cry…" Might as well just tell them to, "Calm down."

So, crying has become a very personal activity. Snot and puffy eyes aside.

As I lay in my bunk in the back of my van, tears streaming for the thousandth time, eyes shut tight against the glare of the light that enveloped me, I heard the words coming from my mouth, from my heart, and for the first time, I didn't feel silly. I wasn't miserable. I wasn't pitiful. I *was* confused. I was aware. I was curious.

And I wasn't worthy.

"I am so lucky… I am so bloody lucky… I have no idea what I did to deserve so much… I'm sorry I'm so unworthy… I'm so sorry… I have no right to be this lucky…"

I accepted the gratitude as mine.

"Thank you... Whoever… Whatever… Thank you… Thank you for choosing me… Thank you for… I have no idea what I'm thankful for…" I blathered on until my voice cracked painfully.

The ball of light began to fill me; I felt it pushing into me, pressing against my ribs, wending its way through my flesh, pushing harder, and harder long after I was sure I couldn't hold anymore. It condensed within me, becoming dense, almost solid, and still, pouring more of itself into me. The gratitude, the light, heating my body, overloading my mind, lighting my spirit on fire.

"Thank you… Thank you… It's not enough… The words are not enough… What do I do?... The words aren't enough…"

My body began to ache with the effort of containing the light within. My muscles were clenched with all the strength they possessed. I willed my body to stay strong, not to fight, but to accept whatever this was, even while knowing that it was more than I was capable of doing. What did it want with me? What was happening to me?

"I'm sorry... It's not enough... The words... They're not saying what I want them to say... There are no words... Thank you sounds so petty... So inadequate..."

My legs began to tremble. I shivered intensely. I couldn't hold on any longer but still couldn't figure out how to make it stop.

I don't know what to do with this!!!

In the next moment, I experienced a power of unimaginable force swirl itself through my very being, blinding me with the white of its light, numbing my nerves with the static of the charge it was building within me. Beyond being absolutely positive that I couldn't go on, having no idea how to stop it, being forced to simply hang on, I finally accepted its power, gave in to its control, yielded to its dominance.

And it erupted. Time stopped as the light exploded from within me, in the absolute silence one hears when sound overloads the senses. I saw nothing but light. I heard nothing but peace. I felt nothing but warmth. All I could smell and taste was Spring. My mind reached out, to the hawk who flew across the heavens, and through his eyes I saw the energy explode from my body, a shock wave of atomic proportion expanding instantly around me, outside of the van, across the parking lot, through the valley, over the glaciers, swallowing the mountains, and spreading beyond my vision over the horizon, with no lessening of power or speed, leaving behind it a shimmer that set the world alight with intense colour, brilliant clarity, and something else. Something deeper. Something bigger. Something profound. A wave of something greater than Absolute Gratitude had radiated across the land, not as a blanket so much as a dome, reaching as high as it had far. It had come from me. I hadn't created it, but because I had allowed it, it had been created. I wasn't the source of this energy, but I was the door through which it had emerged. I could see the aftermath of its passing as clearly as I could see the feather in my hand. It had coated everything it touched with something that left it shining, standing taller, stronger, with more life in it than it had before.

Somewhere in the back of my consciousness, I was sure I heard something, a whisper of a something, an echo of a whisper, a something that sounded like, *thank you.*

I have no idea what happened. I can describe what happened, but I can't explain it.

Whatever I had just done, I'd shared it with the world.

In time the light calmed. Not a dimming, even though at some point I noticed the sun had set. I might have slept. But I didn't move. My mind emptied. I just *was*. I was existing on a level with the universe that I had no way of understanding. Yet I accepted the confusion easily, part of me excited without knowing why, part of me reassured that there was more to come: more of *what* I didn't know or feel bothered about. As the world around me seemed to glisten with the afterglow of whatever I'd cast out over it, I was left with a lingering feeling of warmth and strength that swirled through my thoughts and memories. I poked around through the photo album of my life.

I recalled three months in bed trying to give my twins the best shot possible at a safe and healthy start while neglecting the son I already had. I had always cringed at the guilt this would stir up. But here, in this moment, the vision that accompanied it saw me sitting on my bed with a curious toddler, watching my belly heave with the kicks and punches of siblings who would grow up to be his best friends, reading books and telling stories, enjoying the abundance of one-on-one time that would soon evaporate into the depth of family. I might not have been able to take Dan to his swimming lessons, but I sure didn't miss out on time with him. I smiled to myself, feeling his sweet chubby cheek, tightened by his infectious smile, pressed against mine.

I shifted to the first time I noticed my mom's memory failing. I'd picked her up for a doctor's appointment. She was ready when I arrived, dressed as nice as she always was, and we chatted pleasantly as we drove off. Stopped at a red light a few minutes later, I was hit with the warning that would signal the beginning of the end.

"Here's a stupid question…" she asked plainly.

"Wouldn't be the first," I pointed out.

"Don't be a smart ass." Moms never lose that power over you. "Where are we going?"

I've watched Jeopardy! with her my whole life. It was a rare feat for me to get a question right at all, never mind beat her to the punch. She still loves to watch the show with me. The feeling was never mutual, but now the reasons were different.

It's unbearably hard watching my mom lose her identity, her independence, and her intellect. But for the first time in forever, I found myself laughing at her sense of humour, which remained undeniably intact. I am forever reminded that I am a Cheeky Beggar.

The last words I, the Cheeky Beggar, had said to Nathan, that I would tell his mother on him if he didn't behave for the doctors, has haunted me terribly. At some point after, I realized that he'd been trying to get my attention, to get them to stop, to tell me something. That thought has caused me more grief than almost anything else. I've never been able to bump into that memory without falling apart from guilt and regret.

But in this moment, with the darkness pushed aside, I could see him clearly, almost panicking, trying to get me to listen. All I could think at the time was to get him inside, to get the help he needed. His best chance at a full recovery, from whatever this was, was inside with the doctors, not outside chatting with me. If I had to do it again, knowing what I knew at the time – because, at the time, as far as I knew, *no one was dying* – I would do exactly the same thing.

If I had known that that was the last time I'd ever see him, I would have hung on to him and never let him go. I would have told him everything that mattered most one last time. I would have told him I loved him, more than anyone else in the world, I loved him, with my entire being. I would have told him I was sorry. I wish I'd been a better wife. A better friend. *I'm sorry I laughed at you cutting your head. I'm sorry. I'm sorry I didn't notice you weren't feeling well. And I'm mad at you for not telling me you weren't feeling well. Were you not feeling well? Did you know?*

At some point, he did know. He knew. When they pulled him out of that ambulance, he knew. And he wanted to say something to me.

I didn't have to guess what it was. There was no doubt.

I love you. I love the kids. Look after them. I'm sorry. I love you.

Nothing I needed to hear.

Nothing new.

All things that I knew like I knew I my own name. They didn't need to be said.

Yes. If I had to do it again, I would do the same thing. I would opt for help over hearing him tell me he loved me. Because there is no way I would accept that he was dying, no matter how sure he might have been.

A tiny black balloon filled with regret floated up from my chest, rising to the heavens until I could barely see it, popping into the non-existence of forgiveness.

I hadn't been able to see it before. Our last words for each other weren't the last words we said. They were the only words we said. Words that never needed to be said. Words that described what we already knew. We loved each other. No regrets.

Morning came with sunshine and clarity. I woke easily, feeling refreshed and energized. I took care to rearrange my living quarters into an organized, tidy, comfortable home. I found a new zippy plastic bag and protectively tucked my trinkets into it, using a straw to vacuum the air out of the bag, sealing my treasures safely within.

I pinched the corner of the bag into the latch of the glove box, securing it for the drive, but leaving it out in the open to accompany me on the trip home.

I hadn't begun to understand what had happened to me. It was as surreal as it was real. A mystery and a certainty. Something I remember clearly, but something I knew I would never be able to fully share with anyone else.

What I did understand, however, was that something had changed. Something had shifted. I had connected with something outside of myself that I hadn't known was there, only to find that it had been inside of me the whole time. I had experienced something that changed everything about how I perceive the world, how I interact with it, how I fit into it. I still didn't know what that *it* was. But whatever *it* was, this wasn't the last time I was going to run into it.

Making Sense Of It All

It occurred to me, as did a great many things over the next few days, that I was going home. Whatever plan I had brought with me when I'd set out aimlessly more than two weeks before, was left behind in the chaos of thought and wonder that had transformed me in the mountains. I'd left the rest stop that morning, driving with a new sense of freedom. Windows down, music on, the steady hum of the tires on the road, I drove, quite uncharacteristically, right at the speed limit, in no hurry, with no pressure. I passed through Banff, avoiding the more touristy stops, soaking in as much of the scenery as my imagination would allow. I would treasure these views, keep them stored in my memory for the rest of my life, realizing I would probably never be back. There was a reason I was supposed to come here. And I was fairly certain I'd found it.

Coming out of the mountains, I could see Calgary in the distance, looking very much like the Emerald City sprung from the Plains. Home was basically straight ahead to Lake Huron and a right turn south to Hamilton, though that would likely take the better part of a week. I smiled to myself, content with the idea of returning, but still not in any rush to get there. So much had happened to me, and I welcomed the chance to try to sort through it in solitude and routine.

For the first time in days – no, actually, weeks! – I thought about the fact that I hadn't talked to my kids. I hadn't called or texted them, nor they me. Five kids, all with cell phones, and not a single text. Camped out in a small flat campground just outside of Regina, I plugged the phone in and checked it. Nothing.

A hint of panic flashed through my consciousness, and just as quickly, melted away. They were fine. Of that I had no doubt whatsoever. Though I was curious as to how not a single one of them even bothered to check in.

I realized that I hadn't either. Which is probably more the issue. It was likely I would be passed over for Mom Of The Year again this year.

It's not like they were little kids. John was still living at home and would be there to keep an eye on Gilda and Nanny. The twins had a car and could check in. Dan was around and would certainly make sure everything was okay. But none of that explained why none of them – not even Gilda – had even texted me an 'I love you Mom.'

I found it curious that I wasn't hurt as much as I was curious.

For a half a second, I considered texting her anyway, checking up on her, but something stopped me.

There were no texts from my sister, either. Okay. Now *that* didn't make sense at all.

On one hand, she would have hunted me down if something were wrong, so it made sense that I hadn't heard from her if everything was okay. On the other hand, I hadn't told her I was leaving or where I was going; surely, she should have missed me by now.

I considered texting her, but just as quickly decided against it.

Oddly calm, I turned off the phone and tucked it away. My fire was hot and ready. I tossed in a giant foil-wrapped potato to bake in the coals and settled myself into my chair to watch it cook, mouth-watering as I anticipated the steak that would join it. Throwing caution to the wind, I cracked open the bottle of Merlot I'd grabbed for the occasion – whatever occasion this would turn out to be – and got a head start on the wine.

The smell of the wood burning, the hot evening air blowing across the tranquil sea of grass that blanketed the Canadian Prairies, the sharp bite of the wine against unsuspecting taste buds, all lulled me into a sense of feeling rooted to the Earth. I kicked off my shoes and let my toes dig through the dirt and grass under my feet. With eyes closed, I let the peace of my day envelope me in a light-as-air cushion of comfort, blocking out the rest of the world and all of its problems. Breathing deeply, I felt the gratitude building again. Not as forceful as it had been the day before, I was both relieved and a little disappointed. But I allowed it in, feeling the crescendo deep in my belly as it collected there, gaining strength and power, filling me easily. More prepared for the experience, I relaxed, welcoming the feeling, letting it take over my mind and heart. The light within me grew once more, threatening to overtake my senses again. I reached out to touch it, just to poke it with a single fingertip. It popped easily, as fragile as a soap bubble, and I felt the wave of emotion spread through me and away from me in a ripple that expanded as far as I could see. Opening my eyes, I was not surprised to see the glimmer that shrouded everything around me, as if the world had been painted with light. Tears dripped silently down my cheeks, as I took in the view around me, bathing in the euphoria left behind by the ripple.

The air smelled sweeter as I watched the sun sink closer to the horizon, flavoured with the scent of campfire. I picked up the appetizing aroma of my potato and hurried to throw my steak on the grill. An hour later I sat curled up in my borrowed lawn chair, wrapped in my sleeping bag, sipping the last of the wine from the bottle, sated, relaxed, and incredibly grateful. And probably a little bit drunk.

I remember watching the fire. And the stars. But I don't remember going to sleep, though I woke up in my bed, rested and ready to face my day.

The sky was clear and blue when I woke up, earlier than I'd expected. Even after taking my time eating and packing up to leave, I was still driving head on into a blindingly bright sunrise. I opened the windows and spent a good hour with my hand 'flying' along behind the side mirror. I know I was supposed to yell at the kids for doing that; it seems there was always one of them learning about aerodynamics as they stuck a hand out and let the wind lift and lower it. I'd forgotten how much fun it was.

Despite being able to easily fall into my driving trance, I was repeatedly distracted from it by cars passing by me, paying far too much attention to me for my liking. I finally pulled my hand in, deciding I still preferred to be left alone. But the attention didn't wane. Car after car passed me, and virtually every one of them contained at least one passenger who turned to look at me as they went by. I found myself watching vehicles approaching to my left in the mirror, forcing myself to keep my focus straight ahead, but failing as I strained my eyeballs to the side, inevitably making awkward eye contact with some curious outsider. It got to the point where I started to get a little nervous that maybe I had a flat tire or something. Nobody had made any kind of motion as if to point out a trouble spot on my van, but eventually the attention got to me and I pulled off to take a look for myself.

I walked around the van twice and saw nothing that should attract any kind of notice from others. I'd been driving calmly, at the speed limit. I'd kept my singing in check with the window open.

Well, whatever it was, it seemed to have nothing to do with me. I stopped inside the gas station where I'd pulled in and ducked in to use the washroom. The lady at the counter was talking to a customer but stopped mid-sentence to say hello while the man she was talking to turned to me and just stared, saying nothing. I mumbled a quick hi and went about my business. Once in the washroom, I checked myself in the mirror. Maybe my hair had fallen out or something.

Again, nothing out of the ordinary. I looked fine.

In fact, I looked pretty good, I thought. My hair was up in a quick ponytail, but wisps had broken free in the wind. I liked the effect. I never wore makeup, but my face had a nice colour to it; I looked like I'd gotten a little bit of sun. I didn't look tired; that was an improvement for sure. But mostly, I just looked like me. On a good day. I finished up and headed back out to the store.

I was pouring myself a coffee when I heard the man from the counter wish me a good morning as if he were standing right beside me. I turned toward the voice, and was surprised to see him standing right there, coffee in hand.

"Good morning," I offered cautiously.

"Nice day for a drive," he added.

"Yes, it is," I agreed, feeling the sentiment a little more fully than I'd expected. It brought a grin to my face as I suddenly felt a wash of gratitude for the beautiful day and the freedom to enjoy it.

The man smiled back, genuinely, looking at me as if he wanted to say something.

"Do you live close by?" I asked, though I had no idea why.

"No, I'm just passing through. Heading west."

"Ahh. I'm going east."

"Vacation or home?"

"Home." Again, the gratitude. The man eyed me with a most peculiar expression. As if he recognized me but couldn't place my name.

I put the lid on my coffee and wished him safe travels. I stopped to pay the woman at the counter on the way out and left, glancing through the window as I passed, somehow not surprised to see the man still standing where I'd left him, watching me go. And yet there was nothing creepy about him. I smiled again, waved, and was on my way.

I drove on until mid-afternoon and decided to stop for the night in a small campground just before Moose Jaw. It was clean and my site was tucked away into a corner, but close to the showers on the other side of a pond with a sandy beach and rows of plastic Muskoka chairs. After a good scrub down standing in the luxury of hot clean water, I parked my butt in a chair to let my hair dry in the afternoon sun and watch some kids playing in the water for a while.

There were three young ones, two wearing inflatable water wings on their arms, and the third, a girl in a bright green swimsuit a little older than the other two, teaching them how to swim. A group of adults out of earshot from me on the beach were keeping a close eye on them. As I watched, I thought the budding instructor wasn't doing too bad a job; the little ones seemed to be catching on. I felt a little catch in my throat as I thought about my own kids at that age, learning to swim, playing in the water. The tiny stab of discomfort melting away as quickly as it came, as quickly replaced with gratitude for the moment. My eyes closed and I smiled openly, remembering. I saw a faint shimmer splash outward from where I sat.

When I opened my eyes again, the little girl with the water wings was standing in the water, turned toward me, staring, smiling. I waved at her and she shyly waved back, shrugged her shoulders with a little giggle and rejoined her friends. For a split second I grieved for the little girl I'd expected to have. But before I could latch on to the feeling, it was replaced with an overwhelming pride for Gilda. Gilda who was bugging to get her driver's license. She'd been studying the book for two years now, and I was running out of excuses. I was going to have to let her try. There was nothing to grieve there. She's caused me as much stress as any other kid could have. Again, the gratitude.

Eventually, one of the moms called the kids out of the water for supper, and I realized I was hungry too. I made my way back to my campsite, smiling, looking forward to dinner.

I woke myself up in the middle of the night, laughing loudly at something that I'd said in the dream I'd been enjoying a moment before. I was still overtaken with mirth as I realized I had no idea what I was laughing at. The dream had faded amidst the confusion of finding myself alone in the dark, now laughing at nothing. However, this, I found outrageously funny, and lost myself all over again in peals of wracking hysterics. The more I tried to stop, the harder it got, until finally, spent, I tried to catch my breath.

Both sliding doors to the van were open, letting what little breeze there was pass through and over me. Somewhere in the distance I heard the grumbling of a woman, the loud zipping of a tent, more grumbling, silence, more grumbling, the loud zipping of the tent again, and then a man's voice, loud and clear.

"For chrissakes Angela, shut up! You're making way more noise than her laughing!"

That set me off all over again. I laughed until my sides seared with the effort. My cheeks seized painfully. I thought I might pop my eyeballs in their sockets. I gave up trying to keep it quiet and just let loose, overcome by the absolute hilarity of waking up some poor woman and pissing her off with my laughter.

If I could have explained to her how new this was for me. If I could have told her how long it'd been since I'd found anything funny. If I could have made her see what a miracle it was that I was laughing for the first time in years, how good it felt, how surprised I was, how much I'd missed it. Maybe she would have understood more and been more tolerant of it.

But then I wouldn't have been laughing in the first place.

I hugged myself tightly, grateful for Angela's reaction, appreciating her sacrifice of peace and sleep so that I could enjoy a few minutes of bliss. I took that little ball of gratitude and invited it to grow inside of me, finally releasing it to the universe, willing it to find her, to cocoon her in its light and warmth, to share my gratitude with her, to give her back her calm and her dreams, to somehow let her know how much I appreciated her, and to give back what I'd taken. In my mind, I imagined her snuggling back into her sleeping bag, tucking into the warmth that welcomed her back to bed, I saw her roll onto her side, relaxing her body into the form she would take for the rest of the night as she fell into a deep and rejuvenating slumber. I have no idea what Angela looked like, but I'm positive I saw her smile as she drifted back into her dreams.

I allowed myself to melt into my own bed, releasing my body parts in stages from the efforts of their merriment. I'm sure there's some kind of scientific chemical reaction that makes one feel so good after a great laugh, but none of that mattered in the face of the euphoria that carried me back off to my own unconscious state that night. I slept with absolute abandon, pure surrender, and perfect trust. I was beginning to understand that, while something had changed dramatically within me, there was something more. Something deeper. Something profound. A tiny part of me opened to the message, knowing without knowing how, that it would reveal itself to me when it was ready. When I was ready to hear it.

I might not have been ready to hear it, but I was ready to listen.

Making A Difference

I drove on the next day marvelling at this bizarre new euphoria I'd discovered. I'd figured out that its energy source was gratitude. But not just a general feeling of appreciation, not just being thankful for something. It stemmed from surrender to Overwhelming Gratitude, which, I was learning, was the difference between a matchstick and the sun.

I'd heard all kinds of gurus touting the benefits of being grateful. At some point I, like countless others, kept a Gratitude Journal, where I took the time at the end of every day to write down three things for which I was grateful. After a couple weeks of that, all I had was pages and pages of the same three things: Nathan, the kids, and our life. That notebook made for good kindling.

It's not like I took my good fortune for granted. I don't think I ever really overlooked the enviable life I was lucky enough to live. But I also don't think I ever really made the effort to explore the details.

We express our thanks at Thanksgiving. We offer up prayers of thanks. We say thank you as part of our habitual manners. We *think* we're grateful.

This is not the same thing.

The Overwhelming Gratitude that I'd been playing with the past couple of days was energy on a whole nother level. It was as if I'd been walking around in the dark my whole life, able to find my way around, with access to everything I needed, and then some. And now someone had turned on the light. I could see colour and texture and distance and shape and size. Water had drained from my ears and what was once muffled now exploded with harmony and rhythm, melody and bass. Everything I touched seemed to touch me back. Scents reached out to me. The air itself felt like the arm of a fierce and powerful protector around my shoulders. My first encounter with it that night in the Ice Fields after finding my feather certainly caught my attention. But since then, I'd been able to call the feeling back to me, without the panic, without the doubt, without the apprehension. Each time it returned, it came with as much power as it had the first time. I'm not sure whether I was able to control it or if I'd just learned how to catch it better. The rush of wellbeing that I experienced each time it took me was equaled only by the fascination of being able to actually see it affect the people around me.

I'd thought it odd that perfect strangers were suddenly making eye contact with me, striking up conversations, interacting with me. I've never been overly amenable to random encounters with others. And I wouldn't say that that had changed. But between my curiosity and the feeling of genuine connection with the majority of the people I was running into, I couldn't say I wasn't enjoying the effect.

I'd noticed it when I was driving the day before, with people going out of their way to make eye contact with me as they passed me on the highway. And there was the Guy Heading West in the gas station. The Little Girl in the pond.

But today, it took on a whole new potency.

I turned off the TransCanada for a quick detour to Qu'Appelle Saskatchewan. I'd gone to school with a guy from there a couple of lifetimes earlier, and I took that connection as close enough to stop in for a visit. Fred had been a good friend and I'd thought of him often over the years. He was a traveller, so I didn't expect to find him there, but still, I liked the idea of seeing where he'd grown up.

I drove around for a bit. Just a bit, because it's a very tiny town, and stopped into a cute little cafe on a corner for lunch. The place didn't look like much from the outside, but the inside was clean and bright and promised a tasty meal. I ordered myself a club sandwich and fries and sat watching the locals while I waited.

It was pretty small-townsy. The staff were friendly and seemed to know everyone. There were people at four other tables besides mine. Of course, the one with the mom and two kids caught my eye first. The kids, one in a high chair and the other in a booster seat, were eating fries and giggling like munchkins as they took turns showing each other the mashed-up mess of fries and ketchup in their overstuffed mouths. Mom was trying to get them to stop and behave themselves, but the cause was lost when they caught me watching and laughing at them. The show was on, and I did my best to rein it in for Mom's sake. When she finally caught me, I gave her my Best Sheepish Apology Face. She smiled warmly at me, understanding, but not giving up the good fight.

A little twitch up the back of my neck and the shiver that came with it redirected my attention to a couple seated in a booth along the far wall, on the other side of the young family. All four elbows on the table, they were both leaned in to each other, speaking in low tones, seriously, oblivious to everyone else in the room. When the waitress stepped between us to place their drinks on their table, they both stopped abruptly, without taking their eyes off each other or acknowledging her. I felt like I'd been hit with a splash of cold water.

I caught the annoyed look on the server's face as she turned away, though she replaced it quickly with her natural smile as she passed the children. I turned back to look at the couple off to my left. As close as they were to each other, he was talking with more force than a casual conversation should allow. His neck was quite red above the collar, and his hands were moving in small but jerky movements, accenting his tone. The woman, still leaning in to listen, was seething. Her jaw was clenched tightly, her brows almost touching each other across the vertical crease they'd created above the bridge of her nose. She tried repeatedly to interrupt him, but he wouldn't let her speak.

I looked around the dining room, surprised to see that no one else seemed to have noticed the pair, let alone be bothered by them as I was. The kids were blowing bubbles through the straws in their milk.

The man barked a too-loud, "No!" immediately quieting his voice once more.

A man's voice carries, its tone can be heard, or rather felt, quite far away. I remembered hearing my parents as a little girl. When we had company, I could fall asleep soundly knowing my dad was downstairs, talking, laughing. I couldn't hear what he said, but I could make out his voice from among many, and I always felt safe. As I got older, he turned mean. Or maybe he was always mean and I hadn't noticed. But I would hear my parents come in late, after a long night at the restaurant, and I could tell by the tone of Dad's voice seeping through the walls whether I was going back to sleep or not. More and more, I spent my nights curled up in my bed waiting for him to finish giving my mom shit for whatever stupid thing he thought she did this time, while knocking a coded conversation on the wall that separated my bedroom from my sister's. This man's voice had that same tone to it.

I cringed inwardly, feeling myself withdraw as I had as a teenager. I've never been good with confrontation; I'm a good thinker and an even better speaker, but not when the emotion kicks in. As I got older, I stood up to my dad, but at great cost to my mom and sister. Confrontation under attack was not my strength.

Determined not to let their quarrel invade my space any more than it already had, I pulled my attention away from them, focusing instead on the chair in front of me. My eyes zeroed in on the red vinyl that lined the back of the seat, dotted with the shiny silver upholstery nails that held it in place. My gaze separated the chair into two, freeing my mind, allowing my imagination out of its cage to soar eagerly around the room.

I hadn't moved, but I was somewhere else. In the same place, but not. I glanced at the floor, recognizing the diagonal pattern of the checkered black and white floor tiles. When I looked back up at the chair before me, Nathan was sitting there looking right back at me, smiling. He reached across the table and took my hands in his, massaging my palms with his thumbs the way he always did when I was stressed. I looked deep into his eyes, recognizing him, seeing him, connecting with him. They closed softly as he nodded, understanding my question.

Yes, he could hear me. His smile never broke. It seemed he couldn't talk to me but didn't need to.

Why are you here?

I understood. *Because I'd called.* I smiled back at him gratefully.

That guy is mad. He's really giving her a hard time.

He looked as concerned as I felt. I'd seen that expression before, when we'd blundered through the agony of Gilda's heart surgery, and understood it immediately. My apprehension turned instantly to compassion for the couple.

His grin leaned to one side.

I smiled back. *Yeah. We did. We made it through. Together.* My eyes closed as the light filled me once more, the gratitude sweeping in, unbidden but welcome. It spread through me, building its strength, preparing its charge. Until I felt ready to release it.

The light flowed from me, encircling everyone in sight, flashes of brilliance streaking around the room, excited to be freed, sharing itself with anyone who was open to feeling it. I envisioned it passing through the man's body, into the woman's and back, willing it to bounce back and forth between them until they both lit with the hope and strength it brought. I forced it into their souls as it had been forced into mine, encouraging it to cleanse them of their fear and anger.

The piercing squeal of a child brought me roughly to my senses, interrupting my trance, jolting me back to reality. I glanced around me quickly, feeling suddenly humiliated that I'd been sitting there having a conversation with my dead husband like some kind of lunatic. Sure that everyone in the place had been watching me, I was surprised to find them all chatting and going about their business like a whole bunch of normal people.

Until I found myself looking directly into the eyes of the man and the woman seated across the room. Identical expressions on their faces, they both sat staring raptly at me, mouths slightly open, stunned into silence. I felt like I should say something, but, seriously, what?

What?

Nobody else had taken any notice of me. So, I hadn't spoken aloud or done anything overly stupid. But these two were fixed on me. Thankfully, the waitress rescued me, stepping between us with two plates of food for them. A moment later, I watched her retreat to the kitchen with the same full plates. Looking back at the table, the pair were now relaxed comfortably back in their seats, hands loosely resting on the table, chatting quietly. They seemed to have forgotten all about me.

The waitress returned with two take out boxes, collected the cash the man was handing her, and I sat dumbstruck as the two walked out the door, together, his arm protectively around her shoulders. The looked tired, raggedly so, but calm, and composed, at ease. I felt none of the anger or resentment I'd sensed earlier. The confrontation was over, forgotten.

My club sandwich arrived, setting off an appetite of impressive proportion. As I ate, I relaxed back into my chair, avoiding serious thought as to what had happened here; there would be time for that later. For now, I was content to sit and eat and watch the people around me. Here in this tiny town in the middle of Saskatchewan, I'd had a very remarkable day.

Making History

I was back on the highway, happily nibbling cold leftover fries out of a cardboard takeout container, dancing in my seat, just enjoying my drive. It was the kind of good mood that comes after accidentally helping someone overcome something they didn't realize was a problem in the first place. They're happy. You're happy. And you go about your business feeling as if you've earned the Lightness Of Being you take away from the encounter. There's a clear and obvious *reason,* a cause and effect, a particular string of events that fell together, quite serendipitously, but that you recognized and reacted to, to ultimately *deserve* a celebration of sorts.

Still smiling, far beyond the active memory of the scene in the café, I waved my good mood in front of me like a flag for all to see. I made eye contact. I smiled back. I said hello. People in the other cars couldn't hear me say hello. But that didn't stop me. I was on a high, and I planned to ride it out.

Seeming to have transitioned from the Escape to the Vacation portion of my journey, I was comfortable slowing down and taking the time to look around. The dogged essence of my departure had ebbed, to be replaced with a sense of peace and calm. I needed to catch my breath.

It wasn't four hours later when I decided to stop for the night. There was still plenty of light left. I wasn't hungry but had a half of a club sandwich if that changed. I looked forward to a relaxing evening in front of a fire, watching the stars.

I checked into a welcoming, private campground and grabbed myself a double scoop of chocolate chip ice cream at the store on the way in. I found my site, pulled in, and managed to set up my lawn chair one handed, plopping myself into the seat to lick away at my cone. There was nothing I needed to do, nothing pulling my attention. It had been a long time since I had enjoyed an ice cream cone so fully! It was an ice cream cone: cold, sweet, tasty - and nothing more.

Once done, I sat peacefully in the late afternoon sun as the feeling slowly returned to my frozen lips. It was the part of the ice cream experience that I liked the most. Once my lips were completely numb, it would take about ten minutes for them to feel normal again. Like being at the dentist but far more pleasant, I ran my tongue across the smooth softness from side to side, the top, the bottom, and back. Coupled with the lingering sweetness of the ice cream, the sensation was one I thoroughly enjoyed.

Weird, sure. Probably more weird to share it. But I can't possibly be the only person who likes to play with my lips like they're someone else's. So, there's that.

I got up and pulled my cooler out of the van, rummaging through it to the bottom, sorting through what was left, collecting a few things that should probably go *in* the fire instead of *over* it. I made enough room for my wine, cracked open the bag of ice I'd bought at the tuck shop, and noisily crushed a bottle deep within it to chill. Still struck with the desire to celebrate, I closed up the cooler and dug through the van for a long-buried grocery bag of forgotten treasure. The marshmallows were quite squished, but that wouldn't matter as they melted with the chocolate amidst some graham crackers.

Party for one, coming up!

I set about arranging my campsite, moving the van twice to get the best angle for star gazing from bed, getting my bunk ready, setting up the fire for later. Once satisfied that I would be camping in luxury this night, I had only to dispose of the bag of garbage before commencing my revelry.

Like most campgrounds, someone would be around in the morning to collect the garbage, but I didn't want a crap bag of trash killing my chi. I walked it down the road back to the gatehouse, passing a dozen other campsites on the way. Most of them were occupied by trailers; it seemed that people preferred to camp in style these days. Regardless, you can't walk by without taking a peek in, and on this night, I found myself squeaking happy hi theres to virtually everyone I encountered. So caught up in the sense of community, I returned to my site the long way, touring the entire resort as I followed the loop of the dirt paved main street. By the time I got halfway back, bbq's, propane stoves, and fire pits were all hard at work cooking dinners of all sorts, and the smell of the place was glorious!

A handful of sites before getting back to mine, I came upon a double site with four tents and a crowd of kids that looked like they could be mine. As I came into view, one of the young men spotted me, his hand coming up in greeting accompanied by a big grin and a hearty, "Hi Mom!!"

It's funny how, no matter how old we get, we still feel like we're eighteen on the inside. My first reaction was, hey, look, friends! Theirs was, Mom!!

It'll happen to them soon enough.

Remembering my station in life, I waved back, throwing in good solid 'Behave yourself' look for good measure.

"We'll try to keep it down tonight, but if we're too loud, just let us know," he offered as someone shoved a fresh beer in his hand.

I laughed out loud at the endless levels of irony in that statement. But I nodded in agreement and continued on my way. Most people of my general life stage would have cringed at the idea of spending the night so close to so many unsupervised bundles of energetic youth, but I figured there was little they could do to surprise me. I was sure it would feel quite homey.

I got back to my site still thinking about my young neighbours. Which got me to thinking about my kids. As I lit and stoked the logs in my fire pit, I wondered again about their complete lack of communication. No matter what my gut was telling me, my mind was wrestling with my newfound neglect. Confident that my mini blaze had grown to independence, I dug out my phone and steeled myself to wrestle with it. Realizing that I had a crowd of experts only a few yards away, I resolved to handle the matter myself, only using their help as a last resort. I could do this.

Concerned a tad that the phone was only half charged, I got over it when I found the camp's free wifi. I logged in and went online to download Facebook.

I'm not a Techy Mom. The kids have tried to get me involved, but, let's face it, why? They set me up a Facebook account that I never bothered with after the first week or so of painful lessons. Mostly it was just a reminder of loss. I had 10 Friends. And five of them were my kids.

While it loaded, I readied a line of smores for cooking, pulled out my wine, and curled up in my chair, with my phone, in front of the fire.

The first thing it wanted was a login name. Well, that was easy enough. I typed in my name.

Then it wanted a password.

That was different matter. What the heck was my password?

I thought back to John patiently explaining things that came so easily to his young mind, trying to fit them neatly into mine. He was a smart kid; he learned quickly, taking information given him and expanding it into conclusions that the rest of us never saw coming. He also understood that not everyone learns at his pace. I think kids who grow up with a sibling like Gilda learn a side of humanity that the rest of us miss out on. It's definitely not a bad thing.

John would have made my password as easy as possible.

I tried 1234.

A little swirly circle popped up for a few seconds and I was in!

I felt a sense of pride that far and away exceeded the measure of my accomplishment. There was an insane urge to tell someone that I, Queen Of The Tech-Inept, had just logged onto Facebook, *all by myself!!!* I wanted to announce it to the world, but the only ones around to hear me would have been the kids down the block, and I didn't want to embarrass myself.

I poked around at a few things, trying to get my bearings, finally, somehow, landing on Gilda's page. She had an iPad, and she knew how to use it. I scrolled down through her timeline and just about fell off my chair.

Gilda Bear
Today at 5:37 PM
Momma did leave Caron Saskkatchwan today
Likes 42 5 Comments

Gilda Bear
Yesterday at 4:02 PM
Momma did stay at Tillebrook Park in Alberta
Likes 187 27 Comments

Gilda Bear
Thursday at 4:30 PM

> Momma is at Columbia Ice Feilds today
> Likes 152 18 Comments

What. The…

I scrolled down, watching an exact itinerary of my journey, day by day, updated, liked, and commented on. She had tracked my entire trip!

I found the first entry, dying to see how she started this. How the hell did she explain to everyone she knew that I'd up and left? I took a deep breath, steeling myself for what I might find. This is the same kid who told all the teachers that I had four boyfriends, I like to lick the ice cream out of the carton, and we don't have toothbrushes in our house. Thankfully, teachers are used to this kind of thing. But Facebook?

There it was. The day I left.

> Gilda Bear
> July 4 at 2:42 PM
> Momma did og on a vacation today Me and Nanny are stay home and have a vacation too Momma is very sad I hope she has a happy vacation Happy birthday Momma! I love you so much too much!
> Likes 198 54 Comments

Dumbfounded.

I let that soak in a bit while I melted a marshmallow and squished it into its chocolate and graham cracker nook, biting into it in sheer ecstasy. The gooey sweetness filled my mouth, sticking to my lip and chin on the way in, covering my fingers in a gunky mess. There is no way to look elegant eating a smore. I let the last of it melt away on my tongue and began licking the rest of it off the rest of me.

How was it that a kid – scratch that – young woman with Down syndrome could connive such a scheme? She had managed to convince literally everyone she knew that I had gone on vacation. That I had left her and Nanny home alone. That they were okay. That I was okay. Finding her posts online raised as many questions as it answered.

I dipped my fingers in my wine, licking them off carefully, figuring the alcohol might cut through the last of the sugary mess. It was actually a little more tasty than I'd expected. Maybe I was onto something.

I clicked on the Comments.

> Awww, that's awesome! I hope she has a wonderful time!
>
> Good for her! We're thinking about you guys all the time. I hope she's feeling better!
>
> Happy Birthday Momma! Have a great trip!
>
> Let me know if you need anything, Gilda! Happy Birthday Momma!

Not a single person questioned my leaving her home alone.

Because she wasn't alone.

I clicked back to the very first comments, finding her brothers.

> Hey! Mom didn't tell us she was going on vacation!
>   Yes she did
> When???
>   She did say I need a vacation
> Oh yeah. I didn't know she was going though
>   Yeah she did.
> I'll be home tomorrow
>   I love you Dan
> I love you too Gilda Bear

Yeah. I didn't even see her leave this morning
You wer asleep
You should have woke me up
I was asleep

We'll be back on the weekend – help with the pool and lawns
The pool is closed come open it for me and Nanny

Do you have groceries Gilda Bear
No you can take me shoping
Okay we'll go tomorrow
Okay Dan

Good lord!!

I couldn't decide if I was the best mom on the planet or if I was going to be arrested when I got home!

Scrolling along past more birthday greetings and well wishes, I spotted my sister.

Where did she go for her vacation Gilda Bear?
Hi Auntie She did go for a drive
How long will she be gone?
When she comes home
Okay then. I'll give her a call
I am watching her phone
What do you mean?
I can see it moving on the road Momma did fix my phone I can watch her phone go

What? No! I fixed it so I could track *her* phone. Not that I'd ever used the feature. But apparently, she had. And it seemed to be working for her. I resolved to get John to fix that for me when I got home.

So you're tracking her trip?
Yes
And Nanny did say don't bother her she's sad
Got it. She definitely needs a break.
Yes Nanny is looking after me

Oh, for the love of.... Nanny bought the kids vibrators for Christmas!!

Good.
And my brothers is coming home tomorrow
You keep me posted. I want to know where she is, okay?
Yes I will post on facebook
You do that. Let me know if you need anything. I'll be by tomorrow too.
Yes

I took a good swig of my wine.

So, they all knew where I was. No one was worried. Nobody questioned that I'd been gone for weeks. They were all giving me time. And space. And for some reason that was completely foreign to me, I was good with that.

I dug into another smore wondering at how very okay I actually was with it.

My family, my friends, everyone I knew, had all stepped back away from me, and the only thing I could feel was grateful. There was no self-pity, no reading between the lines, no woe-is-me tiny voice in my head blowing it out of proportion. I was glad of the chance to have been able to run away as far and for as long as I needed to work things out. For myself.

Truth be told, I'd had to go pretty far.

I had travelled halfway across the continent and back, alone, unprepared, in search of *what* I didn't know at the time. I'd thought I was finished. I'd believed that I'd been left for waste, only biding my time until I could be done with this world. Yet here I was calmly cooking smores over an open fire remembering clearly the pain and heartache that had taken me into the darkest of places, without so much as a tear. No hesitation, no foreboding, no avoidance. Only for a moment, because I didn't dare stay long, I tapped into the pain of losing Nathan, of losing myself, and I understood exactly how I had come to be so desperate.

I suddenly understood that the pain would always be there. It had become a part of me. It would come to shape me into a person very different from the woman I'd started out as. It would never go away. But maybe I would get better at taking care of it. The tragedy was permanent. It would be up to me as to how much I let it hurt me.

My neglected marshmallow melted and fell into the fire. I stabbed another one and started over.

It was going to be a long time before I could make any sense of all of this. But I knew, deep down, like I knew I was still breathing, that I had the time. I had been given the time that Nathan had been denied, and it was up to me what I chose to do with it.

And I'll be doing a lot more than what I thought before!

I made my smore and chomped into it happily. And, *SHIT!* The sticky marshmallow could very well have still been on fire for the searing flash of pain it shot across the back of my tongue. I tried to spit the whole mess out, but it stuck, forcing me to take a deep breath to try again. Except that a chunk of chocolatey marshmallow broke free and shot down into my esophagus instantly triggering my gag reflex. I coughed once, violently, and shot the sweet chunk straight up into my sinus. Eyes watering, tongue crying, ribs aching, I coughed and hacked until finally managing to dislodge most of the offending matter from the nooks and crannies of my oral cavity, save the one lost lone chunk now firmly embedded up my nose. I sat back in my chair, exhausted from my efforts, grateful for not having met my death By Smore.

Laughing didn't help the pain in my face, but it did help me see the situation for the comedy it was. Glad no one was around to witness it, I chalked it up as one of those experiences better kept to myself.

I turned to gather up the rest of my smore fixin's and discard them vengefully into the fire when I realized that they were all gone. I half hoped someone had stolen them while I was barely conscious, but I knew the truth.

I'd mostly recovered, though there was still a hint of chocolate wafting in the warm night air and was enjoying the warmth of the fire on my feet, sipping away at the last of the wine when I was struck with a thought.

I pulled my phone back out and, without too much trouble, found John's timeline. He could do things with computers that astounded me. Chances were, there was more on his page.

No disappointment there. I scrolled through the month I'd been gone. I'd thought I couldn't be more surprised than I'd been with Gilda's feed. I was wrong.

I found a picture of Dan and the twins sitting in the garage. It was nighttime and the overhead door was wide open to the outside, where the rain was falling so thick and heavy I could barely make out the streetlight on the curb. The three boys were smiling widely into the camera, thumbs up, soaking wet. And for some reason, they'd filled the garage with pool hoses.

> So our driveway slopes down to the garage and it's raining outside like crazy tonight. Gilda Bear kept saying it was raining in the garage. We finally went to check and the drain at the bottom of the driveway was plugged

> and the water was up to our knees when we opened the door and flooded the garage. We panicked for a second and then remembered the pump and hoses for the pool cover. So we've been pumping the water from the garage through the house and out the back door! The garage is soaked but not a drop in the house. Hope Mom's having fun on her vacation – cause we're having an adventure at home!!

You can't help but be impressed with that kind of ingenuity!

A couple posts later there was a photo of Gilda and Nanny sitting on Nanny's couch, both buried in blankets they'd pulled up over their heads. All I could see of them were two smiling, happy faces.

> When you hear your sister and Nanny screaming like they're being murdered, brothers come running from all directions. Took a few minutes to figure out they were okay - except for the bat. We figured out how to get it outside and saved the day! Mom's still away missing all the fun with the local wildlife!

It's hard to find a cell phone in the dark that's fallen into the dirt and sat there long enough to turn itself off. Especially when your ribs hurt from laughing so hard. My battery was down to 5% but I couldn't resist one more scroll.

A shot of a cute little shed caught my eye: vertical wood siding, paned windows, complete with bright yellow flower-filled planters under each, bookending a barn door. A shiny black weather vane topped the gable. I quite liked it but wouldn't have thought it John's cup of tea at all. The caption simply said, "DONE!!!"

I looked at the picture more closely, wondering what it had to do with my son. It wasn't the shed that finally tipped me off; it was the dog in the distance behind it that did it. I used two fingers to magnify the picture. Yes, that was Murphy back there, lying under the oak tree in the corner of the yard.

So, if that was my dog, and my tree, and my yard…

The shed was standing where the shed should be standing but didn't look anything like it should look. This one was nothing like the old metal creaky piece of crap I hated so much.

I checked the comments and found a long string of way-to-goes and you-guys-are-awesomes, but no explanation as to what happened and why they replaced the shed. The only hint at all that I found that it had actually been my kids who did it was a quick question asking how Eugene's thumb was, to which John had simply replied, "It's good. Now…"

This Facebook thing was turning out to be pretty handy.

My phone died, and I tossed into the open door next to me. I'd seen everything I needed to see.

So, my kids had had an adventure, too. It looked like they'd faced some pretty big challenges while I was away, yet not once did anyone call me or need my help. Again, I wondered how that didn't bother me. I was liking the freedom of not being needed.

They would have had to work together to overcome all of those things; none of them were one-man jobs. They must have used the emergency bank card to pay for everything. But they'd managed everything beautifully from what I could tell.

I was sure there was a lot more to the story than what was posted, and I was looking forward to hearing it. I imagined getting home and sitting out back with all five of them while they took turns giving me all the details of what they'd been through. They'd bounce from kid to kid, not in any particularly chronological order, each mind being reminded of something by whatever the last one had said. Their stories were always full of energy and enthusiasm, if a little work to piece together. We could sit out around the fire pit like we were camping. Like we did when they were little.

Like we did when Nathan was here.

It seems I hadn't quite lost *everything*.

As much as I was sure I was supposed to go away to figure out my shit, I suddenly realized that I needed to go away so the kids could figure out theirs. While I was gone, they'd had some big challenges themselves. They'd had to work together to get through them and did a great job of it. They'd started their new history together. A new history that started with their *new* family. They'd had to overcome their differences to find their way back to each other. It was a new beginning for them.

And for me as well. I would go be going home to a family that I wanted to be a part of again. It was going to be as different as life could make it. But there would always be things that would tie us together: a past that included Dad, and a future that didn't. I think I was finally ready to let that happen.

I fell asleep that night, face up to the stars, grateful for the day that had brought me here, for the kids down the road and their exuberance for life as they pulled out a guitar and sang for hours through the darkness, for my kids and their amazing ability to look after themselves and each other, and for the tiny bit of wisdom I'd found to be able to appreciate it all.

Making Pacts

There was no sign of life amongst the four tents as I passed the kids' campsite on my way out just before noon. I wished them all safe travels while I drove by as quietly as possible, making my way through the resort and out to the highway.

It looked like it might rain, but the crisp smell of ozone in the air made the possibility of a good soaking a welcome thought. I headed east under ominous clouds, cozied up in a hoodie with the heat blowing on my bare legs, and drove until the downpour made squinting through the rhythmic deluge across the windshield too hypnotic to be safe. I stopped at a strip mall in Kenora and hit the dollar store for a notebook, some pens, and some snacks, deciding as I almost drove away to duck back into the pizza parlour for a large pepperoni with double cheese. There'd be no campfire tonight.

I wrapped the pizza up carefully in a plastic bag and tucked it into my sleeping bag to try to keep some of its heat and headed east another hour until I found a sleepy little campground to hunker down for the night. Once parked in my site, there was no need to get out. I climbed into the back, snuggled into my pre-warmed sleeping bag and sat munching away on the cheesy goodness, taking the time to savour both the flavour in my mouth and the sublime feeling of being sheltered in the middle of a rainstorm.

When we were kids, my dad would take us outside to sit on the bench on the covered front porch to watch a storm as it would boast its power through blinding light that would paint bizarre streaks of fury and might across a black canvas as big as the universe, only to skip our very heartbeats like a stick in the spokes of a bicycle wheel with the physical wave of sound that would pass through our tiny bodies with each clap of thunder that followed. We would sit curled up with Dad feeling both safe and terrified, awed and excited. To this day, I will still stop my life in progress to experience a thunderstorm.

As I sat chewing happily on my third slice, the first of the flashes that would light the sky that night heralded a dousing that had me wondering how close I still might be to the impressively pervasive Assiniboine River and its floodplain. I'd driven past the campground that had threatened to wash me away overnight so long ago, just outside of Winnipeg about an hour into my drive that afternoon. I hadn't recognized the landmarks, only the sign that assured me of its identity. What had been a sprawling resort along a river two weeks before was now a lake, filled with trunkless trees and rooftops, walled in by the shoulder of the highway on which I drove. I slowed reflexively as I passed, wondering how it was that whoever owned the place would ever be able to recover their losses. It was something to hear about the threat; it was something else entirely to see if for myself.

Comfortably nestled into my van with blankets and pizza and snacks, I felt the warmth of my circumstance, appreciating the gifts of shelter, of food, of safety, of privacy, of memory,

I scrambled awkwardly into the front seat and released my baggy of trinkets from the glove box. For the first time since I stashed them there, I unzipped the bag and took them out.

I opened the notebook and folded it back to a clean white page and splayed them across the sheet evenly, seeing their silhouettes fairly clearly in the dim evening light. I opened the package of pens and used one to trace the outlines of my trinkets onto the page. Moving them out of the way, I doodled away, filling in the details of each one as best I could. I'm no artist.

I sketched away, tackling the objects one by one, trying to convey shape, texture, and tone and wasn't doing too badly, I thought. I could certainly tell what it was I was drawing and was fairly sure that anyone else looking at my objets d'art could identify at least one, maybe two of them.

I held the bear's claw up beside its image, the shadows of weather and evening lending some compassion to the comparison. I thought back to me squatting in the woods against the threat of that giant beast. A shudder ran up my back. One day I might look back at the encounter with a clear sense of reality, but for now, I was still seeing it as the most spiritual experience I'd ever had. And I'd had quite a few lately.

My ears twitched as I recalled the sound of the bear's claws scraping on the rock, inches away from my head. That had been when he'd broken it off. He had to have felt it, painfully, but hadn't reacted in any way I noticed. Albeit, my experience in bear behaviour up until that moment was limited. He'd calmed though, and eyed me carefully, connecting with me on some level. At the time I'd wondered if he was trying to ask me a question. Thinking back now, it wasn't a question so much, as a confirmation. An assurance. An agreement of trust.

If I let you go, if I give you your life, what do you offer in return?

I recalled my thoughts of afterward, my realization that I'd acted out of pure reaction, and not fear. Silly, I thought now. Of course there was fear. *Idiot. You'd have to be dead not to feel it.* But I'd controlled it, the fear. It had sharpened my senses, awakened my instinct, cleared my thoughts. The fear had allowed me to act in a way that I wouldn't have expected to. I tucked my forefinger into the claw again, marvelling at the size of it.

The fear hadn't stopped me. I'd used it to help me. A tool in my skillset to strengthen my own abilities. The fear told me to be cautious, but it did not tell me to stop.

I touched the claw to my lips, eyes closed, and made my offer.

I will not avoid fear. I will welcome it. I will use it to strengthen me. I will listen to it, but I won't let it control me.

A single tear rolled down my cheek and onto the claw. My first thought was to wipe it off. My second thought was to rub it in. And as I did, I felt the weight of my commitment to the bear. I would live my life with a sense of intent, an attitude of determination and resolve, understanding that there was nothing that could stand in my way as long as I respected the fear, using it to guide me, but never letting it derail me.

As I placed the claw neatly in place over its picture, I was sure the bear would be satisfied with our contract, as I was.

I lay back, listening to the rain, watching the fogged windows flash with the lightning outside. My mind wandered aimlessly through my brain, looking for something to latch onto. I wouldn't say I was bored, but I was certainly open to ideas. I had the pebble in my hand without realizing I'd reached for it.

The dragonfly had creeped me out some at the time. But here alone, in the dark of my cozy cave, I only remembered the shimmering blue of her body, blurred by the movement of her wings. I thought about how she'd watched me, a creature who could have stepped on her and ended her without any effort whatsoever, and still, she'd stood up to me, held her ground, and, I assumed, protected what mattered to her most. She risked everything to win her case.

Her persistence against all odds had caught my attention then, as it did now. So much tenacity crammed into such a small body!

But what struck me now was her absolute and unshakable expectation of success. She hadn't flinched or faltered for a second. She took me on from the moment she found me there, and fought me the entire time. She wasn't intimidated. She wasn't discouraged. She decided on a course of action and saw it through.

I held the cold pebble to my lips and spoke my oath to her aloud.

I will learn from your example of perseverance. I will not play the victim. I will not give in to my weakness. I will make your purpose my own.

I spoke the words with such conviction, so much emotion, that, again, a tear fell, and I rubbed it into the pebble sealing my oath.

Exhausted, I slept deeply until startled awake by a clap of thunder that shook the van. Pulse racing, my first thought was of my treasures, which I found calmly resting on the picture I'd drawn as if nothing had happened.

Inanimate objects: funny things.

I took the tip of the feather's quill between my thumb and forefinger, holding it up against the dim light of the window. My throat squeezed around the guilt of the damage I'd caused it while I tried to focus on the gratitude for the fortune that had brought it back to me. The warmth spread through me as I felt a wave of forgiveness for my actions, much like a hug from Mom after I'd done something she'd warned me against, but still loved me anyway.

I hoped the hawk would forgive me as easily. The hawk who carved his way through thin air with such finesse and ease. Who could fly as fast and as high as he wanted. Able to watch us mere mortals as we fumbled and failed our way through our ridiculously complicated lives. His life was far less cumbersome. From his vantage point in the clouds, he could see everything, yet he could target in on something as small as a chipmunk, attacking it with unbelievable speed and accuracy. He might not hit his mark every time, but from the looks of him, it was close. He had the skills of timing and implementation that marked him elite. He could see the big picture, but he could focus on the one tiny piece of it he needed to overcome. He had excelled in order to survive, but had the potential to impress anyone watching with his effortless execution.

I envied that level of promise, the ability to push the self to the mastery of something bigger than basic talent should allow. He could have simply gone for the chipmunk; but he'd made a show of it. It wasn't enough to just fly. He'd been flying with genius.

I held the feather to my lips, pledging to the hawk as I had done the others.

I will dream bigger, reach further, aim higher. I will fuel my hope with your vision. I will strive to do more than I think I can, raise my expectations, and leave my mark on this world.

I felt the feather's ripped quill against my lip.

Even if I fail in the attempt, I added, feeling the impact of that admission to my core. I placed a kiss on the feather, sealing my oath, confirming my own promise, and swearing my pact before the universe.

I placed the feather gently back with my other trinkets, feeling the weight of the responsibility I'd been given along with them.

The word trinket didn't sit well with me. They weren't baubles to be played with and mishandled. They weren't treasures of any worth to anyone but me. And the bear, and the dragonfly, and the hawk.

They were gifts. Gifts given to me by Nature, by Nature's messengers. But the true gift was in the lesson that each one carried. My gifts were actually symbols of those lessons, reminders of the experiences, the wisdom, and the vows that were borne of them. The gifts of Strength, of Purpose, and of Hope. Mine to keep, to use, to share. Mine to guard and cherish and appreciate.

They were gifts that would see me change my life in ways I hadn't begun to envision.

Making Up With Old Friends

The next morning had that dewy, wet, refreshing feeling that comes after the world has taken a long shower. The trees glistened with leftover rain that would spray generously over unsuspecting campers every time the wind moved their leaves. It was a warm morning that promised to turn into a humid day: the kind that takes you from clean to sticky somewhere around noon. I drove off with the windows open, determined to enjoy the freshness of the world before it all turned into a stinky armpit.

Ontario is huge. Google said I still had more than nineteen hours of drive time to Hamilton. That's virtually the same distance from home to Disney World in Orlando. I was home, but nowhere near close.

In keeping with my decision to wind down and take my time, I was limiting my driving now to about four hours a day, with a rest stop about halfway, and I was beginning to enjoy the relaxed pace of my travels. When I saw the sign for Kakabeka Falls, I did a quick calculation and made that my destination for the day. It would be nice to meet up with familiar for a change.

I stopped and bought some dry firewood and stocked up on supplies on the way in and wasn't surprised to be assigned the same campsite I'd stayed at when I was here before. Settled in and not hungry yet, I went for a walk to spend the hour before suppertime building an appetite. I headed for the falls by sound, finding them easily. I followed the maze of wooden walkways around the park, stopping to take in the rainbow down in the gorge. There was a misty spray in the air, but not the soaking I remembered. On this day, the colours were exaggerated under the bright blue sky, setting off the countless shades of green through the trees, and accenting the rusty brown of the rock beneath the crest of the falls. The best part of the whole scene was the almost complete lack of other tourists, hotels, and traffic.

I stopped in at the Visitors' Centre and had a look around, learning a little about the area and its history. There's a story about an Ojibwe Chief's daughter who, to protect her people from an attack by the Sioux, led the warriors, and herself, over the falls to their deaths. Legend has it that you can still see Princess Green Mantle when looking down into the mist. I wandered back over to the falls and stood searching for a bit but saw nothing. My stomach grumbled loudly, and I turned back in search of a meal.

Passing through the larger sites that housed the trailers and RV's, I stopped, gawking at the bumper of a mid-sized unit with a very familiar bright green Saskatchewan Roughriders bumper sticker. I didn't think it was possible but took a couple steps back to get a better look and see. I recognized the voice laughing through the open window and smiled at the memory, far more excited at the coincidence than I'd have expected. I hesitated for a half second and went ahead and knocked on the door. The voices within stopped immediately, creating an uncomfortably long silence while, I imagine, the two sat looking at each other trying to figure out who could be knocking on their trailer door.

There must have been a mimed conversation, the result of which was a bit of grunting and umphing before Roger's face appeared through the screen.

"Hi," I started cheerfully.

"Well, if it isn't The Neighbour From Hamilton," he announced, looking surprised but not unwelcoming. "Nancy, look!"

A moment later, Nancy was pushing past Roger and the out the door, grabbing me into a full-on hug the likes of which loved ones returning from the dead could only hope for. She took my arm and led me to the picnic table, sitting me down on the bench and squeezing in right beside me.

"You look amazing!" she shone enthusiastically.

Not what I'd have thought to start with, but I managed a thank you, not accepting that there could be much of a difference in two weeks.

"Where have you been? What have you done?"

I smiled warmly. There was no five-minute answer to that question. "I made it to the Yukon. Had a bit of an adventure. And now I'm heading home." That pretty much covered it.

She covered the gasp with both hands before reaching out and taking my hands in hers. "You're going home. Oh, that's wonderful! I've been so worried about you."

"Worried?" I asked, both confused as to why and flattered, just because.

"Oh yeah darlin'. You were so lost. So lost," she squoze my hands tightly. "You've had some time to think, I think?"

I looked at her, deep into her eyes. I saw a level of understanding and compassion that startled me a bit, and I realized that she knew. She'd known where I was and where I was going. She probably even knew what I was up to. Even before I did. I smiled and squeezed back, relieved for some reason. Maybe that she knew. Maybe that I didn't have to explain.

"Yeah," I nodded happily. "A LOT of time to think. And figure things out."

"I think you had a lot on your plate." She beamed at me, still holding tight, shaking her head in a disbelieving kind of way.

The door popped open and Roger muttered a quick, "Here," as Nancy jumped up and grabbed a stack of plates and utensils from him. Before I knew it, she and I were dealing out place settings and chatting like old friends. We'd barely finished when Roger busted back out the door with a giant bowl of Caesar salad and a full tray of steaming lasagna. I was instantly starving!

We sat and ate, laughing and chatting well into the night. They'd circuited Lake Superior since I'd seen them last, and had quite the adventures of their own, not the least of which was finding a skunk in their camper! Nancy carried most of the conversation, which seemed to suit both Roger and myself quite well. He was obviously used to providing the punctuation for her, and I wasn't quite ready to figure out how to tell anyone any of the things that had happened to me. By the time I headed back to my own makeshift camper, I'd been filled with food, fun, and friendship to last me quite a while. Nancy had been thrilled to add me on Facebook, and I accepted the request after I'd tucked in for the night and before I drifted off on waves of Overwhelming Gratitude that I swept back over to the camper from Saskatchewan, wishing them safe travels, warm spirits, and happy hearts.

I was still smiling when I left the next day, having stopped back in to say goodbye to my new friends. They made me promise to come visit them in Saskatoon after their kids had moved back out, and I offered a genuine invitation to them to visit me and my kids at home. They seemed quite happy with the idea, and I actually found myself hoping that they'd show up on my doorstep one day.

Passing through town around mid-morning, the Kakabeka Falls Gift and Amethyst Shoppe caught my eye and I pulled over to take a look. I was betting on them having exactly what I was looking for.

I roamed through the store enjoying the abundance of Canadian, Kakabeka, and Native crafts and souvenirs for sale, but I was in need of a wooden box, exactly the length from my wrist to my fingertip and as wide as my hand, lined, with a latch or lock. My gifts deserved a more permanent home.

My expectation for success panned out, and the box I found was well-made with dovetailed joints and a soft deep blue felt lining. There was a picture painted on its lid of the Northern Lights over The Falls. I bought it on the spot.

With gifts safely stowed in their new niche, I tucked the box safely under the seat and continued my travels along the northern tip of Lake Superior before stopping once again to spend the night at White Lake. Familiar was working for me. I'd stayed here the night before I ran into that shmuk in Walmart. I wondered for a second how he was doing, and with uncharacteristic empathy, I closed my eyes and wished him well.

Making Sense Of It All - Part 2

It was a night as clear as any starry sky could be, and even with the fire going strong, it was easy to lean my head back and just gaze. My entire field of vision was filled with twinkling lights against an as yet moonless black backdrop. I leaned back into my chair, staring up, past the flickering light of the fire, through the endless needle laden pine boughs that reached into my field of vision to wave hello to me, and up to the heavens themselves. The longer I looked, the more stars appeared, until I could easily make out the swath of speckled light that was our galaxy itself. The Milky Way spanned from horizon to horizon as far as I could see, bigger than anything I'd ever seen before, and yet only a glimpse of the whole. It occurred to me that as small and trivial as I was in comparison, I was also a strong and vital part of it all.

I thought of my time by the water earlier, as the last vestiges of sunlight were absorbed into the night, and accepted into my being that I had, indeed, awakened to my role in the universe.

I'd gone for a walk through the campground after getting settled in too soon before dinner. The roadways through the park were mostly canopied by towering pines that grew in such density as to filter out all of the bright light save the hour or two it took for the sun to pass directly overhead. It made for an invigorating infusion of sight, sound, and smell, filled with singing birds and rasping cicadas, green walls and brown floors, woody campfires and succulent mosses. I stepped off the road into a clearly used, if narrow, trail, and followed it up, down, and around through the ferns and ivies that reached out in feeble attempts to connect with passersby, until it opened up to a small piece of rocky shore with a full view of what would be the tail end of White Lake.

Something about Ontarians, coupled with the abundance of rocks through our wilderness along the Canadian Shield, made the idea of Inukshuks intensely appealing. Originally an Inuit design to guide travellers in Arctic areas where permanent landmarks were few and far between, modern Ontarians had adopted the tradition as their own. Stickmen of all sizes, from the height of my knee to the stature of a tree, all made of rocks collected locally and stacked solidly, could be found in every place where people had ever been, and more than a few places where I wouldn't think they could get to. Granite outcroppings along highways were littered with them where kids would venture out at night for bush parties, leaving a memorial totem behind. They were quite literally Northern Graffiti. But they could also be found along trails and shorelines, on ledges and in fields. And I, like anyone else who came across one, always felt the welcoming friendship these faceless statues offered. The Inukshuk here on this rocky bit of beach was about three feet tall. Its legs were short, its arms were wide and inviting, and its head was as blank as any other rock, except that it had been placed carefully so that a crooked crack that marred its surface ended up exactly where a smile should be. I smiled back and said hello.

The water was calm and crystal clear. I could easily see rocks of a size that I could lift scattered like crumbs just inches below the surface, separated by lines of them gathered in places where they'd collected with the movement of water and ice to fill the deep and rigid cracks along the rocky floor. I took off my shoes, tucking my socks neatly into them, before wading out a half dozen steps across the icy smooth hardness to sit in a comfortable crouch on an island boulder just big enough for one.

Surrounded by water, supported by the earth, warmed by the sun, cooled by the breeze, I closed my eyes and let the energy of the beauty around me flow through and within me. Time stopped. Reality faded. I began to blend into the world, becoming one and the same, joined, connected, inseparable.

My face relaxed into a warm smile as I fell into the hypnotic trance of my melding seamlessly into Nature, and I welcomed the serenity of it deep into my heart.

The gratitude grew within me, a force unto itself, without my help or encouragement. It swirled around me, teasing and tempting, passing through me, filling me, changing me. Changing me into something more. Accepting me as a welcome friend, someone with whom it could visit whenever it wanted, knowing that I would welcome it, care for it, respect it. The flow consumed me, spilling over in a gentle wave. It reached the trees and the water, the ground and the sky around me, passing through me as it went, painting me into the landscape. This wasn't a gift. It was an acceptance. I had accepted the Force Of Gratitude within me, and it was now accepting me back. I was now a vessel, a carrier.

A messenger.

The word came clearly and strongly.

I was now a Messenger. And in its acceptance of me, I was agreeing to carry its message.

Without hesitation I thought about how easy it would be to spread a Message Of Gratitude. It would be effortless to share something that I'd adopted as my own.

But there was a hesitation in the thought, in the breeze around me.

That's not The Message. Gratitude is just the means; it isn't the message. It's the means to *hear* the message. The message is so much bigger.

I laughed at that, because in my small mind I couldn't imagine anything bigger than the force that I'd discovered.

And then I heard it. As if someone spoke the word standing right beside me.

Joy.

Gratitude is the price you pay. Joy is the value you receive. Pure and absolute. Overwhelming and all encompassing.

Joy.

I thought the sun had reached down from the sky to light me on fire.

I had thought I understood. I had thought that gratitude was the answer.

When it was just a suggestion. It was an invitation. It was the attraction.

And I saw now that it was the secret room, the hidden path. Because the true reward was Joy. I saw clearly now that the light that had built within me, that had exploded from me, was Joy. A force so powerful that I was able to share it, so abundant that I could give it to others without losing it myself. In fact, giving it away only made it stronger for me.

The Gratitude I'd been feeling was only the flint. I was the spark. Come together to light the fire that would set my heart ablaze. How long I sat there trying to wrap my head around the enormity of that, I don't know. But I do know that finding my way back to my campsite in the dark was not an easy task.

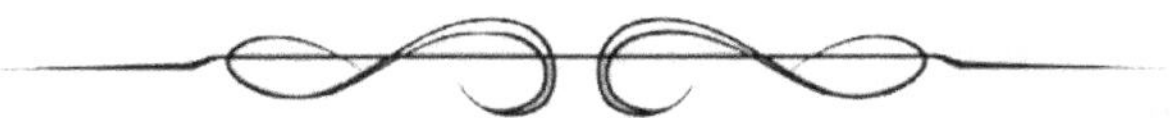

Once I'd found the main road through the park, it was easy enough to find my way back, even if I did manage to keep taking wrong turns at every chance. I was starved when I arrived, munching away on a box of cereal while my infant fire took its sweet time cooking my burgers. The odd one or five people passed by and said hello. I managed to wave pleasantly, reminding myself after my initial greeting to put the Cap'n Crunch down first. Appetite finally assuaged by the best double cheeseburger I'd ever tasted, I kicked back in my chair to watch the stars.

Following the dense mass of tiny white lights to its edges, I felt at once both humbled by my smallness and empowered by my association with such vastness. I was as powerful as I was pointless. As important as I was invisible. I may not be much, but without me, the whole is not the same. For better or worse.

Much has and will be written postulating on the underlying energy that fuels the universe, but on this night, in this place, with my entire essence open to the possibilities of infinity, its name was Joy. And I felt it like I was glowing.

Not for the first time, I wondered how I could be so happy, when I was hit with a remarkable revelation.

Happy is not Joy.

They are not even related.

Happy is an accident.

The stars align, the mood lights up, the circumstances mesh, and for a moment, and just a moment, the delirium of happiness descends on us and we find ourselves in the middle of a bubble where everything is right in the world. We're laughing, we feel good, even great, and everyone around us is having fun.

But Happy is unpredictable.

How many times have I gone to a function I absolutely dreaded, only to find that once I got there, somehow, with no change of heart on my part, I end up having a really good time? And yet at other times, I've planned and plotted, spent money and time, to put together all of the things most likely to produce a happy event, only to have the whole thing fall apart, sometimes, for no discernible reason whatsoever.

It's like ooooooh!!!! We're gonna have fun!!! And somebody shows up and sucks the life out of the room. Or the opposite with ooooooh!!! This is gonna suck!!! And somebody shows up and changes everything.

We have no control over this. There is no guarantee of Happy. It's luck.

Happiness can be bought. With money we can have a better shot at providing the entertainment and environment most likely to produce a happy event. At minimum, we can buy a good distraction. But it's not for sure.

Happy is a fluke. When you find it, you want it to go on forever. You're visiting friends and having a wonderful time. Everybody is. You swore you'd leave by ten but you're still going strong at three in the morning. You go back to their place a week later, excited. They're excited. The expectations for more fun are through the roof. And for some reason no one understands, you're going through the drive-thru on the way home at eight.

I concluded that we should take happy when it comes. Enjoy it while it lasts. Do our best to seek it out, make the most of it. But in the end, it plays by its own rules.

Joy is different.

Joy is earned.

Joy is real.

I was discovering that I could create Joy. Out of nothing. Using only my thoughts and Gratitude to do so. In fact, I could focus my energy and grow my gratitude to the point where it overwhelmed me, where I was met with a Joy that dissolved every other emotion I could feel into something that had no power over me.

Never before that moment on the lake had I ever considered the power of Joy. It had only ever been a word. Something I used in conversation. I was probably joyful when I got married, and when I had my kids. I thought about that for a minute. Yes, that's probably the closest I've ever come to actually experiencing Joy, because I couldn't think of a time when I'd felt more grateful, even if I didn't recognize it at the time. But never did it occur to me that I could create it, harness it, or give it away. Until now.

Only now, it didn't take a life-changing event to be able to create it.

I looked at the fire, felt it warm my feet right through my shoes, wiggled my toes inside my soft new socks, and felt the Gratitude build.

I thought of my dinner, the hot meal had tasted so good, filling my empty belly, leaving me lumped in my chair in a bit of a food-coma. And the Gratitude grew.

I smiled remembering the smile on the couple's faces as I'd waved happily at them with a box of cereal, unable to manage more than a mumbled hello without spitting little yellow sugary treasure chests at them. The cereal, the people, the greeting. The Gratitude filled me and blossomed into the Joy that I was quickly coming to crave.

No, I didn't need a house to fall on my head to find Joy.

But it had taken a life-changing tragedy to open my mind and heart to it. It had taken my complete surrender, my own personal and absolute abandon of control of my entire existence to be able to find it. And now that I had, it was up to me what I was going to do with it. It seemed to be hovering around me all the time now, as close as the next wave of Gratitude. It seemed to be making a difference in how others perceived me. And in how I saw them. I doubted it was going to make everything perfect, or to wipe out my grief, or fix anything, for that matter. But it was already changing how I felt about me, about my life, and about my future.

It was the Strength of the Bear, the Purpose of the Dragonfly, and the Hope of the Hawk that had opened my heart to the power of Gratitude. It was the surrender to Overwhelming Gratitude that showed me a sense of Joy that I'd never before encountered. An abundance of Joy that encompassed every nuance of my existence: my body, my heart, my mind, and my soul. A gift that would ultimately turn the worst thing that ever happened to me, into the best thing that ever happened to me.

Making A Second First Impression

I left White Lake as I'd found it, and a bit more reluctantly than I'd expected. I experienced a massive revelation here and would remember it fondly for the clarity of thought it had brought me. As I pulled back out on the highway toward home, I concentrated on the feelings I was taking with me because the details were far too distracting to make for a safe drive. As it was, the residual Joy I'd found was still fresh in my heart, and I was aware of driving along with a smile on my face and chattering away to myself as if I hadn't seen me since forever. At some point, as traffic had backed up to a crawl in a construction zone, I noticed the driver in front of me watching me in his rearview mirror. Unable to explain and not wanting to look like a moron, I made eye-contact, tapped my ear twice, and started talking and laughing in earnest as if I were on the phone. He didn't bother with me again.

But I had to laugh at the sheer Joy that filled me, just because.

Thoughts I hadn't thought about before, if at all, popped into my head, with none of the baggage that I would have expected to accompany them.

I remembered the mountains of food that kept coming to the house long after we ran out of room for it all.

I recalled giving my speech at the funeral.

I remembered agreeing to the organ donation.

There were several conversations with the wonderful people at Trillium Gift of Life Network. I had asked the doctor in the emergency room if there was anything of Nathan's body that I could donate. He'd seemed surprised at the time, and honestly, I don't know what made me think of asking, but I did. He told me he'd see what he could do, but probably not, as the blood thinners they'd given him would have rendered most of his organs unviable.

'Unviable' was not a word I'd ever heard before. The fact that I remembered clearly the doctor saying it surprised me.

Two days later I received a call from a woman from Gift of Life. It had taken quite an explanation from her, for me to figure out who she was, and why she was calling me; it just wasn't registering. But the second I clued in, I was eager to speak with her. I made my excuses to everyone in the house at the time and locked myself in my room to be able to talk freely. It wasn't something I'd spoken to anyone else about, and I didn't want to get into it with them just then.

It took two days and three extended phone calls with them, I was recorded and questioned, with different people, confirming and agreeing on the record, but I was able to donate his eyes.

The fourth call I received from them was on a beautiful Spring day in April when they were able to tell me that, because of our gift, two people had received successful corneal transplants, had been given the gift of sight in time for Easter, and how did I feel about meeting them should they be interested in meeting me.

The Joy in the memory of that news, as I drove along, was stronger now than what I'd felt that day three years before, now that I could feel it for the miracle it was and not the loss. I hadn't thought about it much since, because the thought of two someones walking around, seeing the world through Nathan's eyes, was too much to bear. But now, it was overwhelming in a completely unfamiliar way. How beautiful to think that someone had been able to see their grandchild, or the stars at night, or the smile of a loved one who's happy to see them, because of Nathan's gift. To bestow upon someone the gift of independence, of freedom, of hope. I hadn't wanted to meet them and now was glad I hadn't; I could imagine any number of different circumstances, each as moving as the last. A gift that would return to me whenever I wished.

That a memory as powerful as that one didn't break me to pieces, that it, instead, lifted me up, warmed me to my core, and sparked a light within me, was as surprising as it was expected. I knew, without knowing how, that my tears and grief for Nathan were far from done. But I also knew that I would now be able to begin the true missing of him. Missing for the sake of missing him. Not missing him for the loss of him. It was a subtle difference, but a big one nonetheless.

It wasn't a lessening of the grief, it wasn't an easing of the pain; I've learned since, that that never goes away. It was an acceptance of it. An agreement that I decided to keep the pain as a part of who I was now, but only a part. I didn't have to be afraid of losing his memory; he would always be with me. As would the hurt. But I was beginning to understand that I could hurt, and I could live at the same time. Like the fear, I could feel it, accept it, listen to it, but at the same time, I could go ahead and live my life anyway. It didn't have to be either or. It wasn't letting go.

It was the same. But different.

Without Joy, the agony of loss was crippling. All day, every day. Everything triggered it. Sleep was a relief. Distraction was addictive. Everything was dark. Everything hurt.

With Joy, the agony of loss was just as strong. Always present. Always devastating. But somehow not debilitating. Not stopping me from thinking. Or from acting. Or from feeling.

There would be times where I would pull the pain out and allow myself to feel it, to go there to that dark place. To let it out of its cage to ravage me. Because to deny it completely is to deny the love that made it possible. To feel the pain on that level is to feel the love that I felt, to remember it, to keep it close. But to keep the pain in check, the love must be locked up with it. They are one, the yin and the yang, the love and the loss. It is impossible to keep only one alive. I can talk about both, openly and freely, with passion and heart, all while seeming perfectly in control of my emotions. And for the most part, I am in control, although sometimes it can leak out a bit. I am fully aware of the both the bliss and the agony, all the time. But I don't allow myself to *feel* them, to let them take me, to surrender to them until I have the time and the privacy to do so fully, completely, and with absolute devotion.

I didn't realize as I was driving that day how very much I'd learned to that point. It would take years after for it all to fall into place. But I was taking my first steps into my life without Nathan.

I recognized Blind River when I saw it, the sign on this side in better repair than the one had been coming in from the other end a lifetime ago. I stopped at a store and picked up supplies I'd been thinking I'd need as I would embark on the final leg of my journey home the next day. Once stocked up, I searched out the little roadside motel I'd stayed in my first night away. I wanted a full-service bathroom and a comfortable bed.

I checked in, finding Motel Guy behind the counter as I stepped inside. He looked up and recognized me quickly.

"Oh, there. Welcome back Mrs. Bullock," he smiled sheepishly.

I didn't have the heart to correct him.

"Hi there?" I looked at him, eyebrows raised for a name. 'Motel Guy' didn't seem fair.

"Harv. I'm Harv. Did you have a good trip?"

"I did, thank you. "

"You'll be wanting a room then? Same as last time?"

"Sure," I smiled warmly at him. He had kind eyes. I hadn't noticed before.

I ran my credit card through the machine and punched in my PIN number. It came up approved and I tucked it back in my wallet while Harv printed out my receipt.

"Checkout's at 11. I'm here all night if you need anything. Just dial '9' on your room phone. Ice machine's fixed if you need any. It's just around the side there," he pointed over his shoulder.

"Thanks, Harv," I offered, earnestly.

"Do you need help with your bags or anything?"

We made momentary eye-contact as we both remembered my last visit and my less than stellar entrance. We both looked away awkwardly.

"No, thanks, Harv. I got it. I've had a little practice since last time."

He grinned and was about to say something but thought the better of it.

I took the key from the counter and headed back out to the van. The number on the palm-sized plastic key ring was number 4. I knew my way.

I parked in front as I had before and managed to pack up my things into backpack and bag and carry them with grace and ease to the door. I let myself in, flipped on the lights, and beeped the van doors locked. Once inside, I spent the next few hours enjoying a DIY Spa Day. I dyed and shaved and exfoliated and plucked and flossed and clipped like I had all the time in the world. I opened a bottle of wine, thoroughly enjoyed the sandwich I'd picked up at the deli, and was relaxing in the last of my clean clothes deciding on something to watch when there was a knock on my door. I muted the tv, not sure I'd heard right. The knock knocked again.

My first reaction was a city reaction: sit and pretend you're not here. I let out a snort of derisive judgment. This was definitely not City Country.

I got up from the bed and went to the door, wondering if I should ask who it was. The knock knocked again with a definite 'clink' to it. Whoever it was had glass in his hand.

I opened the door and felt my face fall into a genuine smile.

"Well then, you look good," he drawled appreciatively.

"Sam."

"Sandra," he said with one eyebrow.

"I don't believe it."

He held up one hand with two dripping bottles of beer. "Come out for a drink?" It wasn't much of a question when both bottles were already opened.

I nodded and he handed me one of the beers, turning away toward our Muskoka chairs. I followed him out and climbed cross-legged into the seat next to him. I hate beer, but, what the hell.

He Cheers!'d me and our conversation started as if we were old friends. He told me about his new grandson. His daughter lived in Green Bay with her husband. He'd finally managed to take time away from his work to go see them and meet the new baby. He was every bit the doting grandfather, and I didn't mind so much looking closely at all the pictures on his phone. Home was Oakville, twenty minutes down the highway from me, and this little motel was about half way to Green Bay. So here he was again on his way home.

"So where did you end up going?" he asked in that hot molasses down my back ooze.

"I made it to the Yukon," I smiled proudly.

"Did you now? Good for you. That's a long trip."

"Yeah. I haven't figured out the mileage yet. I had to get an oil change in Kamloops." I'd got an oil change at some point because the light came on, but I wasn't sure where exactly. That didn't matter. "I always figured if you have to do laundry while you're away, you're not on vacation anymore. But an oil change? That's a bit much," I laughed.

"You're probably gonna need new tires, too," he added.

I looked at him, surprised by the idea. He was likely right about that.

"So, did you see any wildlife out there?"

I hmphed at that.

"That's a no?"

"Oh no. I saw some wildlife alright!"

"Bigger than a raccoon?"

"Bigger than a car!"

"A moose, then?"

I looked at him, not sure how much I wanted to tell him. Finally, I grinned. And went for it.

Well, most of it, anyway.

"I saw a full-size adult male grizzly bear."

"You did not."

"I did. I was taking a pee on the side of the road in the bushes, and he came right up to me."

"Like hell!"

"Dead serious."

"What did you do???"

"Besides the obvious?"

He barked a laugh, and I waited for him to stop coughing on the beer he'd just choked on.

"I just sat there. What could I do?"

"Hell, I don't know. Pray?"

"Maybe if I'd thought about it."

"What'd the bear do?"

"He danced around a bit, yelled a lot, then he went away."

"Just like that?"

"Just like that."

"Well, shit."

"Yeah."

"Wow."

"Yeah. I guess he wasn't hungry."

He laughed aloud at that. "Lucky for you!!"

"Yeah," I took a swig of my beer, which was not the worst beer I've ever tasted. I figured it was the company.

"A bear, eh?"

"Yep," I smiled smugly. Even half of the story was a good one.

"Too bad you couldn't have got a picture or a souvenir."

"Just the memories," I lied. I felt guilty for a half a second, not showing him my claw. But the bear had gifted it to me, with a purpose. And that purpose didn't include making a spectacle out of it. Not everything has to be shared with everyone.

I told him about the flood in Winnipeg and the fires in the mountains. About driving through the mountains and sleeping in the Yukon. I'd been rambling on for some time when I realized he was just sitting there staring at me.

"What?" I asked with a tinge of self-consciousness.

"You've changed."

"Really. Well, I had a little spa day in there," I pointed to my room.

"No. I saw that when you opened the door. You look really good."

I'm pretty sure I blushed like an idiot.

"I mean, you're different."

"I don't know if that's a good thing or not." But I knew. I knew I'd changed in the most amazing way possible. I just couldn't figure out how he could see it.

"It's definitely good. I mean, I thought you were pretty interesting when I met you here last time, but you were more closed. It's like you had this giant 'Don't Fuck With Me' sign on your forehead."

"And now?"

"Now? Now it's more like 'No Offence But I'd Think Twice About Fucking With Me If I Were You.'"

"What??" I cried in my best interpretation of indignant offence.

He laughed at me. "I don't mean it as an insult at all. It's more like the warrior blew through here a couple weeks ago all fired up and ready to kill someone. Now it's like you've fought your battle, won, and you're coming home with the spoils."

Wow. That's pretty damn close.

"You didn't kill anyone, did you?"

"No, I didn't." Technically, no I didn't. But in reality, I managed to do away with angry, frustrated, lost me. I wasn't about to get into that.

"Good. I couldn't be friends with a murderer."

My turn to laugh. "Glad to see you have standards."

We talked on into the night, the intimacy of our last meeting returning, welcoming us once again into the comfort of just sitting together. At some point, we both seemed to notice that we had very little in common. In fact, we seemed to be polar opposites of each other. Trying to find something we agreed on, we got a little silly, a condition very much enhanced by my third beer.

"Okay, okay. Favourite colour. Blue," I offered.

"Grey."

"What? That's not even a colour!"

"Hey don't judge. Grey is a very versatile and useful colour. And I like it."

I doubted that, but I was trying to be open-minded.

"Pop," I decided. "Coke."

"Pepsi."

I squinted at him.

"Books," he said.

"Oooh. Historical fiction"

"Autobiographies."

"Ugh. Pizza."

"Ham and pineapple."

I just stared at him.

"You're judging."

"Because, ewww."

"And?"

"Pepperoni."

"You probably like vanilla ice cream, too."

"There is no such thing as bad ice cream," I swore.

"Chocolate."

"You like chocolate or don't?"

"Chocolate is the only flavour that matters," he declared.

I laughed at him; he was serious. "You know they make chocolate out of all the leftover other stuff because the chocolate and brown covers it all up, right?"

"I. Don't. Care."

We sat for a few minutes. At this point, I think he was as determined as I was to find something we both liked.

"Women," he said shaking his head. His tone was a comment on our entire gender's ability to frustrate his, but I couldn't resist.

"Nope. Men," I clarified.

He looked at me, a number of responses running through his mind before deciding on, "Well, that one might actually work."

I had to agree.

"Aha!" he declared.

I looked at him expectantly.

"Beer!" he announced, holding up his empty bottle.

He waited patiently for me to stop laughing.

"You mean to tell me that you've been sitting here drinking my beer this whole time and you said nothing??"

"No, I'm not telling you that! Besides, this isn't the worst beer I've ever had," I argued.

He grunted and got up complaining about creaks in his knees, went into his room and came back out with another beer and handed me a bottle of water. He was killing me!

We finally gave up our game and the conversation turned serious, its end becoming apparent.

"So, you're heading home tomorrow."

"Yes," I told him happily. "I've been gone a long time."

"Me, too. But I'm going home to an empty house. Are you excited to see your kids?"

"Yeah," I smiled. "I can't wait to hear their stories."

"That's gonna be some homecoming."

I just nodded, feeling the Gratitude build and turn instantly to Joy. I took a deep breath and met his gaze.

"Something about you has really changed," he smiled with his eyes.

"Thanks, I think."

"So, are you driving all the way?"

"As opposed to what?"

"Taking the ferry?"

"What ferry?" I was instantly intrigued. I'd never been on a ferry before.

"The Chi-Cheemaun. It goes from Manitoulin to Tobermory across the straight between Georgian Bay and Lake Huron."

"I like the idea of the ferry," I agreed. "Are you taking it?" I asked, thinking I sounded a little too hopeful.

"No. I'll be driving around the Lake. I left the dog at a friend's place; I didn't want to take him over the border. And with the baby and all. It was easier."

"How is it we talked all this time, and I didn't know you had a dog?"

"You like dogs?"

"Well yeah! I've got two-year-old Newf."

"A three-year-old Bernese."

We grinned stupidly at each other, realizing that we'd finally found something we have in common. He clunked my water bottle with his beer bottle. We were good.

With that success behind us, we both seemed to accept the understanding that it was time to turn in for the night. I hated to leave him, but this was what it was. And it had come to an end.

I stood to say goodnight, and he stood with me. Without another word, he stepped toward me, took me in his arms and held me closely, nuzzling his face in my hair as I reached around his shoulders and hugged him as tightly as I dared, feeling his chest, warm and solid against me, his heart beating strong and in time with mine.

"Drive safe," he breathed into my ear.

"You, too," I promised.

He kissed my cheek firmly, his beard tickling my face, his lips soft on my skin.

He stepped back, wished me a good sleep, and turned into his room, closing the door quietly behind him.

My insides skipped over Gratitude completely as the Joy within exploded around me, seeming to light the dark night everywhere I looked.

I stepped back into my room, and went to bed, alone, but not lonely, not invisible, and not anonymous. I had seen and been seen, accepted and been accepted, reached out and found someone reaching back. I slept a deep sleep, filled with dreams of lakes and mountains and giant dogs.

When I woke in the morning, Sam was gone. I felt a tinge of disappointment, though I knew that's what I'd wake to. I packed up my things, tidied up, and locked up the room. I loaded up the van and climbed in to drive away. I'd started the engine before I noticed the paper in the wiper. I climbed out to get it.

It was a piece of the motel's stationary, folded in half.

On one side was a phone number. A phone number with the same area code as mine.

On the other side, in bold, slanted, even lettering, it read:

When you're ready.
If you're interested.
And not just sex.
Sam.

Making My Way Home

I backed away from the building and let the vehicle creep its way slowly along, listening to the popping of the gravel under the tires as I went, to the driveway that would take me back to the two-lane highway that had brought me there more than three weeks before. Without hesitation, I turned left, toward home.

It was two and a half hours to the ferry port at South Baymouth on Manitoulin Island, through some of the most beautiful landscape this side of the Rockies. Some ancient elementary school art lesson made it all look a little familiar, and I felt a strange urge to try my hand at painting when I got home. I stopped to take some pictures along the way in case I was serious.

After miles and miles of natural beauty and perfect isolation, I was surprised to roll into a bustling little port town.

I asked the first person I could stop about getting a ticket to cross and was pointed to the terminal to wait in the stand-by lane. I'd just missed the first crossing of the day, so my chances of getting aboard on the second were pretty good. I was worried only because I had suddenly decided that I wanted to get home. I would have to wait for the ship to finish its crossing to Tobermory, and return: a two hour wait and another hour boarding, but I would still be home well before dark. I left the van parked in the line-up and went for a walk.

Wholly dedicated to the locals and tourists alike who simply passed through the port every day, South Baymouth was a pretty little place with all of the souvenir and craft shops I could want, without the pressure and crowds a bigger town would have thrown in my face. I happily strolled through all of the shops and cafes the place had to offer. Two hours later, souvenirs and knick-knacks all wrapped and stowed, I sat in the van waiting to see if I would be boarded. My Expectation Of Success was fairly high, and I was not disappointed as men in orange vests with yellow reflective tape waved me along. Approaching the entry ramp, I was surprised at the size of the ship. Far bigger than I'd expected, its nose was tipped up to allow even the biggest trucks to drive straight in. Once inside, I was guided to park between tight yellow lines on the floor, and ushered quickly to the sides of a huge, clean, well-lit interior parking garage. I followed my fellow passengers along, squeezing between side view mirrors at times, until making our way up a staircase to the upper decks.

As much as I was intrigued by the layout of the ship, the cafeteria, the lounge - the washrooms! – there was no way I was missing the views from the outside. I roamed the deck until I had a spot along the rail to watch the crew finish the loading, astounded at how much they could fit inside. Leaning over, I could just make out the nose of the ship closing, heralded by a loud siren that warned anyone in the way to get out of it.

There was a divide amongst the passengers. Half of us were bored and blasé with their umpteenth crossing. The rest of us were like kids waiting for the tooth fairy. It was obvious from the start who was who. We kids just about crapped our pants when the ship blew its whistle announcing its departure. En masse, we moved from one side to the other, bow to stern, as the ship turned about and maneuvered its way out of the harbour. I stood on the deck, high above the water, the floor humming solidly beneath my feet, and watched the shore, the shops, the lighthouse, pass by before finally finding a seat at the bow, wrapping myself tightly into my hoodie, and settling in to sit and watch Lake Huron for two hours.

I often think back to that ride on the ferry three infinite years ago. It was the last first in a series of firsts that changed my life. It was the last leg of a journey that changed me - in ways that still leave me humbled by their impact.

I'd left home one morning, lost before I'd even hit the road. I still remember it clearly. The shit on the carpet. The fury of my departure – I'd been yelling and crying the whole time while everyone in the house slept on. Whether they heard me or not, I'd been ignored. The cat. (There are no words for the remorse I carry for him. I make regular and generous donations to the local SPCA to this day to try to lessen the guilt. It hasn't worked yet.) It was my fiftieth birthday. And I believed with my whole heart that that was as far as I was going in this life.

I can still feel the desperation and hopelessness that suffocated me that day. It was real. It was powerful. And I couldn't see through it. I would like to be able to say that I would do things differently, but the fact is, at the time, I truly believed I had no choice. I had very logically, very deliberately planned to kill myself. And I was absolutely convinced that there was no possible acceptable alternative. I knew like I knew that I knew, the world would be better off without me.

I do think about that. Every day. When I wake up, it's pretty much my first thought.

I'm still here. I'm not sure how. But I am. And I am glad of it.

The Gratitude follows. And the Joy carries me through the day, no matter how sideways it goes.

And it does still go sideways. I am not immune to all of the dramas and traumas that life has to offer. The heartbreak of my godson David's constant struggle with his mental health and legal problems continues on, relentlessly, callously, deviously. His parents are tortured, day after day by the uncertainty and fear, as am I, though one step removed. Good days for my mom are now few and far between, and I desperately try to sweep away the impatience and frustration to focus on whatever good I can find, knowing that time is not on our side. The loss of Appa, who had been with us for so long, had been such a beloved member of the family, had been my guardian angel, watching over us and our home so that I could sleep, calm, and think, had been unbelievably difficult for all of us, felt doubly when grief lands on top of grief.

Even with Joy, some days are still bloody hard to get through, because the Gratitude is out of reach. I know what I'm looking for, and how to find it. It's just that some days, I can't seem to be able to do it. It's not a perfect science.

Some of those days, I've learned to gift myself permission to just wait it out. It's okay to hang out in pajamas, eat junk, and watch tv all day. Sometimes, we need to take the time to breathe, to recharge, to heal. Eventually, I find myself in *other* days.

Other days, *most* days, I want to fight it. I want to take charge and own my life force. I want to be strong. I want to look shit in the eye and scream *Bring It On Fucker!!*

I keep, under my bed, within easy reach, a small wooden box with a painting of the aurora over the falls. And in it, tucked safely away, are my keys to the power that fuels my spirit. Locked in the quiet and privacy of my bedroom, I can take them out, whenever I feel the need, and I can use them to connect once more to the elements that speak to me in a way that lights my soul on fire. Always, the Strength, gifted to me by the Bear, the Purpose, revealed to me by the Dragonfly, and the Hope, entrusted to me by the Hawk, are close at hand, connecting me to the universe that calls me its own.

I had originally planned to give the box's contents to Gilda, in the tradition of family adventures before and since. But in a newfound attention to me, to what I need most, to what's most important to me, I kept them to myself. I have never shown them to anyone, nor told anyone about them. Not everything needs to be shared with everyone. Although I did change my will to leave the box, and the story of how I came to earn the Gifts within, to Gilda. *A great way to take first steps in overcoming guilt*, I thought. She still ends up with them in the end.

My connection with Joy isn't as sporadic as it was in the beginning. These days, it's just always there.

Always.

It hasn't *fixed* anything. I still struggle with a bit of road rage. Patience is still not one of my strong suits. I wrestle with my temper constantly. And I am the Queen Of Saying Stupid Shit. The car breaks down. I worry about the kids when they struggle.

But still, the Joy is there.

Joy is still there when there's no Happy. It's still there when shit hits the fan. It's still there in the dark.

It's still there at the funeral home as I say goodbye to my husband. Because as much as I'm wrecked, I have collected decades of incredible memories, built a life with him, created people with him, and I wouldn't trade any of that for anything. All of that is mine to keep, and for that I am deeply and truly Grateful. And there's the Joy.

It's still there in the social worker's little Ugly Room, on your worst day, because as much as I'm hearing how hard things are going to be for my new baby girl, and for us, I have a daughter. A tiny person who will grow up to amaze me every day with her determination and love. A young woman who has taught me more about being human than anyone else ever has. And for that I am Overwhelmed with Gratitude. And there's the Joy.

It's still there when the bills come in, because I can pay them. When the groceries run out, because I can buy more. When the furnace breaks down, because it can be fixed.

It's as readily available as the ability to simply sit back, consider your luck, and open yourself to how bloody lucky you are to have that. And it doesn't matter what *that* is.

These days, I can tear up over a toilet. *Seriously, indoor plumbing is humanity's greatest luxury. Think about it. Really think about it. I'm crying.*

We used to sit around the Thanksgiving table and go person to person telling everyone what we were thankful for. Now, I sit watching my kids as they eat and talk and remember and joke and I am often caught off guard as the Gratitude tackles me head on. The kids are used to seeing me, just sitting looking at them, and dissolving into tears. There was a time when that would upset them. Now, all I get are hugs and a bunch of, "Me too!"s.

Not so much with people who don't know me as well. I've left more than a few people unsettled, uncomfortable, and at a complete loss as to what to do when I've just been overwhelmed by the Joy I've suddenly encountered, and that they happen to have got caught up in. It's hard to explain that you're actually happy while you're blubbering like a freshly melted brook in Spring.

The work of life only comes in finding my way back to a State of Gratitude when I've strayed. Once I've reset my tired soul, Overwhelming Gratitude is right there, often without my bidding. It hovers around me like the hazy glow around a humid summer's full moon. Close enough for me to touch whenever I feel the need to connect.

I have played with the Gratitude, and the Joy, for more than three years since that trip. And I have learned so much.

I realized that it didn't matter that I had no one to thank. Only that I was thankful. I have never reconciled with God. I've never been able to forgive Him. Maybe one day, but not now, not yet. I question religion. And though I'm not giving up Christmas, I'm not a good Christian. But I don't think that matters.

What matters is that I believe in something greater than me. I believe that we are all connected, by Gratitude, by Joy, and by Love. Those of us who are here, those of us who have moved on. We are all One. And I think that's the point.

I visit Nathan. Not often, really, but still. Usually when I go to bed. There is a secret portal in my backyard, where his world and mine intersect. I will leave my body tucked soundly under the covers, while I walk through the house, out the back door and across the yard. When I pass through the portal, I enter our diner, finding myself in a small alcove where there's a payphone just to the left. I can see through the doorway to the other end. There's a counter along the left, with a half dozen stools spaced along it; sometimes there's people there. Along the right side, against the window, are three booths, with red vinyl benches. There are usually people in the first two. There's a door at the other end. I can see myself walk along the aisle, across the black and white tiles, checkered on the diagonal, and I take my seat in the last booth, facing the wall. Sometimes he's there waiting for me. Sometimes I have to wait for him. Sometimes he doesn't show up. Sometimes we'll have a coffee. He always manages to bump my knees or step on my foot under the table. Same as before. We can hold hands; I can feel him squeeze mine, as I can hold his tightly. I talk to him, and he listens. He laughs, he looks concerned, he'll shake his head in disbelief. He hears me. But he can't speak. He can't talk to me, and that bothered me at first. But eventually, I was just so glad to see him that I stopped worrying about it. Eventually, I learned that I've gotten really good at understanding him without words. If I listen carefully, I can still hear him despite the silence. Truthfully, this is a step forward for me.

Once my heart had been opened, it welcomed the possibility of new people, I began to find the most incredible friends. Although, it could be more that they found me.

Out of the blue one day I decided to jump in on a Book Club. I knew no one there. But I'd found them online and was interested in the book. So, I went. There are five of us, now two years into the most intense and rewarding friendship any of us have ever known. They are my sisters, my rocks, my sanity, my cheerleaders, my therapy, my role models. They have listened and supported and suggested and hugged and loved me, helping to shape me into the person I truly want to be. They help fuel my Gratitude when I'm just too tired to go it alone.

At some point, I realized, too, that I never really was as alone as I thought I was. I had fallen into a hole so deep and dark that I couldn't see the hands reaching down to help me up. They were right there the whole time; it was me who had walked away from them. Not the other way around. But no one can tell you that at the time.

Yes, the Joy is always with me. I only consciously build it to a crescendo when I feel I need to share it with someone. Although, my natural state with it seems to affect anyone around me who's open to it.

Being the Messenger, however, has been a bit of a challenge. Because, let's face it, people think you're nuts. And maybe I am a little.

But those who are open to the idea, whether they have already experienced it or not, will listen raptly as I share, absorbing the meaning of my words as well as the feeling behind them. There's an intense release for me when I am able to share it. I can't believe I was given such a life-changing gift to keep to myself. So, I'll tell anyone who'll listen. To mixed reviews.

In the end, I don't care. When the naysayers walk away, I can't help but shoot a little Joy juju their way. It can't hurt.

What I've come to learn these past few years, what I've come to accept, to believe, is that Joy is the meaning of life. To live a life of Joy, to be able to share it with others, to use it to help others, to spread it to others and to teach them to find it so they can use it themselves and for their loved ones, is the most fulfilling way to live it. Because when we have strength, when we have purpose, when we have hope, we have everything.

I was lost when I left home that day.

Little did I know that the more lost I became, the closer I was to finding my way home.

I turned onto my street, coasting slowly past the houses I'd passed a thousand times before, but noticing that Number 18 had planted some new roses. Number 27 got a new car; his standard issue plates started with BASS and I always wondered if he was a fisherman. Or in a band. Or neither. The kid at 35 got a new bike. It was sitting in the driveway with a helmet hanging from the handlebar. Mr. 48, the guy who drove me to the hospital that fateful day so long ago, was watering his lawn. He looked up and waved, smiling broadly. I waved back, grinning like we were old friends.

Turning the last bend before my house, I stopped, just for a moment. I lived in an incredible place, this home of mine. Nathan and I had worked so hard to get here. We'd been ridiculously choosy in our search for a new place to live. He'd get the itch to move every February, making the kids pack up and stage the house for sale, and he'd be off house hunting with the focus of a dog on steak. After years of this, the kids dug in their heels, refusing to unpack last year's boxes, let alone pack more this year, and I couldn't disagree with them. Enough. I bailed on the search and left him to it by himself.

A week in, I couldn't take it. Watching him go it alone was unbearable. The struggle was real.

I sat him down and talked him into making up a wish list. I had to remind him of my previous success with the idea before he agreed to work with me. By the time we were done, he sat looking at the List as a Quest Of The Impossible. He wanted an ensuite bathroom; I wanted a pool. He wanted a fireplace; I wanted a dead-end court. He wanted a yard; I wanted a price limit. And a location. And a minimum number of bedrooms.

He skulked off in search of the Impossible Dream. I forgot about it.

Two days later, he handed me a listing, "What do you think about this?"

I took the paper from his hand; skeptical didn't begin to describe me.

I read it through. Twice.

Resourceful did begin to describe him.

We moved in three weeks to the day later, on our anniversary. Of course, it helped that we were already packed. Our first night in the new house, and we were beside ourselves with how perfect it was for us.

He lived there for a year and a half.

When I think back to the things that happened during the couple years before he died, to the things that were put in place when we had no idea what was coming, to how perfectly we were preparing for an inevitable ending that neither one of us could have expected, I am once again overcome with Gratitude. How lucky I was. Because things could have been so very much worse.

Here I was pulling in. Again. A lifetime after the first time. And it wasn't lost on me how incredibly lucky I was to live here. The Gratitude filled and overwhelmed me, bringing me to tears. I accepted the Joy of it, welcoming it home with me for the first time, here, where I belonged. I gave in to it, letting it use me to bloom until it burst from me, leaving me warm and welcome. Yes. This is where I was supposed to be.

I wiped my face on my shirt, took a deep breath, and moved forward, around the bend, my house coming into view. We couldn't have chosen better. This house that Nathan gifted to me, my family, this life. I was going to spend the rest of my life trying to spread the Joy it all brought me so that I didn't drown in it!

Parked in the driveway was the twins' car. Dan's was on the street out front. My sister's was on the other side. It looked like everyone was here. And expecting me. That Sneaky-Pete Gilda. I would surely be keeping a better eye on her.

I pulled up to my driveway, not surprised to see that there was no sign of my departure almost a month earlier. Grateful not to have the reminder. I rolled the van up over the sidewalk and into the driveway next to the boys' car, cutting the engine and setting the brake.

I'd had one hell of an adventure. I'd set out on a journey into the unknown. And I'd come home changed. Ready – no, eager – to start the second half of my life. Excited to meet the challenges and accomplishments that awaited me.

Overwhelmed. Grateful. And overflowing with Joy. I began to cry once more. There was no help for it.

I heard Murphy's giant woofing in the house. I'd been announced.

The inner front door opened. I couldn't see a face through the reflection in the glass of the storm door, but I had a good guess as to who it was.

I was home.

The End

A Note from The Author

While this is not a true story, parts of it are real.

My husband, Paul, passed away suddenly at the age of 49. We have five kids. And the loss to me, our family, and the community was felt deeply and wholly. A year and a half later, what remained of my family was lost, disconnected. I threw caution to the wind, packed all six of us into a 31' RV, and traveled the 13,000 km from our home in Hamilton to Yukon, Vancouver, and back. We brought Nana figuring she might be the voice of reason in an otherwise impromptu, unplanned, chaotic journey into the unknown. Coming home a month later, we'd begun our new history together, as a family of six. I'd cemented my family back together after the tornado of grief had quite effectively torn us apart.

My personal journey through grief, while still very much in progress, has been a story I've wanted to share simply because, as

I've learned in the process, it is such a universal tale. Nobody gets through this life without the struggle and pain that comes with it. My hope is that deep insight into another's thoughts and challenges might provide answers, support, and hope for others.

The problem was, my emotions were far and away too thick to sift through with any kind of formal mode of communication. I tried to write a chronological accounting. That turned into something even I didn't want to read. I tried something more autobiographical but couldn't get anywhere and still respect my kids' privacy. I tried a self-help kinda thing. That flopped fast.

I got curious about all the comments that I'm constantly hit with about how strong I am and how well I'm doing. In my mind, and sometimes out loud a bit, I am fascinated at how easy it is to fool people. But I did get to wondering about what the alternative is.

What would happen if I simply fell apart?

I decided to play around with the idea of running away from it all. And in the telling of it, I decided to remove myself one step further and hide behind a fictional character. I think, up until the first word on the first page, she is me. But the moment she's in motion, I let her make the story her own. In fact, it very quickly turned into her story, as writing it in the third person just wasn't working. I'm not big on first person stories. Especially ones where I'm expected to worry after the character: does she live or die in the end? Because, obviously, if she's telling the story, there's your ending. But there was no way around it. The story is hers. She stopped being me on the first page.

I lent her our trip to the Yukon. I had a map over my desk the entire time I was writing, where I'd drawn out the route we'd taken, and fully intended to keep her on the same itinerary. She made quite a few changes along the way.

I gave her a family similar to mine but changed up some of the kids a bit. Mostly, it was easy enough to connect with her on the ups and downs of having a big, busy family.

I encouraged her to speak her mind. There were times I wasn't sure about her honesty. But that's where the alter-ego effect comes in and lets me communicate ideas that I couldn't otherwise. So, I did nothing to shut her up.

Though, truth be told, she wouldn't have listened.

As for her potty mouth, I've taken a bit of flack for that; there are a lot of people who don't agree with her language. I considered trying to write around it, but the fact is, until she discovers her Joy, she is angry: enraged, hellbent, infuriated. Her outbursts carry the excruciating weight of her inability to control her world. The frustration over her circumstance is real. This I know. To shut her up is to deny her reactions and her right to have them. The fury she feels fuels her words, and yet for her, still doesn't offer the release of emotion she craves. An f-bomb, for her, isn't strong enough. And if it's too strong for the reader, I envy either the level of self-control it takes to seethe so quietly or the lack of heartache that would make such expression necessary. In this matter, I won't apologize for her choice of words. Nor mine.

She stole a few things from me – a few things that are intensely private and personal – and insisted on making them her own. Try as I might to convince her otherwise, she's a stubborn bugger and left me no choice.

She doesn't have a name. She didn't have one from the beginning. I asked a few times, but she just ignored my requests. I would have liked for her to have some kind of moniker, other than 'She.' But I've come to accept that it's not up to me to know it.

The lessons she learned on her travels are the same ones that I've discovered on my own personal journey. Whether they came to me in exactly the same way or time is something I'll keep to myself, but suffice it to say, the results are remarkably similar.

True or not, private or not, the details will remain locked with me. She's had her say. And not everything needs to be shared with everyone.

(As I sit here typing these words, in this moment, there is a red-tailed hawk sitting in the tree just outside my window, watching me. He's been around a lot lately. He's new around here; I never noticed him before a couple weeks ago. But he has a habit of sitting there looking in my window at the most conspicuous times. He won't let me take his picture. And he never stays long. But it makes my day when he stops by. My Gratitude is real.)

I've subtitled the book at times with:

How the worst thing that ever happened to me
turned into the best thing that ever happened to me.

I am positive that there are people out there who would find that statement offensive on a variety of levels. And, taken out of context, I can see that. But it all comes back to the fact that things are what they are, and there is absolutely nothing I can do to change it.

Given that fact, and considering the life I've been able to build for myself, I, quite seriously and without hesitation, consider myself to be the luckiest woman on the planet. Add to that the fact that I get to spend the rest of my life in a state of euphoric joy, at will, regardless of what life throws at me, and I can't imagine ever wanting or needing more. I do move forward without fear, with purpose, with hope. Fuelled by Gratitude. Inspired by Joy.

It doesn't get any better than that.

EDIT:

I need to add this. I finished the first draft and sent the manuscript to print with such an incredible sense of accomplishment and pride. To be able to tell a story, as important as this one has been to me, has been both a privilege and a pleasure. But there is one truth that I want to add, because it is so fresh, and the coincidence, for me, is too great. And because it has incredibly deep and profound meaning for me.

Five minutes after I closed my laptop on the order for the printer, I went to celebrate being done with my family. Stepping

over my dogs – a 9-year-old Shepherd Cross, Henry, and a 2-year-old Newf, Gilligan, I was bouncing around all over the place planning an evening with everyone where I could finally be present, and not somewhere west of here.

On my fifth or sixth climb over the beasts, I finally got fed up with their lazy bones and shooed them up and out of the way.

Except that Henry couldn't get up.

Two hours later, as I sat on the floor with his head in my lap at the emergency clinic, I said my final goodbye and sent him on from this life to the next, home with Paul.

I wrestle with losing him right on top of finishing this book. And I can't release this story to the universe without thinking of him. Henry has been my protector, my confidant, my companion, without whom I never would have survived these past years without Paul, with any kind of sanity. The simple luxury of being able to sleep, deeply, knowing that I can because someone is on guard, watching over me, to alert me should I need to be wakened, is one of my most treasured. I am beyond grateful for the gift of his life and devotion and am filled with Joy because of it. Even now, as my heart breaks with the loss of him, I couldn't be more thankful for the memories he leaves behind.

I wrote this book to help others who are struggling with loss. I could not have known that the very first person I would be helping would be me.

Acknowledgements

While there are countless people who have come and gone throughout my own personal Road To Joy, there are three whom I would like to acknowledge simply because, without them, you wouldn't be reading this right now.

The first is the artist who created cover art for me.

I awoke one fine morning to find an odd little sketch in my bedside notebook. It was a penned outline of two hands holding a bear claw, a pebble, and a feather. Or, at least, that's what I thought it was. If it was a pair of hands, the thumbs were on the inside, and the scribbles within *seemed* to be those items. Above the sketch was the name Trevor.

At this point in time, I still wasn't sure if my Alter Ego was going to survive her trek, or not.

But my tiny drawing in the corner of a blank, lined page, drawn, I assume, by me, in the middle of the night, sowed the seeds for the rest of the story. It became my plot outline.

As the drawing began to make sense, it occurred to me that it had to be the cover of the book. I draw, but this was outside my skill set – I couldn't even get the thumbs in the right place. I had to find an artist.

Enter Trevor Gustafson (www.TrevorGustafson.com). I had taken a drawing class with him a little while back and knew him to be a skilled artist. I figured it was a good place to start.

He sat with me for most of a morning, asking questions I hadn't thought relevant at all, looking at my pathetic sketch – without judgment, by the way, something I enjoyed with new respect for his tact! – and agreed to give it a go.

His first draft blew me away. It was as if he'd taken a photo of the image I'd developed in my mind, and I was looking at my book cover. We made a few back-and-forths from the drawing to the narrative, matching the descriptions to the imagery, and the cover came to life. Given its contribution to the story, I couldn't close my story without thanking Trevor for his incredible insight and talent.

The second is an old friend whose talents and expertise I hold in a level of esteem that I'm sure would surprise and probably embarrass her. In addition to being an inspiration as a woman, wife, mother, and friend, she happens to be a professional publisher. And I wrestled with the idea of contacting her about this book for a long time.

I finally decided to ask her for help in finding an editor to polish this story so I could self-publish it. Without any judgement or hesitation, she repeatedly offered great advice and direction, until agreeing that I was finally *editor-ready*. I sent her the manuscript so she could take a look through it to find the right person.

When she got back to me, the message started with, "To be honest Alex, I read the first few pages of the book,…"

It took me three days to get up the courage to read the rest.

The traditional publishing process is a lengthy one. It can take months to years to see the release of a book to the market. And I've created a timeline that didn't allow for the wait. I have my reasons, but I had a tight and self-imposed timeline.

I was quite confident in my work when I sent it out, and I won't out Noelle until I prove her right, but what I was too afraid to read that first day, turned into some of the most exciting encouragement I've ever received. It is absolutely my intention to *put this out there and look good doing it*!

In the meantime, I would like to thank her for her time, and her efforts, and her kind words to someone who is going out on a limb, baring her soul, and, as Brené Brown would put it, Daring Greatly.

The third person I would like to thank is my daughter, Maggie.

Maggie is my Gilda.

Two years ago, she attended a summer camp where she set a goal to be able to stay home alone for one hour.

Overshooting that goal completely, over the last six months she has proved an invaluable roommate. She is the last of my five kids still at home, and she has excelled at the running of a household. From making sure that she, Nana, and Gilligan all eat regular meals, to doing dishes and laundry, getting herself to school, making grocery lists, and just generally picking up all the slack I've left for her, there is no way I would have been able to put this story together without her.

I am at a complete loss as to how to repay her for all of her patience and support. She asks nothing, gives everything, and I am beyond grateful for the privilege of being her mom.

Maggie, I can say thank you, but you need to know that I mean so much more.

One last thank you, and that goes to you, Dear Reader. Thank you for sharing this journey with me. It is my deepest hope that in reading this story, you have been able to find a piece of yourself, or someone you love. I wish you all of the Strength and Purpose and Hope that you need to find your own life filled with Joy. And know that I am truly and deeply enriched by the time and spirit that you have spent in connecting with me.

With Overwhelming Gratitude,

Alex

Alexandra Stacey is a Canadian writer who loves nothing better than the surprise of learning something new just when she starts to think she knows it all. She firmly believes that life will throw sticks in her spokes when she least expects it, knowing that her plans will be end up seriously and irrevocably sidetracked. She therefore does her best to choose her own challenges, lest one be chosen for her.

Readers can contact Alex through her websites at

www.ARoadToJoy.com

and

www.AlexStacey.com